From The Roman Invasion To The Present Day

By

Emile Cammaerts

**With 36 Illustrations
And 9 Maps**

Contents

Preface 1
Introduction 2
Chapter I The Coal Wood 9
Chapter II From Saint Amand To Charlemagne 13
Chapter III Lotharingia And Flanders 18
Chapter IV Régner Long Neck 21
Chapter V Baldwin The Bearded 26
Chapter VI The Belfries 29
Chapter VII The Golden Spurs 37
Chapter VIII The Cathedral Of Tournai 43
Chapter IX The Great Dukes Of The West 52
Chapter X The Town Halls 59
Chapter XI The Adoration Of The Lamb 67
Chapter XII Hapsburg And Burgundy 77
Chapter XIII The Last Stage Of Centralization 87
Chapter XIV Antwerp 91
Chapter XV The Beggars 96
Chapter XVI Separation 100
Chapter XVII Dream Of Independence 110
Chapter XVIII The Twelve Years' Truce 115
Chapter XIX Rubens 119
Chapter XX Political Decadence Under Spain 125
Chapter XXI The Ostend Company 133
Chapter XXII The Brabançonne Revolution 137
Chapter XXIII Liberty, Equality, Fraternity 146
Chapter XXIV Black, Yellow And Red 153
Chapter XXV The Scrap Of Paper 159
Chapter XXVI Neutral Independence 166
Chapter XXVII Economic Renaissance 174
Chapter XXVIII Intellectual Renaissance 182
Chapter XXIX Conclusion 188

Emile Cammaerts

Preface

We possess happily, nowadays, a few standard books, of great insight and impartiality, which allow us to form a general idea of the development of the Belgian nation without breaking fresh ground. The four volumes of Henri Pirenne's *Histoire de Belgique* carry us as far as the Peace of Münster, and, among others, such works as Vanderlinen's *Belgium*, issued recently by the Oxford University Press, and a treatise on Belgian history by F. Van Kalken (1920) supply a great deal of information on the modern period. To these works the author has been chiefly indebted in writing the present volume. He felt the need for placing the conclusions of modern Belgian historians within reach of British readers, and believed that, though he might not claim any very special qualifications to deal with Belgian history, his knowledge of England would allow him to present his material in the way most interesting to the English-speaking public.

Belgium is neither a series of essays nor a systematic text-book. Chronological sequence is preserved, and practically all important events are recorded in their appointed time, but special stress has been laid on some characteristic features of Belgian civilization and national development which are of general interest and bear on the history of Europe as a whole.

The author wishes to express his sincere thanks to his friend, Professor Van der Essen, who has been good enough to revise his work. He is also indebted to Messrs. Van Oest & Co. for allowing him to reproduce some pictures belonging to *l'Album Historique de la Belgique*, and to the Phototypie Belge (Ph.B.), Sté anonyme, Etterbeek, Bruxelles, and other holders of copyright for providing him with valuable illustrations.

Introduction

The history of the Belgian nation is little known in England. This ignorance, or rather this neglect, may seem strange if we consider the frequent relations which existed between the two countries from the early Middle Ages. It is, however, easy enough to explain, and even to justify. The general idea has been for a long time that the existence of Belgium, as a nation, dated from its independence, and that previous to 1830 such a thing as Belgian history did not even exist. All through feudal times we are aware of the existence of the County of Flanders, of the Duchy of Brabant, and of many other principalities, but, in no official act, does the term "Belgique" occur. Even after the unification of the fifteenth century, when the country came under the rule of the Dukes of Burgundy, the notion of a distinct nationality, such as the French or the British, remains hidden to the superficial student, the Netherlands forming merely a part of the rich possessions of the most powerful vassals of France. Through modern times the Belgian provinces, "les provinces belgiques" as they were called in the eighteenth century, pass under the rule of the kings of Spain, of the emperors of Austria and of the French Republic, to be finally merged, after the fall6 of Napoleon, into the Kingdom of the Netherlands. The word "Belgium," as a noun, is only found in a few books; "belgique" is a mere adjective applied to the southern portion of the Netherlands.

It must be admitted that the Belgian official historians of the old school did very little to dispel this wrong impression. In their patriotic zeal they endeavoured to picture Belgium as struggling valiantly all the time against foreign oppression. They laid great stress on Cæsar's words: "Of all the Gauls the Belgians are the bravest," and pictured the popular risings of the fourteenth and fifteenth centuries in the same light as the 1830 revolution. If we are to believe them, the Belgian people must have been conscious from their origin of their unity. They considered national princes, such as the Burgundian Dukes, in the same light as Philip II or the Austrian Emperors, and, instead of clearing the air, added to the confusion. Their interpretation of history according to the principles of national liberty of the Romantic period could not be taken seriously, and the idea prevailed that, if the Belgian nation was not merely a creation of European diplomacy, its existence could only be confirmed by the future, and rested on but frail foundations in the past.

This idea was strengthened by the knowledge that the country possessed neither strong natural frontiers, like Great Britain, France, Italy or Spain, nor the bond created by unity of language like Germany. Other European countries, it is true, like Holland or Poland, did not constitute strong geographical units and lacked definite boundaries7 but their people talked at least the same idiom and belonged, as far as the word may be used in a broad sense, to the same race. Others, like Switzerland, were divided between various languages, but possessed geographical unity. Belgium could not claim any of these distinctive features. Her boundaries remained widely open in all directions. From the cultivated plains of Flanders to the wild hills of the Ardennes she offered the greatest variety of physical aspects. What is more, her people were nearly equally divided, by a line running from the south of Ypres to the north of Liége, between two different languages, two different races. According to recognized standards, the very existence of the Belgian nation was a paradox, and though the history of mankind presents many similar contrasts between the hasty conclusions of the untrained mind and the tangible reality of facts, these cannot be recognized at first, and require a deeper knowledge of the past than that which can be provided by the study of warlike conflicts and political changes.

It was therefore left to the modern school of Belgian historians, and more especially to Professor Pirenne, of Ghent, to place the study of the origin of the Belgian nation in its right perspective and to show that, in spite of diversity of race and language, lack of natural boundaries and centuries of foreign domination, Belgian unity was based on deep-rooted traditions and possessed strong characteristics in every department of human activity which could be recognized from the early Middle Ages to the modern period. By a close study of8 the economic and intellectual life of the people and of their institutions, Pirenne and his disciples made evident what every artist, every writer had already realized, that, in spite of all appearances, Belgian unity had never been impaired in the past by the language barrier, and that both parts of the country presented common characteristics, common customs, and common institutions which no foreign rule was able to eradicate. They showed furthermore that these characteristics, determined by the common interests and aspirations of the whole people, were so strong that they inspired the policy of many foreign princes who, by their birth, would naturally have been led to disregard them. They may still be found in the country's old charters, in ancient chronicles, in the works of the so-called Flemish School of painting, and in every monument of the past which has survived the devastation of war. To these witnesses Belgian historians will not appeal in vain, when they endeavour to show that the origins of Belgian national unity may be sought as far back as those of any other nation in Europe, and that if more exposed than her powerful neighbours to the vicissitudes of war, Belgium always succeeded in preserving, throughout her darkest days, some living token of her former prosperity and of her future independence.

If, as we trust, the reader is convinced after reading this short sketch of Belgium's history that Belgian nationality is more than a vain word, and that the attitude adopted by the Belgian people9 in August 1914, far from being an impulsive movement, was merely the result of the slow and progressive development of their national feeling throughout the ages, he will also realize that this development has received many checks, and is therefore very different from that which may be traced in the history of England, for instance, or even in that of France. Nowhere would the familiar image of the growing tree be more misleading. Belgian history possesses some remarkable landmarks, under Charlemagne, for instance, at the time of the Communes, under the rule of the Dukes of Burgundy, under Charles V, and during the recent period of independence. But, between these periods of prosperity and even splendour, we notice some periods of stagnation due to internal strife or even complete decadence, when the country became a prey to foreign invasion. Few peoples have experienced such severe trials, few have shown

Belgium

such extraordinary power of recovery. Peace and a wise government coincide invariably with an extraordinary material and intellectual efflorescence, war and oppression with the partial or total loss of the progress realized a few years before, so that the arts and trades of Belgian cities which shine at one time in the forefront of European civilization seem totally forgotten at another. In more than one way Belgium has lived under a troubled sky, where heavy showers succeed bright sunshine, while the towers of Ypres, Ghent, Bruges, Antwerp, Louvain and Brussels appear and disappear on the horizon.

How can we explain the tragedy of these abrupt changes? How can we justify these sudden alternations in the life of a hard-working and peace-loving people who never indulged in any dreams of imperialism and foreign conquest?

A look at the map will help us to solve the mystery. The plain of northern Europe may be divided into two wide areas, the French plain, whose waters run from East to West into the Atlantic, and the German plain, whose waters run from South to North into the North Sea and the Baltic. These wide expanses are connected by a narrow strip of territory through which all communications skirting the hills and mountains of the South must necessarily be concentrated, and whose waters follow a north-westerly direction towards the Straits of Dover. This small plain, only 90 miles wide from Ostend to Namur, constitutes a natural link between Germany and France, and plays, from the continental point of view, the same part as the Straits, on its northern coast. Even to-day, in spite of the progress of railway communications, the main line from Paris to Berlin passes along the Sambre and Meuse valleys, through Namur, Liége and Aix-la-Chapelle, and the events of August 1914 are only the last example of the frequent use made of this road throughout history, by invaders coming from the East or from the South. For peaceful and warlike intercourse, Belgium is situated on the natural highway connecting the French and German plains. This geographical feature alone would suffice to influence the historical development of the country. But there is another.

It so happens that by an extraordinary arrangement of the map, which one may be tempted to call a coincidence, the sea straits are placed in close proximity to the continental narrows, so that the natural route from Great Britain to central Europe crosses in Belgium the natural route from France to Germany. This appears all the more clearly if we take into consideration the fact that the seventeen provinces extended in the past from the Zuyder Zee to the Somme, and that Bruges, and later on Antwerp, benefited largely from the trade of the Thames. This then is what is meant when Belgium is spoken of as being placed at "the cross-roads of Europe." Most of the continental communications between Great Britain and Germany or Italy, on the one hand, or between France and Germany on the other, were bound to pass through her provinces. She was, and is still to a certain extent, the predestined meeting-ground of British, French and German culture, the market-place where merchandise and ideas from the North, the West, the East and the South may be most conveniently exchanged, and she derives her originality from the very variety of the influences which surround her. The division of languages and races helped her in her task, and, instead of proving an obstacle to national development, contributed to it whenever circumstances proved favourable. The original contribution of the people to this development may be somewhat difficult to define, but the result is no less evident. Belgian, or as it is sometimes called, Flemish culture, though intimately connected with France and Germany, is neither French nor German, still less English. Its characteristics are derived from the combination of various European influences strongly moulded by long-standing traditions and habits. "The will to live together" which, according to Renan, is at the root of every nationality, and proves stronger than unity of race and language, finds nowhere a better illustration than in the strange part played by the Belgian nation in the history of Europe. Common interests, common dangers, common aspirations produced and maintained a distinct civilization which, according to all the laws of materialistic logic, ought to have been wrecked and swamped long ago by the overwhelming influences to which it was subjected.

As early as the ninth century, under the rule of Charlemagne, these characteristics began to show themselves. The Emperor chose Aix-la-Chapelle for his capital, not only because he possessed vast domains in the region, but also because, from this central position, he was better able to keep in contact with the governors of a vast Empire which extended from the Elbe to Spain and Italy. Aix-la-Chapelle, "the Northern Rome," became the metropolis of commerce as well as the political capital. The various intellectual centres created in the neighbourhood, at the monasteries of Liége, Tongres, and Maesyck attracted English, Irish, French and Italian poets, musicians, lawyers and theologians.

Later, in the twelfth century, when the free Communes developed all over Western Europe and succeeded in breaking the power of feudalism, it was left to Ghent and Bruges to raise the free city to a standard of independence and prosperity which it did not attain in other countries, placed under a stronger central power. In the shadow of their proud belfries over 80,000 merchants and artisans pursued their active trade, and Bruges, "the Venice of the North," became the principal port of Europe and the centre of banking activity.

The part played by the Burgundian Dukes in European politics during the Hundred Years' War is well known in this country, but the importance of their action in unifying the seventeen provinces of the Netherlands is not sufficiently realized. In fact, in spite of their foreign origin, their policy was so much inspired by the interest of the country that they may be considered as national princes. The "Great Dukes of the West" did for Belgium, in the fifteenth century, what Louis XI did for France, and what Henry VIII did for England, half a century later. They succeeded in centralizing public institutions and in suppressing, to a great extent, local jealousies and internal strife which weakened the nation and wasted her resources. Under their rule the Belgian provinces rose to an unequalled intellectual and artistic splendour and gave to the world, by the paintings of the brothers Van Eyck and their school, one of the most brilliant expressions of the early Renaissance.

This prominent situation was maintained, in spite of the fall of the Burgundian dynasty, when, through the marriage of Mary of Burgundy with Maximilian, Belgium passed under the sway of the Hapsburg dynasty. Under Charles V, Antwerp inherited the prosperity of Bruges, and became the principal centre of European commerce. It was visited every year by 2,500 ships, and the amount of commercial transactions made through its exchange was valued at forty million ducats per year.

Belgium

Even after the disastrous wars of religion which separated the Northern Netherlands, or United Provinces, from the southern provinces, and ruined for two centuries the port of Antwerp, there was a short respite, under the wise rule of the Archdukes Albert and Isabella (1598-1633), during which the art of Rubens, Van Dyck and Jordaens threw a last glamour on Belgium's falling greatness.

This rapid sketch of the happy periods of Belgian history would not be complete if we did not allude to the wonderful recovery made by the country as soon as the Powers granted her the right to live as an independent State after the unhappy experiment of the joint Kingdom of the Netherlands (1815-1830). Her population increased twofold. The Scheldt was reopened and Antwerp regained most of its previous trade. At the time of the German invasion modern Belgium occupied the first rank in Europe with regard to the density of her population, the yield of her fields per acre, the development of her railway system and the importance of her special trade per head of inhabitants. In spite of her small area, she occupied the fifth rank among the great trading nations of the world, and the names of Maeterlinck, Verhaeren, César Franck and Meunier show that she had reconquered a great part of her former intellectual prestige.

There is one striking resemblance between all periods of Belgian development. Whether in the ninth, the thirteenth, the fifteenth or the nineteenth century, they express the civilization of the time, and succeed in producing a typical example of essentially European culture, imperial under Charlemagne, communal in the Middle Ages, centralized under national princes during the Renaissance, highly industrialized and colonial in modern times. This trait must be considered when Belgium is represented as the "kernel of Europe," as combining the spirit of the North, East and South. It is not enough to say that the country seems predestined to this task by her geographical position and her duality of race and language bringing together the so-called "Germanic" and "Latin" tendencies; it must be added that, whenever historical circumstances allowed it, the people made full use of such advantages. Whether under local princes, or under foreign princes who understood Belgian interests, given peace conditions at home and abroad, the country never failed to rise to the occasion.

But these periods of greatness were short-lived compared with the periods of decadence which succeeded them. After the division of the Empire of Charlemagne the Belgian counties and duchies found themselves plunged in the throes of feudal disputes and divided between the Kings of France and the Emperors of Germany. The power of the suzerain was nowhere weaker than in these distant marches, and the Belgian princes were left free to pursue their quarrels with complete disregard of the common interest. The prosperity of the Communes in the thirteenth and beginning of the fourteenth centuries, was rapidly undermined by internal strife and by the difficulties the Counts of Flanders experienced in trying to conciliate their duty to their French suzerain with the interest of the people which prompted an English alliance. The fall of Charles the Bold provoked a fresh outburst of the spirit of local independence, which greatly endangered the country's peace, and, if the situation was restored, under Philip the Fair and Charles V, during the first part of the sixteenth century, the second part of this century witnessed the gradual exhaustion of the Southern Netherlands divided against themselves and subjected to the attacks of both Spanish and Dutch.

Emile Cammaerts

The seventeenth and eighteenth centuries, which are for other countries, like France, a period of exceptional national prestige, mark the deepest stage of Belgian decadence and humiliation. The Scheldt was closed, trade and industry were practically dead, foreign troops, French, Dutch, Spanish or Austrian, ceaselessly pursued their work of devastation. A foreign possession, open to the incursions of her possessors' enemies, sacrificed by her masters at every stage of the peace negotiations in order to save their native country, Belgium lost Dutch Flanders, Northern Brabant and part of Limburg to Holland, French Flanders, Franche Comté and Artois to France. The Treaty of Münster sealed the fate of Antwerp, and the Treaty of the Barriers left the Dutch in possession of all the country's most important fortified positions.

Though it gave back to Belgium her natural frontier in the North and reopened the Scheldt for a short time, the French régime did not greatly improve the economic situation. After the union with Holland (1815), the political struggle which followed prevented the people from enjoying the full benefit of the change, so that we must wait until 1830 before being able to notice any considerable improvement.

This general survey will suffice to show that Belgian history may be divided into periods of progress and decadence. The same may be said, it is true, of the history of all nations. But nowhere else is the difference between the higher and lower levels so pronounced and the intervals between the acts so protracted. As we have already said, the country passes suddenly from the brightest limelight of fame to the darkest recess of mediocrity and oblivion. Some of these contrasts, such as those existing between Charlemagne's united Empire and feudal divisions, are shared by the rest of Europe. Others, at the time of the Renaissance and the Reformation, and when the country came under Spanish, Austrian and French rule, are peculiar to Belgium. To the slow development of national unity, her history adds the obstacles of foreign domination and foreign invasion. The exceptional situation of the country on the map gives equally great chances of ruin and recovery. The same conditions which bring about Belgium's downfall contribute largely to her restoration, the same roads which bring wealth in time of peace, are followed, in time of war, by foreign armies. She is not only the cross-roads of Europe, she is the battlefield of Europe. From Bouvines (1214) to Waterloo and Ypres, almost all the great battles which decided the fate of Europe and determined her balance of power were fought on Belgian soil. Sometimes the inhabitants took a share in the struggle, oftener they were not even given the chance to interfere, while the Powers settled other quarrels at their expense.

The Belgian people have acquired a remarkable reputation for their sturdiness and their power of recovery. But, while they are entirely irresponsible for their weakness, which can only be attributed to the small size and the defenceless character of their country, they cannot be considered as entirely responsible for their strength. A port like Antwerp, if at all accessible, is bound to prosper under any circumstances. A town like Brussels cannot fail to benefit by its unique situation, from an international point of view. With her rich coal mines among her fertile fields, Belgium, considering her size, is perhaps more richly endowed by Nature

Belgium

than any other country in Europe. But such exceptional advantages have been more than compensated in the past by the heavy risks which this richness implied.

BELGIUM IN ROMAN TIMES.

Chapter I The Coal Wood

It is usually assumed that, while human conditions alter throughout the ages, natural surroundings remain sensibly the same. This may be true with regard to people whose history is only affected by the streams which cross their land and the hills and mountains which protect them by natural barriers. When dealing with a country like Belgium however, widely open on all sides, we cannot be content with such wide generalizations. We must ask ourselves if some important physical features have not been altered by the work of man and if some natural obstacles, which have since disappeared, did not affect the earlier stage of Belgian history.

The traveller who crosses the country to-day from Ostend to Arlon will at once recognize its main features: first a low-lying plain, between the sea and Brussels, then a district of smooth hills, as far as Namur, and finally, beyond the Meuse, the deeply cut valleys and high plateaux of the Ardennes, reaching an average of 1,500 feet above sea-level. In this last region only will the aspect of the country suggest to him the idea of some natural obstacle to free communications, though it could in no way appear forbidding when compared to the mountains of Scotland and Wales.

But at the time of the Roman conquest (57 *B.C.*), Belgium, that is to say the country peopled by various tribes designated by Julius Cæsar under the name of "Belgæ," was very different from what it is to-day. The flat coast, unprotected against the incursions of the sea, was bordered by wide marshes, while all the southern part of the country was covered by a thick forest, the "Silva Carbonaria," which merged in the wild plateaux of the Ardennes and formed, at the time, a serious obstacle to any incursion coming from the north or the east.

These physical conditions must have favoured the guerrilla warfare waged for four years by the various Celtic tribes against the Roman invader, and it is no doubt partly to them that the old "Belgæ" owed their reputation of courage and fortitude. These tribes, occupying the Scheldt and Meuse valleys, formed the rearguard of the Celtic wave of invasion which, coming from the East, had spread across Western Europe. At the time of the Roman conquest they were already closely pressed by a vanguard of Germanic tribes which had settled in Zeeland and on the left bank of the Rhine, so that even at this early stage of Belgium's history we find the dualistic character of Belgian civilization marked in the division of the country into two Roman provinces, "Belgica Secunda," in the west, and "Germania Inferior," in the east.

ROMAN INFLUENCES

The immediate effect of the Roman conquest, which was far more rapid than in Britain, was to stop for a time the influx of German tribes by the establishment of a solid barrier along the Rhine. The colonists of German origin were soon absorbed by the old inhabitants of the country, and were subjected with them to the powerful influence of Roman culture. Celts and Germans alike became Belgo-Romans, and adopted the trade and the institutions of their conquerors.

Belgium

As far as we can make out from the scanty documents at our disposal, Roman civilization moved along the Rhine towards Cologne, whence a great Roman highway was built towards the West, crossing the Meuse at Maestricht and, following the edge of the Coal Wood, through Tongres and Cambrai to Boulogne. This road, known through the early Middle Ages as the "Road of Brunehaut," was for a long time the main way running from east to west in a country where all the important streams, such as the Meuse, the Scheldt and their tributaries, ran from south to north. The extent of Roman influence may be gauged by the position which the various parts of the country occupied towards this highway. Tongres and Tournai still possess Roman remains. The foundations of Roman villas are found in the provinces of Namur, Hainault and Artois, while all traces of Roman occupation have disappeared from Flanders. The sandy and marshy nature of the soil in Northern Belgium may to a certain extent account for this fact, and we know that, in some instances, the stones provided by old Roman structures were used, in the Middle Ages, for the construction of new buildings. But it can nevertheless be assumed that, generally speaking, communications remained the principal factor of Roman civilization in these far-away marches of the Empire, and that Roman influence, so strongly felt on the Rhine and along the Meuse, became gradually less important as the distance increased. The country was almost exclusively agricultural, but it is interesting to note, in view of later developments, that, even at this remote period, the Menapii, who dwelt in Flanders, had acquired a reputation for cattle breeding and manufactured woollen mantles which, under the name of "birri," were exported beyond the Alps.

Though strongly influenced by Rome in their trade and methods of agriculture, the Belgo-Romans had retained their language and religion. Romanization, in the full meaning of the word, only began during the last years of the third century, under the influence of Christianity. During the third century, the bishopric of Trèves included the whole of "Germania Inferior." A special bishopric was established subsequently at Cologne, and, about the middle of the fourth century, at Tongres. Others appeared later at Tournai, Arras and Cambrai. This gradual spread of Christianity, which moved along the same roads as Roman civilization, from Cologne towards the West, only reached Flanders half a century later.

The Christianization of the country must have been far from complete when the incursions of the Germanic tribes, greatly encouraged by the gradual decline of the Roman Empire, brought a sudden and dramatic change in the life and development of the two Roman provinces.

THE FRANKS

During the third and fourth centuries, the pressure of the Germanic tribes, which had been considerably delayed by the Roman conquest, reasserted itself. The Rhine frontier was subjected to repeated assaults, which the depleted legions were no longer in a position to repulse effectively. The Franks attacked from the east and the north through Zeeland, while part of the Saxons who attacked Britain raided at the same time the Belgian coast. In spite of the military successes of the Emperors Constantine and Julian, the situation became so threatening that a second line of defences was fortified on the Meuse and along the great Roman highroad running from Tongres to Tournai. In 358, Julian authorized the Franks to settle in the sandy moors east of the Scheldt (Toxandria), and when, at the beginning of the fifth century, Stilicon recalled the legions in order to defend Italy against the Goths, the German tribes, finding themselves unopposed, invaded the country of the Scheldt and the Lys, reducing into serfdom the old inhabitants who had escaped massacre. The Rhine ceased henceforth to be the Empire's frontier. The latter ran now along the great highway from Tongres to Arras. Before their second line of defences the Romans, under Ætius, put up a last fight, but they were defeated by the Frankish king Clodion, who extended his kingdom along the coast as far as the Somme and established himself at Tournai (431), where his grave was discovered twelve centuries later.

LANGUAGE FRONTIER

It seemed as if the Franks, in their irresistible advance, were going to wipe out from Belgium and Gaul all trace of Roman civilization, and such a catastrophe would no doubt have occurred, if a natural obstacle had not broken their impetus. We mentioned above that, south of a line running from Dunkirk to Maestricht, the country was covered with a thick forest, the "Silva Carbonaria." This wall of wood did more to stop the invaders than the heroic efforts of Ætius. It sheltered the Celts from the Franks in Belgium as the mountains of Wales and the hills of Cornwall sheltered them from the Saxons in Great Britain. Conquests were pursued by the Frankish kings and their nobles, but the invasion stopped. The movement ceased to be ethnical and became political. The Franks reached the clearings of the forest and nominally subjected Gaul to their power, but they were now in a minority, and the conquered soon succeeded in absorbing the conquerors. It is significant that the "Lex Salica," the oldest document in which the name of the Coal Wood is mentioned, describes it as "the boundary of the territories occupied by the Frankish people." To the north of this boundary the country was entirely in the hands of the invaders; to the south, the "Wala," as the Franks called the Belgo-Romans, succeeded in maintaining themselves and in preserving to a certain extent the Roman language and civilization. The old limit, running in a northerly direction and dividing in the past "Germania Inferior" from "Belgica Secunda," had been bent under the pressure of the Frankish invasions, and ran now from east to west, but the dualism which we noted above had not disappeared. The Franks settled in the north, the romanized Celts or "Walas" occupied the south. The first are the ancestors of the Flemings of to-day, the second of the Walloons, and the limit of languages between the two sections of the population has remained the same. It runs to-day where it ran fourteen centuries ago, from the south of Ypres to Brussels and Maestricht, dividing Belgium almost evenly into two populations belonging to two separate races and speaking two different languages. The ancient forest has disappeared, but its edge is still marked on the map. We cross it to-day without noticing any alteration in the landscape, but the distant voices of the peasants working in the fields remind us of its ancient shadow and impassable undergrowth. The traveller wonders, one moment, at the change, then takes up the road again, adding one further unanswered question to his load of unsolved problems. The historian evokes the terrible years of the fifth century, when the fate of Europe hung in the balance and when the surging waves of Pagan Germanism spent their last energy along that leafy barrier which saved Christianity and Roman civilization, and incidentally gave the Belgian nation its most prominent and interesting character. The singsong of a Walloon sentence may thus suggest the rustling of the leaves and the piping of early birds, while the more guttural accents of a Flemish name remind us of the war-cry of wild hordes and the beating of "frameas."

The Frankish invasions of the fifth century may be considered the most important event of Belgium's early history. Whether the unity of the Belgian nation is questioned or upheld, we must inevitably go back to the cause of its real or apparent division. If such division, from being racial and linguistic, had become political or economic—that is to say, if the language boundary had coincided with some of the boundaries which divided the country at a later stage—the idea that Belgium was born in 1830 and constituted an "artificial creation of European diplomacy" might not be groundless. Here, as in many other countries of Europe, nationality would have been determined mostly by race and language. This, however, is not the case. At no period of Belgian history did any division follow the linguistic frontier. On the contrary, most of the political and ecclesiastical units created during the Middle Ages included both elements of the population, and, through frequent intercourse and common interests, these two people, speaking different languages, became gradually welded into one. When in the fifteenth century the various duchies and counties came under the sway of the dukes of Burgundy, national unity was realized, as it was realized in England or in France at the same time, through the increasing power and centralizing action of modern princes. A few prejudiced writers have vainly endeavoured to exaggerate the racial or linguistic factor, and contended that, in the eyes of science, Belgian nationality could not exist. The duty of a scientist is not to distort the manifestations of natural phenomena in the light of some more or less popular idea. His duty is to explain facts. The development and permanence of Belgian nationality, in spite of the most adverse conditions, is one of these facts. The existence of the Swiss nation, far more deeply divided than the Belgian, shows that it is not unique. But even if it were unique, it ought to be accounted for. It is far easier to indulge in broad generalizations than to devote oneself to a close study of nature or man. It is not the rules, it is the exceptions which ought to retain our attention, for only exceptions will teach us how imperfect are our rules.

Chapter II From Saint Amand To Charlemagne

Pursuing their conquests in Gaul, the Frankish kings soon abandoned Clodion's capital and established themselves in Paris. Clovis and his successors, surrounded by their warriors, could not resist the Gallo-Roman influences to which they were subjected. They gave their name to the country they conquered, but adopted its customs and paid but scant attention to their old companions left behind as settlers on the banks of the Scheldt. With the Belgo-Roman population, Christianity had been swept from Northern Belgium, and it took the Church two centuries, after the baptism of Clovis (496), to reconquer the ground she had lost.

This long delay is easily accounted for. The conversion of Clovis and of his followers, which affected so deeply the course of French history, scarcely reacted on the creeds and customs of the Pagan Frankish tribes established in the northern plain. The organization of the Church, which had had no time to consolidate itself, had been utterly shattered by the invasions. Between the fourth and the seventh centuries, the shadow of Paganism spread again across the land in Northern Belgium as in Britain, and when St. Amand arrived in Flanders, he found the Franks as little prepared to receive him as the Saxons had been, a few years before, to receive Augustine.

In Northern Belgium, as in Britain, the work of rechristianization had to be undertaken from outside. The regular bishops, confined to their towns, could not possibly cope with it. Their influence was limited to a small area, and their frequent change of residence suggests that their situation was rather precarious. During the sixth century, the bishops of Tongres established themselves at Maestricht, those of Tournai at Noyon, and those of Arras at Cambrai. Later, Maestricht was abandoned for Liége (early eighth century). The old titles of "episcopi Tungrorum" and "episcopi Morinorum" had lost all meaning since the disappearance of the old Celtic tribes, but the bishops, in preserving them, showed that they still hoped to increase their influence towards the north.

This ambition would have remained an empty wish but for the action of a few ardent missionaries who undertook to convert the German conquerors, in the seventh century, as the vanquished Celts had been converted in the third. We have already drawn the attention of the reader to the simultaneous events occurring on both sides of the sea, in Britain and Belgium, during the early stage of their history—Roman conquest, German raids, retreat of the Celtic population among the forests and the hills—but none of these concomitant events is more striking than the appearance, almost at the same time, of St. Augustine in Kent and St. Amand in Flanders.

ST. AMAND

The latter's mission, however, was not official. On his way to Rome, he saw in a vision St. Peter, who ordered him to preach the Gospel to the Northern Pagans, and forthwith he established himself at the confluence of the Lys and the Scheldt. In this place he founded two monasteries, which were to be the origin of the city of Ghent (610). Emboldened by his first successes, he attempted, supported by the king, to render baptism compulsory, which caused the Franks to revolt against him. After long wanderings among the Danube tribes, he came back to Flanders as Bishop of Tongres in 641, but soon gave up the cross and the mitre to resume the monk's habit, and sought martyrdom among the Basques. The palm being refused him, he again took the road to Belgium, where he died at the monastery of Elnone, near Tournai, towards 661.

For fifty years, with some intervals, he had worked unceasingly, as a monk and as a bishop, for the conversion of Northern Belgium. His efforts were not nearly so systematic as those of Augustine. He did not organize in the same way his spiritual conquests. He contented himself with bringing Pagans into the fold of Christianity, but did little to retain them there. His burning enthusiasm, however, set an example to many disciples and followers, who wandered after him through the country—St. Eloi along the Scheldt, St. Remacle along the Meuse, St. Lambert among the barren moors of Toxandria and St. Hubert through the forests of the Ardennes. Beside these, English and Irish missionaries took a large share in the conversion of Northern Belgium. The fruit of these individual efforts was reaped by the various bishops who had never ceased to claim the northern plain as an integral part of their dominions, according to Roman tradition. All that was necessary, after Christianity had been reintroduced, was to render again effective a bond which for four centuries had remained purely nominal. The bishopric of Liége extended between the Meuse and the Dyle, within the limits occupied formerly by that of Tongres; that of Cambrai, between the Dyle and the Scheldt (Nervii); that of Noyon, between the Scheldt and the sea (Menapii); and that of Térouanne, along the Yser valley (Morini). Thus were re-established, through the action of the Church, the old frontiers of the Celtic tribes, adopted by the Roman "civitates," long after the disappearance of the Celts and the fall of Rome. Liége was attached to the archbishopric of Cologne, the three others to Rheims, reviving, for ecclesiastical purposes, the old division between "Belgica Secunda" in the west and "Germania Inferior" in the east. This division never changed until the sixteenth century, when the northern part of the country ceased to be under the religious influence of the episcopal cities of the south.

BISHOPRICS

It will be noticed that none of the ecclesiastical boundaries which we have mentioned run in an easterly direction. Instead of coinciding with the language frontier, they cross it everywhere, uniting in the same religious community "Walas" and "Dietschen," Celts and Germans. For eight centuries the Church, which was at the time the supreme moral influence, unconsciously devoted all its energy to bringing together the two groups of population. They met in the same churches, they prayed before the same shrines, they joined in the same pilgrimages, they studied and meditated within the walls of the same monasteries. No wonder if such intercourse succeeded finally in uniting those whom nature had so strongly separated, and in creating in Belgium a new type of civilization neither Celtic nor Frankish, neither romanized nor germanized, but combining some of the strongest qualities of both races and well prepared to act as a kind of intellectual, moral and artistic link between them. This rule suffers only one exception. When the progress of Christianity permitted the foundation of a new bishopric at Utrecht, this religious metropolis was not subjected to any Romanic influence. It remained purely Germanic in character, and, already at this early stage of the history of the Netherlands, gave a distinct character to their extreme northern districts, which reasserted itself so strongly at the time of the Reformation.

The Merovingian kings gave a kind of sanction to this gradual separation of the Salian Franks, established in Northern Belgium, from the bulk of the Germanic tribes. It is significant that the limit which for a time separated their kingdom into Neustria in the west and Austrasia in the east, and which followed, in Eastern Gaul, the language frontier, assumed another course in Belgium, and, instead of running from east to west, as might have been expected, ran north and south along the frontier separating the bishopric of Liége from that of Cambrai, bringing Walas and Franks together on both sides of the line. Another proof of the romanizing influence of the Church may be found in the fact that the Franks established in Belgium forgot their tribal affinities. While in the seventh century Ripuarians, Alamans and Thuringians constituted themselves into so many distinct duchies, no attempt was ever made to found a Salian duchy in Northern Belgium. The very name of Franks ceased to be applied to the Walas' neighbours, and it is as "Dietschen," or "Thiois," that they were known through the Middle Ages.

It ought not to be assumed, however, that the movement was one-sided and that the ancient Franks adopted the religion and, to a certain extent, the language of the southern people without influencing them in their turn. The romanization of the Franks was accompanied by the germanization of the Walloons, who adopted the laws and customs of their conquerors. The latter became, in many instances, the great landowners of this part of the country, while the Frankish settlers, in the North, preserved the economic tradition of their native country and remained small farmers. Even this last contrast gradually disappeared under the influence of powerful landlords and through the foundation of rich monasteries, which gradually drew towards them, as tenants or clients, the bulk of the population in both parts of the country. So that, when the Carolingian dynasty superseded the Merovingian, and when Charlemagne received the imperial crown from the hands of the Pope (800), the work of unification was very nearly accomplished. Through reciprocal influences, Dietschen and Walas lived under the same economic, political, religious and judicial régime. The linguistic distinction, on both sides of the Tournai-Maestricht line, was the only notable difference, and even this distinction tended to disappear through the common use of the Roman dialect.

CHARLEMAGNE

One thing only remained to be done in order to crown the work accomplished during the two last centuries: the creation of a strong centralizing political power. The country was prepared to play the part which she was predestined to play through natural and racial conditions in the history of Europe, but she was still without guidance, a mere borderland, forgotten and neglected, on the fringe of the Frankish kingdom. The instrument was ready, but no artisan could yet use it. As long as the centre of political activity remained on the Seine, the characteristics of Belgian civilization could not be revealed. As long as the balance between Germanic and romanized culture inclined steadily towards the West, the European qualities of this Germanic, semi-romanized people could not be tested. It would be perhaps too much to say that Charlemagne founded Belgian nationality, in the same way that Clovis established French nationality in unifying Gaul, or that Alfred revealed the English to themselves in his triumphant struggle against the Danes. But, by carrying the frontiers of his Empire as far as the Elbe and establishing his headquarters in the centre of his old domain, at Aix-la-Chapelle, in a central position midway between France and Germany, Charlemagne gave at least an opportunity to almost every trait of Belgian social life to assert itself.

During the first part of the ninth century the region of the Scheldt and the Meuse became a beehive of activity. From every part of the world, merchants, theologians, artists and musicians crowded towards the new economic and intellectual centre of Europe. Arnon, a pupil of Alcuin, came to Elnone, the Irish Sedulius to Liége, the Italian Georgius to Valenciennes, while the schools of St. Amand, under Hucbald, acquired a world-wide reputation. Everywhere new monasteries were established, new churches and palaces built. The arts of illuminating, embroidery, carving and stained glass were brought to an unparalleled degree of perfection and refinement. Bishops and abbots competed in attracting to their courts and monasteries the best-known doctors and poets of the time. We have lost most of the artistic treasures and manuscripts of the period through the subsequent Norman invasions. Every vestige of Carolingian sculpture and architecture in Belgium has been destroyed. But, through the works accomplished in other countries and with the help of a few documents such as the inventory preserved in the *Chronicle of St. Trond*, we are able at least to appreciate not only their intrinsic value, but also the interest they awoke among clerics and laymen. That the great emperor encouraged this movement and took a direct part in it in attracting to the various centres of learning the best masters in Europe is sufficiently shown by his letter to Gerbald of Liége. Under his direction, European civilization was definitely established in the northern plain of Europe and Aix-la-Chapelle became indeed the "Northern Rome." The capital, with Tongres, Liége, St. Trond and other neighbouring cities, formed a centre from which civilization spread east and west towards Germany and France, just as it had spread, a few centuries before, from Central Italy towards the Eastern and Western Mediterranean.

FRISIAN CLOTH

The old Roman road, along which the monasteries founded many hostelries, was followed by streams of travellers of every description. The Meuse, Scheldt and Rhine were dotted with the sails of many ships bringing foreign wares and taking away the products of home industry. The most important of these was a special kind of cloth, "the Frisian cloth," for which the northern plain, covered with rich pastures and producing great quantities of wool, was already renowned. It was a specialized industry, the natural development of the ancient clothmaking of the Menapii mentioned above, and the predecessor of the cloth-weaving for which Flanders acquired a world-wide reputation during the subsequent centuries. The "Frisian cloth" was already exported, by the Rhine, as far as Central Europe and, by sea, towards Great Britain and Scandinavia. Pieces of money from the ports of Sluis and Duurstede have been found in both countries, and the frequency of intercourse with the North was such that a monastery was established at Thourout, near Duurstede, for the special purpose of training missionaries for the conversion of the Danish traders.

It is true that the prosperity realized under Charlemagne was short-lived, and that, a few years later, Northern Europe, and more especially Belgium, became the prey of the Normans, who destroyed most of the literary and artistic treasures accumulated with such enthusiasm during his reign. It is true also that Belgian unity was destined to break up, and that the country was to be divided between Germany and France and their respective vassals. But if Charlemagne came too soon, at a time when ethnographic conditions had not yet been sufficiently stabilized, and if his Empire did not survive him, his influence has nevertheless been felt through many centuries. If his dream of a European Empire could not be realized, the mission assigned to Belgium, as a natural link between East and West, remains even to-day one of the main features of European politics. History has shown that no annexation, no territorial division, of the dualistic country could ever guarantee peace between France and Germany. Such a peace is only possible, if the intervening nation is allowed to play its part in the concert of nations, and it has only been realized, when this part has been played. Belgium will never be what Charlemagne made it, the nucleus of a great Empire; but, unless it remains a free factor in the history of Europe, as it was for the first time under the great emperor, conflicts between the two rivals, abruptly brought together along the same frontier, become inevitable. There is a big jump from the ninth century to the Congress of Vienna, between the glory of Aix-la-Chapelle and the establishment of Belgian neutrality; there has been a great deal of ground covered since, but there is a kind of permanency in human affairs which cannot vainly be disregarded, and the policy of Charlemagne teaches us lessons which no modern statesman ought to ignore.

DIVISION OF CHARLEMAGNE'S EMPIRE.

Chapter III Lotharingia And Flanders

The central position occupied by ancient Belgium, which had been the cause of its efflorescence in the first years of the ninth century, was also the cause of its decadence after the death of Charlemagne (814). From the competition which arose at the time date the age-long rivalries between France and Germany and the tribulations of the territories lying between them, which, though claimed in turn by both Powers, and including a half romanized and half Germanic population, were neither French nor German, but possessed an individuality of their own. If these territories had been widespread and strongly defended by nature, like ancient Italy in the Mediterranean world, they might have become the seat of a new European Empire, or at least played the part of a strong third partner with which both French and German rivals would have had to reckon. This would have entirely changed the course of European politics and perhaps greatly increased the chances of a peaceful and stable régime. As it was, the intermediate country, widely open in the East and in the West, too weak to resist foreign aggression, became, at best, a weak buffer State, and, at worst, a bone of contention between two powerful hereditary enemies.

FEUDAL PRINCES

The wars and treaties which brought about the division of Charlemagne's Empire show plainly that the creation of a central Power was doomed to failure, this third Power being too vulnerable to resist combined attacks from East and West and being far too heterogeneous to maintain its unity. The treaty of Verdun, in 843, divided the Empire between Charlemagne's three grandsons. Charles received France, Louis Germany, and Lotharius, the youngest, the rich region lying between both countries and extending from Holland to Italy, including the largest portion of Belgium, with the title of emperor. After the death of Lotharius I, his son, Lotharius II, inherited the northern part of his father's domains, which, for want of a better name, was called "Regnum Lotharii"—Lotharingia. But both Charles and Louis were already endeavouring to conquer their nephew's possessions. Soon after his death, they met at Meersen, near Maestricht (870), where the partition of his lands was decided, Charles obtaining the whole of present Belgium, as far as the Meuse. The death of Louis was the signal for a new conflict. Charles was defeated at Andernach by Louis III (876), and the frontier between France and Germany was fixed on the Scheldt, Charles retaining Flanders, Louis obtaining Lotharingia (879). After the short reign of Charles the Fat, who restored for a few years the unity of the Empire, these two parts of Belgium remained thus separated for three centuries. It is important to notice that both included Flemings and Walloons, and that, on either side of the frontier, there was a strong tendency not to let Lotharingia or Flanders be drawn into the circle of German or French policy. The spirit of independence remained alive, and when, in the eleventh century, political conditions became more favourable, an entente between the Belgian princes on both sides of the Scheldt was the natural result of the weakening of the central power. Such an entente brought about finally, in the early days of the fifteenth century, the complete reunion of both parts of the country. So that the history of Belgium, from the tenth century to the early Renaissance, may be considered as the history of a small part of France and a small part of Germany, which, after struggling for independence against their respective masters, gradually joined hands in order to submit themselves to the rule of common national princes.

It would be an error to attribute the separatist leanings of the nobles in Flanders and Lotharingia to national feeling, at a time when this feeling scarcely existed in Western Europe. No doubt, the resistance offered by the Belgian nobles to their foreign sovereigns might be simply represented as the direct effect of the feudal system and of the jealous pride which every vassal entertained towards his suzerain. But, if local ambitions became supreme in Europe in the tenth century, we may at least point out that, owing to the mixed characters of language and race prevailing in Belgium, and to the peculiar position occupied by Flanders and Lotharingia, nowhere were those tendencies more evident than in these distant marches of France and Germany. Just as, at a later stage, Bruges and Ghent became the most accomplished types of the independent mediæval communes, the counts of Flanders and the princes of Lotharingia offered the most perfect examples of the restless feudal princes.

The origin of feudalism is well known and is common to all European countries. It springs from the weakening of central authority, after the death of Charlemagne, the increasing influence of the big property-owners and the gradual subordination of the small owners to the nobles who gave them the benefit of their protection. Its development was greatly hastened, in Belgium, by the invasions of the Normans. These were particularly severe in a land which had become, under Charlemagne, the richest in Europe, and which was easily reached from the sea, owing to the navigable character of its rivers. They coincided with the Danish invasions in England and with the Scandinavian raids on the coasts of Germany and France. It seemed, at one time, as if the invaders were going to settle in Holland, as they settled later in Normandy. In 834 they established themselves at the mouths of the Meuse, the Rhine and the Scheldt, and, from this centre, pursued their systematic expeditions almost unhindered. Great camps were organized by them at Louvain and Maestricht, at the farthest navigable limit of the Dyle and Meuse, where all the treasures of the surrounding monasteries, churches and palaces were accumulated.

Lotharius II allowed Ruric to establish himself on the lower Meuse, and Godfried, another Norman chieftain, received Friesland from Charles the Fat. When the victory of Arnulf of Carinthia at Louvain (891) put a stop to their activity and compelled them to retreat, the Normans left behind them only barren deserts dotted with ruins, separated by a series of entrenched camps where tenants dwelt under the protection of their masters' strongholds.

THE NORMANS

The Normans not only hastened the advent of feudalism, they wrecked Carolingian civilization as effectually as the Franks had wrecked Belgo-Roman culture. Once more the threads had to be picked up one by one, and the fabric of European civilization patiently rebuilt, and once more the Church became the most important factor in this work of reconstruction and succeeded in preserving the spiritual heritage of St. Amand. For the third time, she endeavoured to bring charity, art and culture into a world of violence and barbarism. After civilizing the Pagan

Belgium

Celts in the third century and the Pagan Franks in the seventh, she had now to civilize the Christians of the tenth century, and this was not destined to be an easier task.

Chapter IV Régner Long Neck

Let us now deal briefly with the general course of events in Eastern Belgium, or Lotharingia, attached to the Germanic Empire since 879. It is merely, as we said, the story of the efforts made by the nobles, who appear, for the first time, as a power in the State, to free themselves from the control of their imperial suzerain. The aristocracy was divided between the partisans of the German emperors and those of the local chiefs, and between these parties no compromise was possible.

It would be without interest for the British reader to follow every episode of this quarrel, but some of its aspects cannot be ignored in the study of the formation of Belgian nationality.

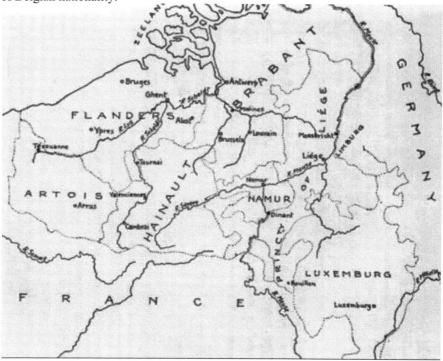

FEUDAL BELGIUM.

LOTHARINGIAN NOBLES

Two features characterize the policy of the native aristocracy: their attachment to the Carolingian dynasty and the way in which they endeavoured to preserve their freedom of action by concluding a series of alliances either with France against Germany or with Germany against France. It is easy to understand that, in these districts, which owed so much to the Carolingian régime, the Carolingian tradition had retained its prestige. The way the descendants of Lotharius had been despoiled of their heritage by Charles and Louis became the pretext for a series of insurrections against the new masters imposed on the country by the second treaty of Verdun. The first of these movements was led by Hugh, a natural son of Lotharius; it failed through the capture of its leader. The second, which was far more important, was led by a native lord, Régner Long Neck, son of one of Lotharius's daughters, who possessed vast domains in Hainault, the Ardennes, the Liége country and on the lower Meuse—that is to say, on both sides of the language frontier. Régner may be considered as a typical representative of this Lotharingian nobility, which, though defeated at first, succeeded in the end in freeing itself from imperial control. Speaking both languages, he was attached neither to the French nor to the German party, but was ready to pass from one to the other according to the interest of his policy, which was merely to preserve his own independence. Régner differed entirely from the other nobles of the Empire, such as the dukes of Saxony, Bavaria, etc., inasmuch as he did not represent any ethnographic group. He was the ideal type of the feudal lord for whom no interest prevails against his own. Thanks to his alliance with the French king, he succeeded in defeating Zwentibold, the son of the emperor, and established his rule over Lotharingia. His capital was at Meersen, near Maestricht, on the language frontier, midway between his Walloon and Flemish possessions. From the point of view of international politics, his son Gislebert is a still more striking personality. Threatened by Charles the Simple, he concluded an alliance with the Emperor Henry, and succeeded thus in shifting his position from France to Germany and from Germany to France no less than four times. He was finally obliged to submit to the emperor, whose power was steadily growing, and married his daughter (925). Having risen against Otto, Henry's successor, he was defeated at Andernach and drowned in the Rhine. Otto experienced further difficulties in controlling his Belgian possessions, and only succeeded by delegating his power to his brother Bruno, Archbishop of Cologne, and germanizing the Lotharingian bishoprics of Liége and Cambrai.

For over a century, the German or germanized high clergy became the strongest supporters of the emperor's influence in the country. Their loyalty never failed, and was emphatically expressed by Wazo, Bishop of Liége, who declared that "even if the emperor had his right eye put out, he would not fail to use the left for his master's honour and service." Bruno and Notger of Liége (974-1005) undertook to reform their clergy and to encourage intellectual culture. Under their guidance, Liége became once more a great centre of learning. Besides theology, grammar, rhetoric and poetry, music and mathematics were taught in the city, which could boast of being a "Northern Athens." The movement reached Cambrai and Utrecht, and one of the most important chronicles of the time, Sigebert's *De Scriptoribus Ecclesiasticis*—a first attempt towards a universal history of Europe—was written in the monastery of Gembloux. The prestige derived from this intellectual movement helped considerably to increase German influence and brought to Liége a number of foreign students from Germany, France, England, and even from the Slav countries.

BALDWIN V

For a time, the resistance of the local aristocracy was overcome. Régner of Hainault, nephew of Gislebert, had been exiled by Bruno, the Carolingian dynasty was supplanted in France by the Capetian, and its last representatives, Duke Charles and his son, lay buried side by side in Maestricht. The descendants of Régner Long Neck nevertheless remained powerful, owing, partly, to the marriage of Régner V of

Hainault with a daughter of Hugh Capet, and to the marriage of Lambert of Louvain to the daughter of Duke Charles. From the first years of the eleventh century, feudalism prevailed not only in Hainault and Brabant, but also in Namur, Holland and Luxemburg, so that the only means the emperor and his loyal bishops had to maintain their power was by provoking rivalries among the nobles. The title of Duke of Lotharingia was therefore not given to one of Règner's descendants, but to Godfrey of Verdun, who succeeded in defeating his adversaries at Florennes (1015), where he was killed. His successors did not show the same loyalty to Germany, and when the Emperor Henry III attempted to divide the duchy in order to diminish the duke's power, he found himself faced by a powerful confederacy, including not only Godfrey the Bearded, the counts of Louvain, Hainault, Namur and Holland, but also Baldwin V of Flanders (1044).

The date is important, for it marks a turning-point in the mediæval history of Belgium. For two centuries Flanders and Lotharingia had remained separated, dependent respectively on France and Germany for their political life. By crossing the boundary established by the Verdun treaty and interfering directly in the internal affairs of Lotharingia, Baldwin inaugurated a new policy and rendered possible a system of alliances between the Belgian nobles which brought about the reunion of both parts of the country under the same sovereign and, ultimately, the foundation of Belgian nationality.

The emperors might have resisted more successfully if they had preserved to the last the support of the bishops, who had been for so long their trustworthy agents. In order to understand how they lost this support, we must describe briefly the conditions of religious life during the tenth and eleventh centuries.

When the Normans left the country, it was again plunged in barbarism. The monasteries were in every way similar to any other feudal residence, and the ascetic rule of St. Benedict was entirely forgotten. The abbots rather distinguished themselves from the other nobles by their greed and violence. They married and indulged in drinking bouts and predatory expeditions. A reform was urgently needed. Once more it was not accomplished by the high clergy, but quite spontaneously by the people themselves, whose faith had survived the ordeal of invasions.

RELIGIOUS REVIVAL

Gérard de Brogne, an obscure nobleman, possessor of the small domain of Brogne, near Namur, after a visit to the Abbey of St. Denys, decided to restore the Benedictine tradition. On his return, he founded an abbey on his own land, gave up the world, and retired with a few disciples to the solitude of the woods. The nobles soon heard of his exemplary life and endeavoured to secure his services. Almost against his will, he was made to go from one monastery to another under the patronage of Duke Gislebert and of Arnulf of Flanders. St. Ghislain, St. Pierre, St. Bavon (Ghent), St. Amand and St. Omer received his visit in turn, and, by the middle of the tenth century, the old rule was re-established from the Meuse to the sea. The bishops of Liége, Cambrai and Utrecht joined in the movement and, with their help and that of the nobility, a number of new monasteries sprang to life in a very short time on both sides of the linguistic frontier. An extraordinary religious revival took place, which was not limited to an intellectual aristocracy, like the reform brought about almost at the same time by Bruno and Notgen in the schools of Cologne and Liége. It was not concerned with science or politics, and was essentially religious and popular in character. The chronicles of the time tell us of many examples of religious fervour. At St. Trond, the people volunteered to bring from the Rhine the stones and pillars for the erection of a new church. Near Tournai, a colony of monks established in the ruins of an old abbey were fed, year after year, by the citizens. At the end of the eleventh century a great procession was instituted in that town, in which the whole population of the neighbouring districts took part, without any distinction of rank or class, the people walking barefoot behind a miraculous image of the Virgin. In order to put a stop to local conflicts, so frequent at the time, it was enough to send a few monks carrying some sacred shrine. At the sight of the relics, the contending warriors laid down their weapons, forgot their quarrels and became reconciled.

Gérard de Brogne prepared the way for the Clunisian reformers, who, coming from Lorraine, spread rapidly during the first part of the eleventh century through Belgium towards Germany. This new movement, however, which became extremely popular not only among the people and the nobility but also among the high clergy, was bound to react on the political situation of Lotharingia at a time when the question of the supremacy of the spiritual over the temporal power was brought to the fore. The Clunisians, like most mystics at the time, were bound to reject any interference of the emperors in the affairs of the Church. They only recognized one power, the spiritual power of the Pope. In the struggle for the investitures, all their influence was thrown against Henry IV and his German bishops. The latter, after a long resistance, were obliged to give way before the popular outcry and the relentless opposition of the feudal lords, who found in the new movement a powerful and unexpected ally. French influence had come once more to their help in their efforts to shake off German hegemony.

GODFREY OF BOUILLON

Against the combined action of the Clunisians, the Lotharingian nobles and their new allies, the counts of Flanders, the emperors were still powerless. After the death of Henry III, Count Baldwin V obtained some territories between the Scheldt and the Dendre (Imperial Flanders) and the supremacy over Hainault, through the marriage of his son to Countess Richilda (1051). The Duke of Lotharingia, Godfrey the Hunchback, the last Belgian supporter of imperial rule, after checking the progress of the coalition, died, murdered in Zeeland (1076). His son, Godfrey of Bouillon, sold his land to the Bishop of Liége and left the country as the leader of the first crusade.

The Belgian princes, talking both languages, in close relations with France and Germany, were bound to take an important part in the great European adventure. They were, as far as the word may be used at this period of history, more European than national lords. And it is no doubt owing to this essentially Belgian character, as well as to his personal qualities, that Godfrey was chosen by the crusaders as their chief rather than other princes who, in spite of their greater riches and power, were not so well placed to understand and conciliate rival claims.

Emile Cammaerts

The same reasons which made Aix-la-Chapelle the capital of Charlemagne's Empire gave the leadership of the mightiest European expedition of the Middle Ages to a humble and ruined Belgian prince.

The first years of the twelfth century mark the triumph of local feudalism over imperial rule. While Henry IV, under the ban of excommunication, found a last refuge in Liége, his son gave the ducal dignity to Godfrey of Louvain. Thus the house of Régner Long Neck, after two centuries of ostracism, came into its own once more.

Chapter V Baldwin The Bearded

While, during the tenth and eleventh centuries, the Lotharingian lords were striving to retain their independence under German rule, the counts of Flanders acquired very rapidly a considerable influence in France, and were practically left free to administer their domains without any interference from outside. No duke, no bishops stood in their way. They were directly dependent on the French kings, and the latter were so weak, at the time, that they could not use the power they possessed. From this point of view the story of the two parts of mediæval Belgium presents a striking contrast. On one side of the Scheldt, an enfeebled and divided nobility struggled against a powerful suzerain; on the other, a powerless suzerain was vainly attempting to assert his authority over one of his most overbearing vassals.

COUNTS OF FLANDERS

There is, however, one characteristic which the house of Régner and that of the Flemish counts had in common. Both owed their initial power to their alliance with the Carolingian dynasty. Just as Régner's father had abducted one of Lotharius's daughters, Baldwin Iron Arm succeeded in abducting Judith, daughter of Charles the Bald, and widow of the English king Ethelwulf (862). This gave him a pretext to intervene in French affairs, of which his son Baldwin II (879-918) made full use. After extending his domains as far as the Somme and annexing Walloon Flanders and Artois, this prince consolidated his power by marrying a daughter of Alfred the Great.

Flanders was definitely established as one of the richest fiefs of the French crown, in close contact with England. Like Lotharingia, it possessed two essentially Belgian characteristics. It had neither racial nor linguistic unity, the north being Germanic and the south romanized, and it was placed between two rival Powers, France and England. The counts, or "marchios" as they preferred to call themselves, sought alliance at one time with their suzerain, at another with their neighbour, according to circumstances. When the power of the French kings increased, they leant more and more towards England, as the Lotharingian nobles had towards France when threatened by the German emperors.

Arnulf I, having secured Douai and Arras, turned his attention towards Normandy, but his progress was soon checked in that direction. His seal, which has been preserved, is the oldest feudal seal known, and the story of his life, the *Sancta prosapia domini Arnulfi comitis gloriosissimi*, was the origin of the collection of annals and chronicles in Latin, French and Flemish which formed, in the sixteenth century, the well-known *Excellente Cronijke van Vlaenderen*. His son and grandson gave up all attacks against Normandy and endeavoured to extend their possessions towards the east and south. Baldwin IV seized Valenciennes, in Hainault, and held it, for some time, against a coalition including the emperor, the King of France and the Duke of Normandy. He was finally obliged to restore the town in 1007, but, a few years later, succeeded in obtaining a portion of Zeeland and Zeeland Flanders ("Four Métiers"). In spite of the efforts made by the emperors to fortify the line of the Scheldt at Antwerp and Valenciennes, his successor, Baldwin V, the Bearded, crossed the river, and, after pushing as far as the Dendre, obtained from Henry II the investiture of the country of Alost and Zeeland. This was called "Imperial Flanders," as opposed to French Flanders, and the count, though nominally subjected to the rule of king and emperor, acquired from his intermediate position a new prestige. Like the dukes of Burgundy, four centuries later, he only lacked the title of a sovereign. "The kings," according to William of Poitiers, "feared and respected him; dukes, marquises, bishops trembled before him." When Henry I of France died, Baldwin was unanimously chosen to act as regent until young Philip came of age. The latter called him "his patron, the protector of his childhood"; he called himself "*regni procurator et bajulus*."

The regency ended in 1065, at a time when William of Normandy, who had married one of Baldwin's daughters, was preparing to invade England. The mere threat of a diversion on the Somme would have prevented this expedition, whose consequences were to prove later on so dangerous to France. But Baldwin acted as a Belgian, not as a French prince. It suited his policy to create a rival to his suzerain. Far from hampering William, he allowed a number of his subjects to take an active part in the enterprise.

BRUGES AS CAPITAL

The marriage of Baldwin's eldest son with Richilda of Hainault and of his second son Robert with Gertrude of Holland suggested the possibility of an early unification of Belgium under the counts of Flanders. According to Gilbert of Bruges, the two sons of Baldwin were "like powerful wings sustaining him in his flight."

The reunion of Hainault and Flanders was, however, destined to be short-lived. Baldwin VI died in 1070, leaving his widow Richilda with two young children; Robert, her brother-in-law, rebelled against her. After his victory at Mont Cassel, where he defeated a French army sent by the king to Richilda's help, he left Hainault to his nephew and took possession of Flanders.

Up to then, the counts had resided most of the time in the southern part of their possessions, where they had their richest domains. Robert the Frisian established his capital at Bruges, whose trade was beginning to develop rapidly, and which had opened relations with England and the Baltic countries. The fact that Robert's first possessions were in Holland might have influenced his choice, but the change marks, nevertheless, an important stage in the evolution of Flanders from a purely agricultural country into an industrial and commercial one. It looked at one time as if war was going to break out between England and Flanders, as the Conqueror, owing to his marriage, had some claims on the country. Robert, who had given his daughter in marriage to King Canute of Denmark, concluded an alliance with him, and even projected a combined attack on the English coast, which, however, never materialized. He proved an irreconcilable enemy to the German emperors, and entered into close relations with the Pope. His pilgrimage to Jerusalem, in 1083, added to his prestige, and the Emperor Alexis, who had received him with great pomp in Constantinople, asked his support against the Turks. The letter which the emperor addressed to him at the time, as to the "staunchest supporter of Christianity," and which was given wide circulation, had a considerable influence in preparing the first crusade, in which his son Robert II (1093-1111) took a prominent part under Godfrey of Bouillon.

The rich and powerful Count of Flanders did not remain in the Holy Land, like the ruined Duke of Lotharingia. His home interests were far too important. He gave up the Danish policy of his father and allied himself to the King of France against the English kings, whose power was rapidly increasing. The French alliance stood him in good stead when, making a pretext of the struggle of the investitures and of his relationship with the Pope, he renewed his ancestor's claim upon the emperor's possessions. More successful than Baldwin IV, he succeeded in detaching the bishopric of Arras from Cambrai, and in spite of the obstinate resistance of Henry IV and Henry V, in obtaining the suzerainty over Cambraisis.

POLICY OF FLANDERS

On the other hand, by encouraging and protecting the first Capetians, Robert of Jerusalem and his son Baldwin VII made a very grave political mistake. Too preoccupied by the imminent danger from England, they did not realize that, owing to its geographical position, this country could never threaten Flanders's independence in the same way as France, which had, besides, the right to interfere in its internal affairs. It is, however, characteristic of the Count's policy that, on several occasions, in 1103 and 1109, they signed separate agreements with Henry I, in which they promised him to use all their influence in his favour in case the French king contemplated an expedition against England, and, if their efforts failed, not to give their suzerain more help than they were strictly bound to. Even at the time when the alliance with France was most cordial, the door was never closed on possible negotiations with England. To call such a policy sheer duplicity would be to misunderstand the spirit of the period and the special position in which the Belgian princes, whether of Lotharingia or of Flanders, were placed. Their diplomacy was the necessary result of the central situation occupied by their possessions. Unless they endeavoured to maintain a certain balance of power between their neighbours, they were in direct danger of losing their independence. Periods of hesitation coincided with a divided menace. As soon as the danger became evident on one side, the Belgian princes invariably turned towards the other. The same reasons which bound the descendants of Régner Long Neck to France soon brought about a closer entente between the counts and communes of Flanders and the English king.

Chapter VI The Belfries

On several occasions in the course of the eleventh century, the constitution of Belgian unity seemed to come within sight. The Scheldt no longer divided the country into two distinct political units. The powerful counts of Flanders were still practically independent of their French suzerain, while the Struggle for the Investitures had ruined the emperors' authority in the Meuse region, where the native nobility was again exerting its supremacy. Both parts of the country were brought more and more into contact by military alliances and dynastic intermarriages. In spite of these tendencies, three centuries were still to elapse before the reunion of the various counties and duchies under the same house and the foundation of what may be considered as the Belgian nation, in the modern sense of the word. While in France and England the central power was making great progress against the separatist tendencies of the feudal barons, in Belgium the work of political centralization was delayed by the considerable influence exerted on social conditions by the towns, or communes.

CLOTH HALL AND BELFRY, YPRES (DESTROYED 1914).
(Thirteenth century.) *Ph. B.*

FIRST COMMUNES

The development of urban institutions in the twelfth century was not peculiar to Belgium. Almost in every European country the progress of trade and industry had the same result, but, just as Feudalism had been more feudal in the region of the Meuse and the Scheldt than in any other part of Northern Europe, Communalism became more communal. The same reasons which favoured separatism from the point of view of the feudal lords allowed the spirit of the guilds to assert itself more energetically than in the neighbouring countries. The very remoteness of any strong centralizing influence, the linguistic and racial differences, favoured the new régime, while the resources of the country and its geographical position on the map of Europe gave to its trade and industry an extraordinary efflorescence. The communes found in Belgium a well prepared ground. Politically, they met with a minimum of resistance; economically, they benefited from a maximum of advantages.

THE CASTLE OF THE COUNTS, GHENT.
(Twelfth century). *Ph. B.*

Up to the twelfth century, it must be remembered, only the lay and ecclesiastical aristocracy had been allowed to play a part in Belgian, and, for the matter of that, in European history. The feudal system had reduced the ancient free peasants to bondage; most of them were tied to the soil and deprived, of course, of all political rights. The foundation of large towns of 50,000 to 80,000 inhabitants, whose citizens possessed their own militia, their own tribunals and their own privileges, was nothing short of a social revolution. The merchants and artisans made their influence strongly felt in the State; they had money and military power, and the impoverished nobility became more and more dependent on them. The spirit of separatism and local individualism passed thus from the castle to the town, and it was only when some balance was re-established between the different classes of society, and when altered economic conditions necessitated a closer co-operation of the whole nation, that unification became possible in the early days of the fifteenth century.

The story of the formation of the first Communes is well known. It is the same in all parts of Western Europe, though the essential characteristics are nowhere more evident than in Belgium. Trade gave the first impulse. It had been practically annihilated by the Norman invasions and the wars of the ninth century. Using the natural waterways of the country and the sea routes, it revived slowly, and we know, through the discovery of Flemish coins in Denmark, Prussia and Russia, that the Belgian coast was already in frequent communication with Northern Europe at the end of the tenth century. The Norman Conquest was the main cause of the rapid progress of trade in the eleventh century. Many Flemings accompanied William in his expedition, many more followed as colonists, and a constant intercourse was established between the Thames and the Scheldt. The development of the trade of Bruges was the natural consequence of the increasing importance of London. Singing the *Kyrie Eleison*, Flemish sailors came up the Thames, bringing to England wine from France and Germany, spices from the East and cloth from Flanders.

MERCHANTS

Meanwhile, great fairs had been established in Southern Flanders at Lille, Ypres and Douai, where French and Italian merchants met the Flemish traders; so that Flanders was kept in close contact with the romanized countries by the continental routes, while the sea brought her into touch with the Germanic world. Wharves and storehouses were built on the main streams where the merchants made their winter quarters, usually in the vicinity and under the protection of some monastery or some feudal castle. Though the commercial settlements were more dependent than the latter on the geographical features of the country, most of the best situated spots, at the crossing of two main roads (Maestricht), at the confluence of navigable streams (Liége, Ghent), at the highest navigable point of a river (Cambrai), etc., had attracted the monks and the barons before the merchants. The new settlements were, however, quite distinct from the old, and their population lived under an entirely different régime. The name given to them at the time is characteristic: they were called either "porters" or "emporia" (storehouses); even after the industrial population had joined the merchants, the inhabitants remained for a long time "mercatores."

The nobles—especially the lay nobles—protected the traders. At a time when landed property diminished considerably in value, they were a source of revenue. They paid tolls on the rivers, on the roads, at the fairs. They provided all lingeries, silks, spices, furs, jewels, etc.; their ships could be equipped for war. These were sufficient reasons for the princes to grant the wandering traders a certain freedom and a privileged position in the State, and even to fight any noble who persecuted them and robbed them of their wares. At the beginning of the twelfth century, trade not only moved from south to north, on Belgium's many navigable streams; it ran also from east to west along a new road connecting Bruges with Cologne, through Maestricht, St. Trond, Léau, Louvain, Brussels, Alost and Ghent, all these places occupying some favourable geographical position. The origin of the prosperity of Antwerp dates from this period, a certain part of the wares being transported to this spot by the Scheldt from Ghent. The Bruges-Cologne road eventually ruined the trade of the latter place, to the great advantage of agricultural Brabant, which was, by this means, drawn into the economic movement then revolutionizing social conditions on the Meuse and the Scheldt.

ARTISANS

Had this movement continued to be purely commercial, social conditions would not have undergone such a rapid change, for the number of settlers would have remained relatively small. But, already in the eleventh century, the "porters" and "emporia" proved a centre of attraction, not only to discontented serfs and would-be merchants, but to skilled artisans, mostly clothmakers in Flanders and metal-workers on the Meuse. From the early days of the Menapii the inhabitants of Northern Belgium had a reputation for working the wool of their sheep. Under Charlemagne, it had already become their principal industry. In the eleventh century, with the conquest of new "polders" upon the sea and the extension of the area of rich low meadows, the quantity of wool increased considerably, and, more raw material becoming available, the cloth industry developed accordingly. From the building of a protective dyke to the weaver bending over his loom and to the ship carrying valuable Flemish cloth from Bruges to London or any other part of the European coast, there is a natural chain of thought. But the progress accomplished along the coast may also be connected with the foundation and development of the first towns and the chimes of the belfries.

In the hills of the south, industry was very likely determined by the presence of copper and tin mines. The latter, however, were rapidly exhausted, and, as early as the tenth century, the artisans of the Meuse were obliged to fetch their raw material from Germany, especially from the mines of the Geslar. The industry, however, remained in Dinant and Huy, and coppersmiths and merchants met in these places, as clothmakers and merchants met in the Flemish towns. So that, in the early Middle Ages, the contrast between agricultural and industrial Belgium was already apparent.

The migration of artisans towards trade centres in the eleventh century is as easy to understand as the attraction exerted in the present day by commerce on industry. But, in the Middle Ages, the union was bound to become closer still, owing to the resistance offered by the old régime to the social transformation and to the necessity felt by the "guilds" (either of merchants or of artisans) to unite against a common enemy.

Though, in some instances, the new towns received their privileges from the princes, who rather encouraged than opposed their development, the burgesses were frequently obliged to fight in order to obtain their liberty. The case of Cambrai is typical. A settlement of traders and artisans had been established close to the walls of the episcopal castle at the beginning of the eleventh century. In 1070 it was surrounded with walls and became a "bourg" (borough). The "bourg" was placed under the jurisdiction of the bishop's officers, who administered it without making any allowance for new conditions, the laws applied to peasants and serfs being vigorously applied to traders and craftsmen. Meetings took place in the "Halle" (Guildhall), and the members of the guilds swore to shake off the bishop's yoke as soon as an opportunity arose. When, in 1077, Bishop Gérard left Cambrai to receive his investiture from Henry IV, the burgesses overwhelmed the soldiery, seized the gates and proclaimed the Commune. It was not a rising of the poor against the rich, for the leaders were the richest merchants in the town, neither was it a rising of Guelphs against Ghibelines, though the bishop had lost much of his prestige owing to his loyalty to the emperor. It was essentially a fight of the new "bourgeoisie" against feudalism, of a commercial and industrial culture against a purely agricultural civilization. The rising was soon crushed, but, a few years later, Bishop Walcher was obliged to grant to the citizens the charters which Bishop Gérard had refused them, and even when, in 1107, the Emperor Henry V tore up Cambrai's charter, the town preserved its sheriffs and magistrates. The burgesses kept up the struggle for two centuries, until they succeeded in taking from the bishops every shred of temporal power and in obtaining the entire control of the city.

NOBLES AND COMMUNES

Cambrai was, with Huy, one of the first communes in Belgium, and the rising had a great influence in Northern France. It is an extreme example of the resistance of the feudal lords to the rise of the bourgeoisie. Generally speaking, this resistance was greater among ecclesiastical than among lay nobles, and in small fiefs, where the prince was in direct opposition to the people, than in larger ones, where the communes frequently supported him against his vassals or even against his suzerain.

While the imperial bishops opposed the movement, for instance, the counts of Flanders encouraged it. During the eleventh century, the merchants had already enjoyed the protection of the counts, and, in the beginning of the twelfth century, the erection of a wall surrounding the "porters" was accompanied by the grant of special privileges. When Charles the Good was killed in 1127, the people rose to avenge his death and besieged his murderers in the castle of Bruges. The count having left no heir, Louis VI of France upheld the claim of William of Normandy, but the burgesses, fearing that the duke would not maintain their privileges, opposed his candidature and selected Thierry of Alsace. A war ensued, during which most of the nobles sided with the first, whilst the towns and free peasants took the part of the second. After his victory, Thierry showed his gratitude by extending to all towns in the country, whether Walloon or Flemish, the same freedom. Strangely enough, it was not the charter of Bruges which was chosen, but that of Arras. The towns enjoyed a kind of self-government. The citizens were judged by their own sheriffs ("échevins"), the prince being represented on their council by a "bailli." They had their own seal, their own hall and archives. They owed allegiance to their prince, and, in case of war, had to give him military help. Their rights were shown by the gallows erected at the gates of the town and by the belfry, whose bell called the burgesses to arms when the city was threatened by the enemy.

Belgium

THE CLOTH HALL AND BELFRY, BRUGES.
(Thirteenth-fourteenth century). *Ph. B.*

In Brabant also the communes enjoyed the protection of the duke, but they developed later, owing to the agricultural character of the region. The importance of Louvain and Brussels dates from the twelfth century, when the Cologne-Bruges road brought commercial activity into the country and when the weaving industry began to spread in the duchy. As for Liége, which was a purely ecclesiastical town, where, for a long time, the number of priests and monks exceeded that of the ordinary citizens, it enjoyed a smaller share of local liberties than the other centres of the Meuse valley where industry was more developed, and the citizens never succeeded in freeing themselves completely from the bishop's authority.

PEASANTS

If the imperial bishops opposed the new movement, it was mainly owing to the influence of the monks, and especially the Cistercian monks, that it spread to agricultural districts and that the rise of the communes coincided with the abolition of serfdom. The direct consequence of the development of trade and industry was the depreciation of the land, and it became necessary to open new districts to agriculture. The Cistercians were pioneers in this direction. They established their houses in barren heaths and marshy districts, and applied their skill and patience to converting them into fertile fields. Unable to carry on the work unaided, they appealed to lay brethren, who established farms in the neighbourhood of the monasteries. These peasants were no longer serfs but free peasants, as had been their forefathers after the Frankish invasion. Under the supervision of the monks and of the stewards of dukes and counts, who soon realized the advantages of the Cistercian method, they created new "polders" along the Flemish coast, cleared the forests of Hainault and Namur, and reclaimed the heaths and marshes of Flanders and Brabant. The reclaimed ground was divided among the workers, so that, at the beginning of the thirteenth century, a new class of free peasants replaced the old class of feudal serfs. The farm produce was no longer for local consumption alone; it was taken to the market-place, where the farmers met the merchants and artisans. The social transformation begun in the town halls spread thence to the country-side, and the whole country began to share the same economic and political interests.

The belfry remains the living symbol of this rapid and widespread transformation, and the few mediæval belfries which remain standing in Belgium date from that period. Those of Ghent and Tournai, built at the end of the twelfth century, stand alone, in the centre of the town, while in Ypres and Bruges (thirteenth century) the tower was erected above the centre of the "halles." In both cases, however, the meaning of these old monuments is the same. They are far more typical of Belgian mediæval civilization than the Gothic churches of the thirteenth and fourteenth centuries, such as St. Bavon (Ghent), Ste. Gudule (Brussels) and Notre Dame (Bruges), and even than the great cathedrals built later in Antwerp and Malines. Belgium's ecclesiastical architecture, though distinct from the French, is strongly influenced by the French Gothic style, while her civic monuments can only be compared to the Palazzi publici of Florence and Sienna. They stand as living witnesses of the heroic times when the alliance of the guilds was sought by the princes and when common artisans did not hesitate to challenge the power of the French kings. The spirit which raised them has left its mark on the people, who still cherish to an extraordinary degree their local institutions, and for whom communal privileges constitute the very basis of social liberty. This "love of the clock-tower" is not only Belgian, or Italian, or English; it is essentially a European trait, as opposed to Asiatic Imperialism, and may even be found in Republican Rome and in ancient Greece.

TOWN CITIZENSHIP

It is not without interest to notice that this European conception of town-citizenship coincided with an exceptional artistic and economic development strongly subjected both to Latin and Germanic influences. While in the thirteenth and fourteenth centuries Ghent became the centre of Flemish-German trade, owing to its privileged position on the Cologne road, Bruges was the most cosmopolitan centre in Europe. It communicated with the sea by a canal, whose great dykes are mentioned by Dante (*Inferno*, XV, 4, 6), and its market-place, deserted to-day, was then crowded with traders from England, France, Spain and Germany and brokers

Belgium

from Lombardy and Tuscany. Seventeen States were represented in the city, where the Hanseatic towns had their main warehouses. Ships, laden with stores from all parts of the world, took with them Flemish textiles, which were celebrated for their suppleness and beauty of colour, and which were exported, not only to all parts of Europe, but even to the bazaars of the East. When local raw material became insufficient, wool was imported from England, and the Hansa of London centralized the trade between the two countries. England and Flanders were thus brought close together, and their commercial relations reacted on the policy of both countries.

In the shadow of the Bruges belfry, amid English, French, German and Italian traders, a new civilization was born, which, combining the Latin and Germanic influences to which it was subjected, was soon to assert its own originality. Belgium had definitely broken down the barriers of feudalism. The same causes which had liberated her people had brought them into contact with the outside world.

Chapter VII The Golden Spurs

The political history of the last centuries of the Middle Ages is entirely dominated by the development of the Communes. Their influence is twofold. On one hand, they prevented the absorption of the country by the French kings; on the other, they delayed its unification under national princes. By safeguarding local liberties, they checked foreign ambitions, but, through their efforts to maintain their privileges and through their petty rivalries, they impeded, for a long time, the establishment of central institutions. During the twelfth and thirteenth centuries they fostered trade and industry by affording due protection to the burgesses and forcing the princes to follow a policy in accordance with the interests of the country. During the fourteenth century they were weakened by internal struggles between classes and cities, and, through their trade restrictions, became an obstacle to the free development of the economic life of the nation.

FLANDERS' INFLUENCE

The cardinal event of the period is the Battle of Courtrai (1302), also called the Battle of the Golden Spurs, owing to the great number of these spurs collected on the battlefield after the defeat of the French knights by the Flemish militia. It was hailed at the time as a miraculous triumph for the commoners, the disproportion between the opposing forces being somewhat exaggerated by enthusiastic contemporary chroniclers. But its influence was not only social, it was national, for it definitely secured the independence of Flanders and of the other Belgian principalities against the increasing power of the French kings, and this rendered possible the unification of the country, which was accomplished, a century later, under the dukes of Burgundy.

SEAL OF THE TOWN OF DAMME (1376).

Belgium

seal of guy de dampierre, count of flanders (1278-1305).

At the beginning of the twelfth century the old distinction between Lotharingia and Flanders had practically ceased to exist. The emperor's prestige, greatly diminished by the Struggle of the Investitures, was no longer strong enough to keep the Belgian princes east of the Scheldt within the bounds of their allegiance. The most loyal of them, the Count of Hainault, would not even depart from neutrality during the war waged between Frederick Barbarossa and the French king. "He was not obliged," he declared, "to put his fortunes in the hands of the imperial troops and to grant them passage across his territory, as that would bring devastation to his country." The development of trade and industry had shifted the centre of interest from Germany, which remained purely feudal and agricultural, to Flanders, which represented a far more advanced civilization, based on the free development of the cities. When the princes of Brabant, Hainault and the other principal cities looked for an example or for some political support, they no longer had to seek it outside the country. Even Liége was gradually drawn within the circle of Flanders's influence. This lead, given by one Belgian principality to the others, over the Scheldt boundary, marks the break-up of the division of the country between-----0 France and Germany inaugurated at the treaty of Verdun, and prepares the work of centralization which brought about the creation of Belgian nationality.

The policy of Flanders was determined by the desire to preserve peace with England and with France, Germany playing only a very secondary part in European affairs at the time. Good relations with England were essential to the Flemish cloth industry, since most of the wool was imported from this country through Bruges. As the power of the French kings increased, the Flemish counts endeavoured also to avoid any conflict with their suzerains, since their northern allies could not bring them sufficient military help to prevent the country's invasion. Counts and Communes tried in vain to remain neutral. Neutrality was impossible, and, whenever it was infringed, Flanders had invariably to suffer from the consequences, either through the ruin of her trade or through the loss of her liberties.

BOUVINES

The House of Alsace came into power at the death of Charles the Good. Its representative, Thierry, had been opposed by the French king, who wanted to give the county to the Duke of Normandy. The Communes, fearing that the duke's attitude would bring difficulties with England, upheld the claim of Thierry, who prevailed after the death of his rival. His son, Philip, acquired further territories in France (Amiénois, Valois and Vermandois). His influence and his prestige were so considerable that the French king, Philippe-Auguste, is supposed to have said: "France will absorb Flanders or be destroyed by it." To his suzerain's policy of "absorption," the Count of Flanders opposed the British alliance, which he, however, broke in 1187, when he thought himself threatened by his ally. Philip of Alsace died in the crusade, during the siege of St. John of Acre (1191). Philippe-Auguste at once attempted to seize his possessions, but his attempt was frustrated by Count Baldwin V of Hainault, who invaded the country and, having been recognized by the Communes, succeeded in uniting both counties.

Baldwin V of Hainault and IX of Flanders preserved a friendly neutrality towards England during the struggle between Cœur de Lion and Philippe-Auguste. When the Count of Flanders, who had become Emperor of Constantinople, died before Adrianople (1205), the French king hoped at last to annex definitely the rich county. He had given Baldwin's daughter in marriage to one of his creatures, Ferrand of Portugal, who thus became the legitimate successor. As soon, however, as he arrived in Flanders, Ferrand recognized that he could only maintain himself in power by pursuing an independent policy friendly to England. Though a foreigner, with little knowledge of the country, he observed the same attitude towards France as his predecessors, concluding an alliance against his liege with the Duke of Brabant, King John of England and the Emperor Otto. The confederates were severely defeated at Bouvines (1214), and, for nearly a century, the hegemony of France became paramount in the Low Countries. Not only did the kings henceforth rule in their own estates of Flanders, but they were able to extend their influence over the whole country as far as Liége. The wishes of their representatives were considered as orders, and the complete absorption of Belgium by France seemed the foregone conclusion of their tireless activity.

Two obstacles, however, stood in the way—the fact that Flanders drew from England most of her raw material and the independent policy of the dukes of Brabant.

Henry III took the hansa of London under his special protection and promised the Flemish traders that they should not be molested even if war broke out between England and France, unless Flanders took an active part in the conflict. The Flemish trade constituted a large source of revenue for the English kings, and it was still as essential, at the time, to the prosperity of England as to that of Flanders. Since the increased power of the French crown had rendered direct opposition impossible, the British kings did their best to favour Flemish neutrality and to enter into close friendship with the only Belgian princes who had preserved their full independence, the dukes of Brabant.

The latter belonged to the last national dynasty ruling in the country and were therefore particularly popular. The Battle of Woeringen (1288), in which Duke John I succeeded in defeating the powerful Archbishop of Cologne and his allies, established his supremacy between the Meuse and the Rhine and gave him the full control of the road from Cologne to Ghent, through Louvain and Brussels, which brought Brabant into line with Flanders's trade and industry. Brabant became thus the national bulwark against foreign influence and the political stronghold of

Belgium, a position which it never completely relinquished, even through the cruel vicissitudes of the seventeenth and eighteenth centuries.

BRABANT

If the prosperity of Brabant did not yet equal that of Flanders, the dukes possessed greater authority over their subjects and enjoyed far more independence. Edward I, when preparing for war against France, fully appreciated these advantages, and gave his daughter Margaret in marriage to the son of John I. Antwerp benefited largely from the Anglo-Brabançonne alliance, since, when the English kings forbade the importation of wool into Flanders, following some conflict with France, the English merchants found a suitable market in the Scheldt port in close communication with the centres of Brabant's cloth industry, Louvain, Brussels and Malines.

The cities of Flanders, however, were not prepared to see their trade ruined to suit the plans of the French. The economic reasons which forbade a hostile attitude towards England would have afforded sufficient ground for an anti-French reaction. The crisis was hastened by internal trouble. The merchants and the craftsmen of the Communes had not remained united. The rich and influential merchants had gradually monopolized public offices and formed a strong aristocracy opposed by the craftsmen. Count Guy de Dampierre declared himself for the artisans, Philip the Fair of France, seizing the opportunity of interfering in the affairs of Flanders, declared himself in favour of the aristocracy. At the same time, he opposed the projected marriage of the count's daughter with King Edward's eldest son. The popular party, or "Clauwaerts" (the claw of the Flemish lion), was not sufficiently organized to resist the "Leliaerts" (partisans of the lily), helped by Philip's forces, and for five years the land remained under French occupation, Count Guy being imprisoned in France. In July 1302 a terrible rising, known as "Matines brugeoises" and led by the weaver Pieter de Coninck, broke out in Bruges, when all the French in the town were murdered in the early hours of the morning. Philip immediately sent a powerful army to punish the rebels, which was defeated under the walls of Courtrai by the Flemish militia, which some nobles, partisans of the count, had hastily joined.

The consequences of the Battle of the Golden Spurs were considerable. It reversed the situation created, a century before, by Bouvines. From the social point of view, it gave a tremendous impulse to democratic liberty throughout Belgium. As a result, the people of Liége obtained, in 1316, their first liberties, symbolized by the erection of the "Perron." The "Joyeuse Entrée" of Brabant was published in 1354 and became the fixed constitution of the central principality. Charters were enlarged and confirmed even in the least industrial districts of Hainault and Namur, Luxemburg remaining practically the only purely feudal State in the country. Duke John of Luxemburg, who became King of Bohemia and who fought at Crécy, was considered at the time as one of the last representatives of mediæval chivalry. The Prince of Wales's motto "I serve" was supposed to have been borrowed by the Black Prince from this noble enemy.

FLANDERS AND ENGLAND

From the national point of view, the Battle of Courtrai is no less important. Had the Flemings again failed in their bold bid for liberty, the principle of Belgian nationality might have been irretrievably jeopardized on the eve of the period when it was to assert itself, and the efforts of centuries towards the reconstitution of political unity might have become useless. It is, of course, entirely wrong to attribute the rising of 1302 to purely patriotic motives, as some romantic Belgian historians have endeavoured to do; but one may legitimately believe that part at least of the blind and obstinate heroism displayed during the struggle may have been inspired by an obscure instinct that Flanders was, at the moment, waging the battle of Belgium—that is to say, of all the lands lying between France and Germany, and which, if permanently annexed by one or other of the Powers, must necessarily upset the balance of Europe and wreck all hope of European peace based on national freedom.

Flanders did not, however, reap the full benefits of her victory. The peace concluded in 1319, after further military operations, took away from the county all the Walloon district, considerably reducing the cattle grazing area and making Flemish industry more dependent than ever on England for its raw material. From the beginning of the fourteenth century, the counts, who had, up to then, sided with the people, went over to the French party, so that, when the Hundred Years' War broke out, Flanders found herself again faced by the cruel alternative of breaking her allegiance and being exposed to the disasters of an armed invasion from the South, or keeping it and seeing her industry ruined owing to the stoppage of her trade with England.

As early as 1336, Count Louis de Nevers having ordered the arrest of English merchants, Edward III, as a reprisal, interrupted all intercourse between the two countries. This measure was all the more disastrous for Flanders because, helped by the immigration of some Flemish weavers and fullers to England, an English cloth industry had been started across the Channel. The English were therefore far less dependent on the Flemings than the Flemings on the English, and it was to be feared that the new industry would greatly benefit from the monopoly created by the stoppage of trade. The prosperity of Bruges was further threatened, since the prohibition did not include Brabant, and Antwerp remained open to British trade.

VAN ARTEVELDE

In 1338 the people rose against their count, and Jacques Van Artevelde of Ghent became the acknowledged leader of the movement. These risings differed from the "Matines brugeoises" in that the aristocracy took part in them as well as the craftsmen. Van Artevelde was not a workman like De Coninck. He was a rich landowner and had great interests in the cloth trade. His aim was not only to preserve the country's independence, but to safeguard its prosperity. Approached by Edward III's delegates, he tried at first to maintain a purely neutral attitude, but, when the English king landed in Antwerp with supplies of wool, he was obliged to side with England. The "Wise Man of Ghent" suggested, however, that in order to relieve the Communes of their oath of allegiance to Philip of Valois, who had succeeded the Capetians, Edward should declare himself the true king of France. The struggle which followed the destruction of the French fleet at Sluis (1340) was protracted, no decision being reached at the siege of Tournai. Edward was called back to England by the restlessness of his own subjects, while the Flemish artisans were unwilling indefinitely to hold the field against the French armies. The departure of the English forces caused great bitterness among the people, who accused Van Artevelde of having betrayed them, and in the course of a riot the once popular tribune was killed by the mob (1345). Froissart, his enemy, pays him a generous tribute: "The poor exalted him, the wicked killed him."

His son Philip, Queen Philippa's godson, vainly endeavoured to succeed where his father had failed. After leading a revolt against the pro-French Count Louis de Mâle, he was defeated by the French in 1382 and died on the battlefield.

All these struggles had weakened Flanders considerably. By chasing German merchants from Bruges (1380), Louis de Mâle had brought about the decadence of this port in favour of Antwerp, where the English were soon to transfer the wool market. Political persecutions had driven a great many of the artisans to England, to the great advantage of English industry. Hundreds of houses in Bruges remained empty, Ypres was half destroyed, and Ghent had lost a considerable part of its population. Civil war had exhausted the country's resources during the last years of the fourteenth century. In the country-side the dykes were neglected, great stretches of "polders" were again flooded by the sea, and wolves and bears infested the woods. The restoration of Flanders to its previous prosperity did not take place before the middle of the fifteenth century, as a result of the wise rule of the dukes of Burgundy.

Emile Cammaerts

Chapter VIII The Cathedral Of Tournai

Literature is perhaps nowadays the most characteristic expression of civilization, just as painting was the most striking mode of expression in the Renaissance and architecture in the Middle Ages. We have seen that, in the Netherlands, civic monuments constitute a typical feature in mediæval architecture, but, though it is important to insist on the conditions which favoured and inspired the building of belfries and cloth-halls, the important part played by churches in the Netherlands, as in France and England, must nevertheless be acknowledged. It is true that, considering the intense religious life of the Low Countries from the tenth to the fifteenth centuries, the number of well preserved old churches still existing is rather disappointing, but this impression would be greatly altered if it were possible to revive the buildings which have fallen victim to destruction or to a worse fate still, wholesale restoration.

SECOND CRUSADE

All through the Middle Ages, Belgium was an extraordinarily active centre of religious teaching and mysticism, and nowhere else perhaps in Europe did the Christian faith penetrate so deeply among the common people. Quite apart from the intellectual and aristocratic movements favoured in the tenth and eleventh centuries by the imperial bishops of Liége and their celebrated schools, from the deeper influence exerted in other parts by the Clunisian monks (eleventh century) and by the Cistercians and Prémontrés (twelfth century), the enthusiasm aroused by the crusades is a sufficient proof of the country's religious fervour. Not only did the nobles play a predominant part, Godfrey of Bouillon, Duke of Lower Lotharingia, being the leader of the first crusade and the counts of Flanders, Robert II, Thierry of Alsace, Philip of Alsace and Baldwin IX, taking a large share in the same and in subsequent expeditions, but the lower classes enlisted with the same enthusiasm and flocked around the cross raised by Peter the Hermit and his followers. It is reported that, during the second crusade, certain localities lost more than half their male population.

Later, with the development of the Communes, the bourgeois and the townspeople endeavoured to nominate their own priests and chaplains, civil hospitals were founded, and, in the thirteenth century, the mendicant orders enjoyed an enormous popularity, owing to the familiarity with which they mixed with the people. They followed the armies in the field, and it was among them that the citizens found their favourite preachers in times of peace.

The great concourse of merchants and artisans in the towns favoured the spreading of heresies, and, for a time, the Manicheans, under their leader Tanchelm, made many converts among the Antwerp weavers; but the Church was strong enough, at the time, not to appeal hastily to forcible repression. The heretic preachers were fought, on their own ground, by Franciscans, Dominicans-----0 and other ecclesiastics, who succeeded in defeating them by their personal prestige. One of these preachers who was honoured as a saint, Lambert le Bègue (the Stammerer), greatly influenced spiritual life in Liége and the surrounding districts. The foundation of the characteristically Belgian institution of the "Béguines," or "Beggards," can, at least partly, be traced to his religious activity.

This institution, which spread all over the country during the thirteenth century, shows once more the success of all attempts in the Netherlands to bring the inspiration of religion into the practice of everyday life and into close contact with the humble and the poor. It was specially successful among the women, and absorbed a great many of the surplus female population. The "Béguines" did not pronounce eternal vows and could, if they liked, return to the world. They led a very active life, settled in small houses, forming a large square planted with trees, around a chapel where they held their services. All the time not devoted to prayer was given to some manual work, teaching or visiting the poor. From Nivelles, the movement spread to Ghent, Bruges, Lille, Ypres, Oudenarde, Damme, Courtrai, Alost, Dixmude, etc., and even to Northern France and Western Germany. The accomplished type of the "Béguine" is Marie d'Oignies, who, after a few months of married life, separated from her husband, spent many years among the lepers, and finally settled, with a few companions, in the little convent of Oignies, near Namur.

ROMANESQUE ARCHITECTURE

Such was the spirit which inspired the builders of the Belgian churches. Certainly the most typical and perhaps the most beautiful is Notre Dame of Tournai, with its romanesque nave, built in the eleventh century, its early Gothic choir (thirteenth century) and its later Gothic porch (fourteenth century). It illustrates admirably the succession of styles used in the country during the Middle Ages and the series of influences to which these styles were subjected from the East and from the South. Most of the romanesque churches of the tenth and eleventh centuries were built either by German architects or by their Belgian pupils. Though the best examples of the period are now found either at Tournai (cathedral and St. Quentin), at Soignies (St. Vincent) and at Nivelles (Ste. Gertrude), the centre of the school was at Liége, where St. Denis, St. Jacques, St. Barthélémy and especially Ste. Croix still show some traces of this early work. The main features of these buildings, in their original state, are, beside the use of the rounded arch, round or octagonal turrets, with pointed roofs, over the façade and sometimes over the transept.

THE CATHEDRAL, TOURNAI.
(Twelfth-fourteenth century). *Ph. B.*

With the decline of German political and intellectual influence, Gothic was introduced into the country by French architects. In the last years of the twelfth century, Tournai thus became the meeting-place of the two currents, and, owing to its favourable position on the Scheldt and to the material available in the district, dominated the whole religious architecture of Flanders. The period of transition lasted over a century and produced some of the most characteristic religious buildings of the country, in which both the rounded and pointed arches are happily combined. To this period belong St. Jacques and Ste. Madeleine of Tournai, St. Nicolas and St. Jacques of Ghent and the pretty little church of Pamele, built by Arnold of Binche (near Tournai) between 1238 and 1242, where beside the romanesque turrets of the façade may be found a short central octagonal Gothic tower. The well-known Church of St. Sauveur at Bruges, begun in 1137, belongs to the same period, but brick instead of Tournai stone has been used for its erection. The same feature is found in a good many Gothic churches in maritime Flanders and Holland, which were too distant from the Hainault quarries.

Tournai again, in the choir of its cathedral, furnishes a good example of Belgian early Gothic (thirteenth century), of which the destroyed cathedral of

Belgium

Ypres, St. Martin, was considered the masterpiece. All trace of the round arch has now disappeared and the columns are formed by massive pillars.

As the Gothic style develops in its secondary period (late thirteenth and beginning of fourteenth century) the windows increase in size, the pillars are fluted and the tracery of the windows becomes more and more complicated. The best examples of this particular Gothic still in existence are the choir of St. Paul at Liége and Notre Dame of Huy (begun in 1311).

BRONZE FONT IN THE CHURCH OF ST. BARTHOLOMEW, LIÉGE (1107-1118).
The baptism of Christ.
St. Peter baptising Cornelius.

GOTHIC CATHEDRALS

The most important and the best preserved Belgian churches belong, however, to the third period of Gothic, when clustered columns replace pillars, tracery becomes flamboyant and spires soar higher and higher above the naves. Brabant is especially rich in fourteenth and fifteenth century churches. Possessing its own quarries, it was independent of Tournai, and can claim an original style altogether free from Hainault or French influence. In this group must be mentioned Notre Dame of Hal; the cathedral of St. Rombaut, in Malines, begun in 1350 and whose flat-roofed tower was only finished in 1452; Ste. Gudule, in Brussels, the oldest of them all, with some parts dating as far back as the thirteenth century, a flamboyant porch and two flat-roofed towers similar to those of St. Rombaut; and, finally, the great cathedral of Antwerp, begun in 1387, with one of the highest towers in Europe and certainly the slenderest, whose various stories mark the transformation of style as they rise to end in a purely Renaissance spire.

COLLEGIATE CHURCH OF SAINTE GUDULE, BRUSSELS.
(Thirteenth-fourteenth century). *Ph. B.*

Most of these romanesque and Gothic churches have no unity of style, owing to the long period covered during their building. From a purely architectural point of view, they lack perhaps the purity of some of their French and German rivals, but they are all the more interesting to the historian and bring him into close contact with the transformation of mind and manners from the Middle Ages to the Renaissance.

In order not to split up our subject we have wandered from the civilization of the Middle Ages into the early Renaissance. Let us now go back to Notre Dame of Tournai, with her five pointed towers, and see what we may learn from her with regard to the intellectual and literary developments of the period. In the same way as the building of its choir, in the early thirteenth century, shows evident traces of French influence, so the use of French, among the upper classes and in the literature of the period, becomes more and more predominant.

During the first centuries of the Middle Ages, French influence in Flanders was particularly noticeable in the monasteries. Almost in every monastery Walloon and Flemish monks lived side by side, and it became necessary that their abbots should be able to make themselves understood by both sections of the community. Thierry of St. Trond was chosen by the monks of St. Peter at Ghent "quoniam Theutonica et Gaulonica lingua expeditus." Examples abound of bishops, teachers and preachers able to express themselves in Flemish and French. The "Cantilène of Ste. Eulalie," the oldest poem written in the French language, was discovered in the monastery of St. Amand together with one of the oldest German writings, the "Ludwigslied." The Clunisian influence tended also to spread the use of French in the northern districts.

BI-LINGUALISM

The same bilingual characteristic may be found among the nobles, who met frequently in the course of their military expeditions or peaceful tournaments. Intermarriages between families belonging to both parts of Lotharingia and Flanders were frequent. Besides, most of the large domains lay across the language frontier. The knowledge of French soon became an essential condition of a good education, and the children of Flemish lords were sent to French abbeys in order to perfect their knowledge of the language. It may be assumed that, at the end of the eleventh century, the majority of the aristocracy was bilingual. It was one of the reasons which gave the Belgian nobles such a prominent position in the crusades. A contemporary writer, Otto of Friesingen, explains that Godfrey of Bouillon was placed at the head of the crusaders because, "brought up on the frontier between romanized and Teutonic people, he knew both languages equally well."

This penetration of French, not only in Flanders, which was nominally attached to the kingdom of France, but also in Lotharingia and even in Liége, the centre of German influence, is all the more remarkable as it implied no political hegemony, the counts of Flanders being practically independent, at the time, and the other nobles attached to the Empire. It was not introduced by conquest, as in England in the eleventh century, or through immigration, like German into Bohemia or into the Baltic States. The race of the northern provinces remained relatively pure, and the adoption of a second language by the aristocracy can only be explained by the intimate relations created between Thiois (Flemings) and Walloons owing to political conditions, to diocesan boundaries and social intercourse.

The influence of French was still further increased during the twelfth century, which is the classical epoch of French literature in the Middle Ages, and during which trade became so much more active owing to the formation of the Communes. It was not only spoken by nearly all the counts of Flanders and used in their private correspondence, but it became, to a certain extent, the official language when Latin was dispossessed of its monopoly. Its use ceased to be confined to the aristocracy and spread to the bourgeoisie, owing to the frequent intercourse between Flemish and French merchants at the fairs of Champagne. All bills of exchange were written in French, and even the Lombards and the Florentine bankers used it in their transactions. Its knowledge was as necessary, at the time, as a knowledge of English may be to-day to all exporters. As late as 1250, it was the only popular language in which public documents were written. It is true that, in Northern Flanders, many Germanic terms are mixed with it, but it exerts practically no influence on the early development of the Flemish language. The linguistic situation in Flanders, during the thirteenth century, is interesting to compare with that existing in England, at the same time, where the imported tongue was progressively absorbed by the native, just as the Normans were absorbed by the Saxons. Again, it is typical of the pacific character of French penetration that when, in the middle of the thirteenth century, Flemish prose, having sufficiently developed, was adopted for public acts, no restriction whatever was placed on this custom. French, however, remained the language used by the counts and by their officers. The documents of the period present an extraordinary medley of Latin, French and Flemish texts.

Brabant was not so strongly influenced, partly because the dukes belonged to the old native dynasty and partly because the dukedom entered later into the current of trade intercourse. French was used at court, and a knowledge of it was considered as a necessary accomplishment for a nobleman. But the dukes used Flemish in their relations with their Flemish subjects, and when Latin gradually disappeared, the popular language took its place in public acts.

PICARD WRITERS

This efflorescence of the French language must be connected with the great prosperity of Walloon Flanders and the development, in Arras, Douai, Lille, Tournai and Valenciennes, of an intense literary movement, including poets, chroniclers and translators endowed with a distinct originality. As late as the thirteenth century these writers, who had adopted the Picard dialect, proclaimed their independence from purely French literature, so that, in their own domain, they play a similar part to that played by the Tournai master-builders in theirs. The counts of Flanders and Hainault, among them Philip of Alsace, Baldwin V and Baldwin VI, patronized native literature and even attracted to their courts some of the greatest French poets of the period, such as Chrétien de Troyes and Gautier d'Epinal. The dukes of Brabant imitated this example and patronized Adenet le Roi, who was considered the most eminent Belgian trouvère. We still possess a few songs composed by Duke Henry III. Nothing can give us a better insight into the intellectual life of some of the nobles of the time than the following lines in which Lambert d'Ardres describes the manifold activities of Baldwin II, Count of Guines (1169-1206). This prince "surrounded himself with clerks and masters, asked them questions unceasingly and listened to them attentively. But, as he would have liked to know everything and could not remember everything by heart, he ordered Master Landri de Waben to translate for him from the Latin into Romance the Song of Solomon, together with its mystic interpretation, and often had it read aloud to him. He learned, in the same way, the Gospels, accompanied by appropriate sermons, which had been translated, as well as the life of St. Anthony Abbot, by a certain Alfred. He also received from Master Godfrey a great portion of the Physic translated from Latin into Romance. Everyone knows that the venerable Father Simon of Bologna translated for him from the Latin into Romance the book of Solinus on natural history and, in order to obtain a reward for his labour, offered the book to him publicly and read it to him aloud."

Translations play a most important part in the literature of the time, and it is significant that Belgium, from this point of view, owing no doubt to her duality of language, acted as a pioneer for France. Just as the Walloon provinces were first to discard Latin in public acts and replace it by French, it is among their writers that the first and most notable translators may be found. The tastes of translators and their patrons were very catholic; science, theology, history and poetry proving equally attractive. Another characteristic of French letters in Belgium is the importance given to history. The first historical work written in French is a translation by Nicolas de Senlis of the *Chronicle of Turpin*, made for Yolande, sister of Baldwin V of Hainault. In 1225 a clerk compiled for Roger, castellan of Lille, a series of historical stories, the *Livre des Histoires*, taken from the most various sources, from the creation of the world down to his own time. Soon original works, dealing with local and contemporary events, replaced translations and compilations. Such are the *Story of Hainault*, written for Baldwin of Avesnes, and the rhymed *Chronicle of Tournai* by Philippe Mousket.

ROMANCES

The bourgeoisie soon became interested in the movement. But the citizens of the towns enjoyed neither courtiers' poetry nor epics and warlike histories. Satire and didactic works were far more to their taste. As early as the first part of the twelfth century a priest, Nivardus, collected the numerous animal stories which were told in his time and in which Renard the fox, Isengrain the wolf, Noble the lion and many more animal heroes play a very lively part. These tales, in spite of their Oriental or Greek origin, had found a new meaning among the townsfolk of the twelfth century, who delighted in the tricks of Renard, whose cunning outwitted the strength of the great barons and the pride of their suzerain. Translations from Nivardus were the origin of the French versions of the *Roman du Renard* and of the Flemish poem of *Reinaert*, written by Willem in the thirteenth century, and which surpasses all other variations of the theme.

The *Reinaert* is the first notable work of mediæval Flemish literature. Willem's predecessor, Hendrick van Veldeke, is merely a translator. One of his most popular poems at the time, the *Eneÿde*, is a Flemish version of the French *Roman d'Enéas*. The number and the success of these Flemish translations of French romances of chivalry, in the thirteenth century, is however, remarkable, especially as it was the means of introducing these stories into Germany, where they received new and sometimes original treatment. From its very origin Flemish literature acted thus as an intermediary between France and Germany. Veldeke was a noble, and his works were only appreciated in the castles. Jacob van Maerlant, who was hailed, in his time, as the "Father of Flemish Poets," was a bourgeois scribe. Though obliged at first to write some translations from the French Romances, he could not but feel that this kind of literature suited neither the aspirations nor the temperament of the people among whom he lived. Turning from these frivolous stories, he sought in the works of Vincent de Beauvais and Pierre Comestor a wiser and more serious inspiration. His ambition was to place within reach of laymen the scientific, philosophic and religious thought of his time, so that they might obtain the same chances of acquiring knowledge as the learned clerics. This is the spirit which pervades his principal and most popular works, *Der Naturen Blume*, the *Rymbybel* and the *Spiegel historiael*, in which the author deals with natural lore and sacred and profane history.

In his impatience against "the beautiful, false French poets who rhyme more than they know," van Maerlant declared that all French things were false: "wat waelsch is valsch is," but one would seek vainly any systematic hostility towards France in the poet's encyclopædic work. On the contrary, on several occasions, he pays a glowing tribute to the intellectual splendour of France, specially as represented by the University of Paris, and it is not without astonishment that we discover from his pen, on the eve of the Battle of the Golden Spurs, a eulogy of the French régime.

VAN MAERLANT

The reason why van Maerlant attacked the French Romances of Chivalry was not that they were French, but that they were Romances. The characteristic of the early Flemish writers, apart from the satiric poetry of Willem, is the seriousness of their thought and purpose. They feel strongly their responsibility in influencing their contemporaries and seldom abandon the tone of the preacher or teacher. The most eloquent verses of van Maerlant may be found in *Van den Lande van Oversee*, in which he preaches a new crusade after the fall of St. John of Acre.

From the very beginning Belgian Flemish literature is distinct from the French, but has many points of contact with the intellectual movement of the Walloon provinces. There can be no question, at this early stage, of disagreement or rivalry, for French was only, at the time, the second language of the aristocracy in Flanders, and, as Flemish letters developed, they naturally penetrated into the upper classes. There are few examples in history of a civilization combining with such harmony the genius of two races and two languages.

Chapter IX The Great Dukes Of The West

There are certain periods in the life of nations and individuals when, owing to a combination of happy circumstances, all their best faculties work in perfect harmony. They give us a complete and almost perfect image of the man or the land. It is towards such periods of efflorescence that we turn when we want to judge a great reformer, a great writer or a great artist, and it is only fair that we should turn to them also when we want to appreciate the part played in the history of civilization by all nations who have left their mark in the world.

THE NETHERLANDS UNDER THE RULE OF THE DUKES OF BURGUNDY.

Such a period of economic, political and artistic splendour may be found in Belgium when the whole country became united under the dukes of Burgundy. The fifteenth century is for Belgium what the Elizabethan period is for England and the seventeenth century for France. Not only did the territorial importance of the unified provinces reach its culminating point and the national princes play a prominent part in European politics, but, from the point of view of economic prosperity and intellectual efflorescence, Bruges, Brussels and Antwerp rivalled, at the time, the great Italian Republics of the Renaissance.

DECLINE OF THE COMMUNES

Considering the common interests linking the various States, and their remoteness from the political centres of France and Germany, the unification of the country under one crown seemed a foregone conclusion. In fact, we have seen that, already at the beginning of the twelfth century, the division of the country between the two great Powers had become purely nominal. Lotharingia ceased to exist owing to the decreasing influence of the Empire following the struggle of the Investitures, and the counts of Flanders were so powerful that they were practically independent of their French suzerains. They began to take an important share in political life east of the Scheldt, and would no doubt have succeeded in uniting the whole country under their sway but for the rising power of the Communes and for the political recovery of France. The Communes substituted economic divisions for the political divisions created by Feudalism. The efforts of the French kings, while unable to crush Flemish independence, succeeded, nevertheless, in checking the power of the counts, while other States, such as Brabant, were allowed to develop more freely beyond the Scheldt.

At the close of the fourteenth century, the Communes, which had proved such a powerful means of liberating trade and industry from feudal restrictions, had, to a great extent, ceased to fulfil their part in the development of the nation. Instead of using their privileges to further economic relations, the large towns oppressed the smaller ones and the country-side was entirely sacrificed. Internal strife, war with France and the decadence of the cloth industry had brought about a state of economic depression and social unrest out of which the country could only emerge through the support of a strong and centralized administration. On the other hand, the French kings were, for the time, reconciled to the idea of an independent Flanders and too exhausted by their struggle against England to make further warlike attempts in this direction. So that when Philip the Bold, Duke of Burgundy, became Count of Flanders, in 1384, the country, exhausted by civil war and independent of foreign hegemony, was at last prepared to submit to parting with some of its local privileges in order to obtain peace and prosperity under a wise central administration.

Philip was the brother of Charles V, King of France, and succeeded Louis de Mâle after marrying the count's daughter. He was supposed to bring back Flanders under French influence, but, as a matter of fact, pursued a policy distinct from that of the French. Once more, as in the case of Guy de Dampierre and of Ferrand, the French king was deceived in his plans, and the interests of the country proved stronger than the personal relations of its ruler. One of the first acts of the new count was to secure Artois, thus reconstituting the bilingual Flanders of the previous century. He then proceeded to extend the power of his house by obtaining, for his second son Antoine, the succession of Brabant in exchange for military help given to the Duchess Jeanne. Such a scheme was opposed to the emperor's projects, but his influence could not outweigh the advantages which the Brabançons expected from the House of Burgundy. It thus happened that, when Philip the Bold died, in 1404, his eldest son John inherited Flanders and Artois, and Antoine acquired

Brabant and Limburg. The latter's possessions were further increased by his marriage with Elisabeth Gorlitz, heiress of Luxemburg.

The two brothers supported each other, and when Antoine died at Agincourt (1415), John the Fearless obtained the lease of Luxemburg. He had previously intervened in the affairs of Liége and received the title of protector of the bishopric. Only Hainault, Holland, Zeeland and Namur remained independent of the Burgundian House when John died, in 1419, assassinated on the bridge of Montereau. Like his father, his policy had been inspired far more by the interests of the Low Countries than by those of France. He resided in Ghent during the greater part of his reign.

PHILIP THE GOOD.
From a portrait by Roger Van der Weyden (Madrid).

PHILIP THE GOOD

Philip the Good, his son, reaped all the benefits of his father's efforts. He completed the work of unification by extending his protectorate over Tournai, Cambrai and Utrecht and buying Namur. John IV of Brabant, son of Antoine and Elisabeth, had married Jacqueline of Bavaria, Countess of Hainault, Holland and Zeeland. When he and his brother had died without heir, Brabant and Limburg reverted to the elder branch of the House of Burgundy. So that, after having dispossessed his cousin Jacqueline of her inheritance, Philip became practically the sole master of all the principalities founded on Belgian soil since the Middle Ages.

No doubt the dukes of Burgundy were helped in their work of unification by a series of most favourable circumstances. Within a remarkably short time, many marriages and deaths occurred which favoured their plans to a very considerable extent. But it would be a great mistake to attribute their success to fate alone. Their power was so great that, through political pressure and offers of money, they might, in any case, have induced the less favoured princes of the country to part with their domains. And, what is far more important, economic and political circumstances were such as to render the old system of local divisions obsolete and to necessitate the formation of a central administration pooling the resources and directing the common policy of all parts of the country. It was not through the process of Burgundian unification that Belgium became a nation. It was because Belgium had already practically become a nation, through the gradual intercourse of the various principalities, that one prince, more favoured than his neighbours at the time, was able to concentrate in his hands the power of all the Belgian princes.

It is not without reason, nevertheless, that Justus Lipsius, the Belgian humanist of the seventeenth century, calls Philip the Good "conditor Belgii," the founder of Belgium. If this prince benefited from the efforts of his predecessors, if he enjoyed tremendous opportunities, he was wise enough to make full use of them. While enlarging his possessions and even contemplating, no doubt, the foundation of a great European Empire, he proceeded step by step and did not launch into any wild enterprise which might have jeopardized the future. While building up a centralized State such as the legists of the Renaissance conceived it, a State independent of local institutions and possessing a distinct life apart from the people and above them, he endeavoured, as much as possible, to respect local privileges, superimposing modern institutions on mediæval ones and preserving, if not wholly, at least formally, the rights of each province and town.

THE GREAT DUKE OF THE WEST

The "great duke of the West," as he was called, "could," according to his own words, "have been king if he had only willed it"—that is to say, if he had been prepared to pay homage to the Emperor. After some protracted negotiations, he preferred to remain a duke and to preserve his complete independence. He was Duke of Burgundy, Count of Flanders, Duke of Brabant, Count of Hainault, "Mambourg" of Liége, etc.; he was, in short, the head of a monarchic confederation in which he succeeded in establishing a few central institutions common to all the principalities, a private Council, the "Council of the Duke," a government Council, "the Grand Council," and the "States General," on which sat delegates of the various provincial States and which the duke called together when he deemed it opportune. The States General's approval was necessary whenever fresh taxes were to be levied or when the sovereign intended to declare war. Following the example of the French kings, the duke was nearly always able to conciliate the States General by giving the majority of the seats to members of the clergy or to the nobility. The latter he succeeded in converting into a body of courtiers by grants of money, land or well-paid offices, also by founding, in 1480, the privileged order of the Golden Fleece.

Philip's external policy was judged severely by his English contemporaries, whose views are no doubt reflected in the First Part of Shakespeare's *Henry VI*, where we see Burgundy abandoning his allies at the instigation of the Maid of Orleans. His "betrayal" was followed by riots in London, during which some Flemish and Walloon merchants lost their lives. Considered, however, from the point of view of the period, when diplomacy and politics were not inspired by a particularly keen sense of justice and morality, the duke's decision is easy to explain. Drawn into the English alliance by the traditional policy of Flanders, which always sought support in this country against France, and by the murder of his father, for which he sought revenge, he never lost sight of the possible threat to his power and independence which an overwhelming English victory might constitute some day. English ambitions in the Low Countries had been made evident by the expedition of the Duke of Gloucester, Henry V's brother, who had championed Jacqueline of Bavaria's cause against the duke. A permanent union of Hainault, Brabant and Holland, under English protection, had even been contemplated. It would, therefore, have been contrary to Burgundian and to Belgian interests, if the power of France had been absolutely and irremediably crushed, since such a victory would have upset the balance of Western power, on which the very existence of the new confederation depended.

Philip's quarrel with Henry VI was, however, short-lived, and, during the last part of his reign, he succeeded in re-establishing the Anglo-Burgundian alliance on a sounder basis. His wife, Isabella of Portugal, a granddaughter of John of Gaunt, used her influence to bring about a reconciliation and the resumption of trade relations. The marriage of Charles, son of Philip, with Margaret of York, sister of Edward IV, which was celebrated in Bruges in 1463 amidst an amazing display of luxury, definitely sealed the bond of union.

Emile Cammaerts

CHARLES THE BOLD.
From a portrait by Roger Van der Weyden (Berlin Museum).

CHARLES THE BOLD

For France had recovered from her trials; and when he succeeded his father, Charles, surnamed the Bold, was confronted by an adversary all the more formidable that, through his impulsive temperament, he literally played into the hands of the cunning French king. Faced, as Philip had been, by the opposition of the Communes and by the separatist tendencies of certain towns, the new duke, scorning diplomacy, tried to impose his will through sheer force and terrorism. The sack of Dinant in 1466 was destined to serve as an example to Liége, where the agents of King Louis maintained a constant agitation. Two years later, the duke obliged his rival to witness the burning and pillage of the latter city, which had revolted for a second time, following the instigations of the French.

Charles might have resisted his enemy's intrigues, if he had limited his ambitions to the Low Countries. Like his father, he entered into negotiations with the Emperor with the hope of acquiring the title of king. His Burgundian domains were separated from the Low Countries by Alsace and Lorraine. Had he been able to join Low and High Burgundy through these lands, he would have very nearly reconstituted the old kingdom of Lotharingia, by unifying all the borderlands lying between France and Germany, from the North Sea to the Mediterranean. The success of such an enterprise might have had incalculable consequences. But Charles was the last man to succeed in an endeavour requiring at least as much skill and diplomacy as material resources. He obtained rights upon Alsace and conquered Lorraine, but fell an easy prey to Louis XI's artifices by launching an expedition against the Swiss. Defeated at Granson and Morat, he was killed before Nancy, leaving the whole responsibility of his heavy succession to his young daughter Mary.

According to Philip de Commines: "He tried so many things that he could not live long enough to carry them through, and they were indeed almost impossible enterprises." But his external policy remained all through perfectly consistent. He was a faithful friend to the House of York and gave his support to Edward IV, with whom he intended to divide France, had he succeeded in conquering Louis.

POSITION OF BELGIUM

Philip the Good, by his work of territorial consolidation, had succeeded in obliterating from the map of Europe the frontier of the Scheldt, which, since the Treaty of Verdun, had divided the country between France and Germany. Charles the Bold failed in reconstituting the short-lived kingdom of Lotharius, which had stood, for a few years, as a barrier between the two rival Powers. Such a dream was indeed outside the scope of practical politics, though, considered from the point of view of language and race, it was not entirely unjustifiable, the population of the Rhine sharing with that of the Low Countries both their Romanic and Germanic characteristics, and asserting from time to time their desire to lead a free and independent life. This desire was never fulfilled, owing partly to the main direction of the line of race-demarcation running from north to south, parallel to the political frontier, and partly to the narrowness of the strip of territory involved. Had such a boundary extended through Belgium along the Scheldt, for instance, instead of being deflected from Cologne to Boulogne, the same result would have occurred. Belgium owes her independent state to the presence of the Coal Wood which, in the fourth century, broke the invaders' efforts along a line running from east to west across political frontiers, not parallel to them. Thanks to the exceptional richness of her widespread plain, easily accessible from the sea, she remains, in modern times, as the last fragment of the great Empire of Lotharius, which, for a few years, gathered under one rule all the borderlands of Western Europe.

Emile Cammaerts

Chapter X The Town Halls

The most characteristic monument of the fifteenth century in Belgium is the Town Hall, just as the most characteristic monument of the two preceding centuries is the belfry, with, or without, its Cloth Hall.

THE TOWN HALL, BRUGES.
(Fourteenth-fifteenth century). *Ph. B.*

GOTHIC TOWN HALLS

It may seem strange that it should be left to great municipal palaces to express the spirit of a period of centralization, when local privileges were progressively sacrificed to the general interest of the State, and when the prince gathered under one sway the various States among which the Netherlands had been divided. When looking at the Gothic Town Halls of Brussels, Louvain and Bruges, with their flowered traceries and luxury of ornament, one might be misled into taking them for the palaces of the prince rather than for the expression of municipal freedom. There is nothing about them of the strength and defiance expressed in the great "halles" and belfries of Ypres, Bruges and Ghent. The latter were, as we have seen, erected for two purposes. They were, so to speak, a central citadel raised in the middle of the town, from the towers of which the sentinel sounded the alarm and called the citizens to arms to defend their privileges and protect their homes against the attacks of any enemy from outside, not excluding the prince himself. Behind their thick walls and battlements, the archives and charters of the towns were jealously preserved. On the other hand, the "halles" afforded a meeting-place for foreign and local merchants and a warehouse where their goods were stored. They constituted fortified covered markets, and the combination of these military and economic characteristics is visible in every outline of the building and reveals the dominant aspirations of an age which succeeded in emancipating the city from the autocratic rule of the suzerain and in safeguarding the trade and industry of its inhabitants.

None of these features is apparent in the "hôtels de ville" of the Burgundian period. Their slender outline and small proportions exclude any idea of defence. Compare, for instance, the graceful spire of Brussels with the proud and massive belfry of Bruges, and the almost feminine aspect of the Louvain Town Hall with the forbidding masculinity of the destroyed Ypres Cloth Hall. Again, the profusion of ornament and statuettes, the delicate flanking towers, especially in Bruges and Louvain, contrast with the austerity of the old "halles." These luxurious mansions were built neither for military nor for economic purposes. They are far too small to be of any use as covered markets. In fact, the new municipal buildings of the fifteenth century only preserved one characteristic of their predecessors. They were still the seat of the "échevinage," and it was within their walls that the magistrates of the town met the duke's representative, the "bailli."

Economic activity had left the central hall and migrated to the Exchange. The achievement of the Hôtels de Ville of Brussels (1454) and Louvain (1463) coincides with the foundation of the first European Exchange in Antwerp (1460). In this transformation of the municipal buildings from the Middle Ages to the early Renaissance, we may read a parallel transformation in political and social institutions. The municipal spirit was still predominant, and the resistance made by Bruges in 1436, and still more energetically by Ghent from 1450 to 1453, to the increasing influence of Philip the Good, shows clearly that the communal spirit was still prevalent, especially in the old towns. But the relatively more modern towns, such as Brussels and Antwerp, were ready to accept the beneficial protection of the princes. The villages and the country, which had suffered for a long time from the tyranny of the large towns, were all on his side. The transformation of industry and trade contributed to break down local mediæval customs and privileges, to the greater benefit of the State. The result was a compromise, and it is that compromise which is revealed by Burgundian municipal architecture. The town was still exalted, but it was no longer the free defiant town which wrested its charters from a reluctant suzerain; it was, if one may so express it, a tamed town, developing its resources under the protection and the control of its master, while still keeping alive its pride by a great display of luxury. The failure of the Ghent revolt marked the decline of the communal militias, which were no longer able to resist the well disciplined ducal mercenary army. The defeat of Gavere (1453) sealed the fate of citizen armies, just as the Battle of the Golden Spurs (1302) had revealed their strength.

POLICY OF THE DUKES

It must, however, be remarked that this success was only obtained by a complete change of policy on the part of the dukes. They no longer, like their mediæval predecessors, opposed the development of the towns by oppressive measures. On the contrary, they did all in their power to protect and expand this prosperity, not only by securing peace and commercial liberty, but also by taking special measures in case of emergency. Philip the Good, on several occasions, attempted to arrest the decadence of Ypres caused by the development of the English cloth industry. In spite of the opposition of Ghent and Ypres, Charles the Bold undertook important works in order to dredge the estuary of the Zwyn, which was rapidly silting up, and thus to keep open, if possible, the port of Bruges. At the same time, the dukes encouraged the trade of Antwerp and gave the first impulse to the maritime activity of the ports of Holland. The Burgundian princes did not live isolated in their feudal castles; they made it a rule to reside in their large towns, either Ghent, Bruges or Brussels, where they held their courts and where they contributed, by their display of luxury, to the general prosperity. This solicitude for the welfare of the large towns was not altogether disinterested. The dukes realized that their power rested not so much on their military forces as on their wealth, and that their wealth depended on the riches of their towns. They understood, according to a contemporary historian (Chastellain), that "in the fullness of substance and money, not in dignities and highness of their rank, lay the glory and the power of princes."

The substitution of the Renaissance Hôtel de Ville for the old Cloth Hall is also the symbol of the decline of the cloth industry. The wool industry in Flanders had passed through three consecutive stages which directly affected the relationships between Belgium and England. We have seen how, during the early Middle Ages, Flemish wool being sufficient for Flemish looms, the cloth industry was almost entirely independent, and how, as the industry increased, Flemish weavers depended more and more on the imports of English wool during the thirteenth and fourteenth centuries. During the fourteenth century, however, owing partly to the immigration of Flemish weavers encouraged by Edward III and partly to the natural course of events, which must induce a country to work up its own raw material, the English cloth industry had become very active, and the quantity of wool available for Flanders consequently decreased, while its price increased, and the Flemish industry was faced by the double difficulty of preserving its market from the import of English cloth, through Hanseatic ships, and of obtaining the necessary raw material. The restrictive measures taken against the import of English cloth proved ineffectual, and Spanish wool, which was tried as a substitute for English, was of inferior quality. Ypres was the first to suffer, in spite of the solicitude of the dukes, who reduced commercial taxes in its favour. Its population fell from 12,000 in 1412 to 10,000 in 1470, and in 1486 one-third of its inhabitants were reduced to begging. Bruges succeeded in maintaining herself for a time through her banking establishments, while Ghent benefited from thestaple of grain, Brussels from the presence of the dukes, Malines from its parliament, Louvain from its newly created university and Antwerp from its rising trade.

LINEN AND TAPESTRY

Besides, when the resistance to English rivalry proved fruitless, in spite of the repeated prohibitions decreed by Philip the Good, the country turned, with extraordinary adaptability, to the linen industry as a substitute for the woollen. Linen replaced cloth, and the same processes and looms which had been applied to the old industry were successfully applied to the new. Clothmaking took refuge either in the Flemish country districts, where the wages were lower, or in some remote parts of the Walloon country. The existence of Verviers as a clothmaking town dates from 1480. The decline of the cloth industry was also to a certain extent compensated for by the introduction in Northern Flanders and in Brabant of tapestry, whose centres, until then, had been in Arras and Tournai.

Belgium

I have already alluded to the ornamental character of Burgundian Gothic contrasting with the severity of the communal period. Luxury rather than strength is aimed at by the architects of the hôtels de ville and other well-known monuments of the period, such as the Hôtel Gruthuse and the Chapelle du Saint Sang in Bruges. This richness is real, and not artificially confined to the prince and the upper classes of society.

At the beginning of the Burgundian régime, under Philip the Bold, Flanders was partially ruined by internal and external wars. Its towns were depleted of their craftsmen, its polders converted into marshes by the incursions of the sea, and wolves and wild boars again wandered through the country as in the early Middle Ages. Brabant, Holland, Zeeland and Liége, though less severely affected, passed through a time of strife and civil war. Fifty years later (about 1430), the Low Countries were again the most prosperous States of Europe, and the historian Philip de Commines was able to call them "a land of promise," while Gachard contrasts them with the southern domains of the duke, "Burgundy, which lacks money and smells of France." Chastellain eloquently vaunts their banquets and gorgeous festivities. The dukes themselves took every opportunity to display their wealth, especially in the presence of foreign princes. It seems as if they wanted to make up for the title of king which they vainly coveted by an ostentatious luxury which no king of the time could have afforded. When, in 1456, the Dauphin Louis visited Bruges with the duke, the decoration of the town amazed the French, "who had never witnessed such riches" (Chastellain), and when Margaret of York entered the town, on the occasion of her marriage with Charles the Bold, in 1469, the streets were covered with cloth of gold, silks and tapestries, and the procession had to stop ten times before reaching the market-place to admire tableaux vivants illustrating the periods of sacred and profane history: "By my troth," wrote John Paston, one of the English gentlemen who attended Margaret's wedding, "I heard never of so great plenty as there is, and, as for the duke's court, as for lords, ladies and gentlewomen, knights, squires and gentlemen, I heard never of none like to it save King Arthur's court."

MANNERS OF THE TIMES

This astounding economic recovery must not, it is true, be attributed only to the beneficial action of the dukes' administration, but it seems evident that a long period of peace, guaranteeing order, security and free communication with other countries, combined with wise administrative and financial measures, contributed greatly to hasten it. Measures were taken to lighten the restrictions and monopolies of towns and corporations and to regulate and control the minting of money. As early as 1483, Philip the Good was able to boast that his money was better than that of any of his neighbours. The right of coining money was no longer farmed out, but entrusted "to notables well known for their wealth, who could provide the country with gold and silver money and exchange any money which might be brought to them by the merchants." In 1469 Edward IV of England and Charles the Bold agreed to call a conference in Bruges to determine a common currency for both countries and to suppress the exchange.

ANTWERP AND BRUGES

These financial regulations are intimately connected with the transformation which trade underwent at the time, and which was one of the main causes of the transfer of the economic centre of the country from Bruges to Antwerp. The reason generally given for this change is a geographical one. It is pointed out that while, at the beginning of the fifteenth century, the widening of the western branch of the Scheldt through inundations in Zeeland afforded a direct road from Antwerp to the high-seas (formerly ships had to go round the Island of Walcheren), all the efforts made to prevent the silting up of the Zwyn from 1470 to 1490 were fruitless. In 1506, it was possible for carts to drive safely at low tide across the end of the harbour. The progress of navigation, increasing the tonnage of ships, and the Spanish and Portuguese discoveries acted also in favour of the deeper and safer harbour, but there are other reasons which might have ruined Bruges in favour of Antwerp, even if the geographical advantages of both ports had remained equal.

From the beginning of the fifteenth century the conditions of trade underwent complete transformation. Powerful companies, disposing of large capital and wide credit, took the place of the old local merchant companies. Transactions became so considerable and involved that mediæval regulations, instead of controlling commerce, only hampered it. Any protective measure detrimental to foreigners became fatal to home trade. Antwerp, which then appeared as a new metropolis, had no difficulty in adapting itself to modern capitalist conditions. At the end of the fourteenth century the town had already lost its Brabançon character and had become almost cosmopolitan. It had adopted economic liberty. Foreign merchants meeting at its fairs were protected by safe conducts. The positions of brokers and money-changers were open to all, and citizenship easily accessible. Bruges, on the other hand, hampered by old regulations and closely attached to its privileges, was not able to adapt itself to the new situation. As late as 1477 measures were taken to prevent foreigners from introducing on the market wares purchased elsewhere, and their position was no longer in accordance with the principle of free trade. It thus happened that, while the population of Antwerp increased by leaps and bounds, from 3,440 families in 1435 to 8,785 in 1526, the trade of Bruges decreased steadily, owing to the emigration of foreign merchants. Protective measures against the import of English cloth estranged the Hanseatic merchants, and, in 1442, the "Merchant Adventurers" established themselves definitely in Antwerp, where they were soon followed by the Italians, Spanish and Portuguese. It is true that Bruges remained, for a time, the centre of banking activity, which accounts for the fact that it preserved its architectural and artistic splendour at the very time when its trade was failing. But in the natural course of events the financiers had to follow the merchants, and at the end of the century the decadence of Bruges as a great seaport was almost as complete as that of Ypres as an industrial centre. It was characteristic of the new trade conditions that no "halles" were built in Antwerp, the mediæval emporium being replaced by a modern exchange.

Antwerp, however, possessed with Bruges one common feature. It was, like its predecessor, the great clearing-house of Western Europe, and derived its prosperity not from the goods either consumed or manufactured in its own country, but from its position as an open market where all merchants could conveniently sell their own wares and buy those of distant lands.

Belgium

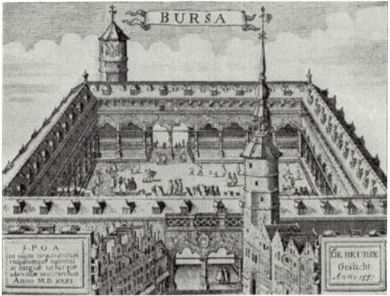

THE FIRST ANTWERP EXCHANGE.
From an old print (1531).

It must also be noticed that, while Bruges resisted as far as lay in its power the centralizing influence of the dukes and of the princes who succeeded them, Antwerp remained loyal to the new political régime which brought it so many advantages. The troubles which arose in Bruges under Maximilian may be considered as the death-blow to the prosperity of the old town.

THE TOWN HALL, OUDENARDE.
(Fifteenth century). *Ph. B.*

The rule of the dukes was equally beneficial to the smaller towns and villages of the country-side. It put an end to the mediæval régime and to feudal and ecclesiastical dues. The nobility had no longer the monopoly of landownership, and many bourgeois enriched by trade bought large estates. This change contributed, to a certain extent, to decrease the number of small landowners and to create a larger class of farmers and agricultural labourers. This was, however, partially compensated for by the reclamation of land from the sea (polders) through the building of dykes and by the impulse given to cattle breeding, which rendered more intensive cultivation possible. It was at that time that the old system of leaving a third of the land fallow was to a great extent abolished through a larger use of manure. With the exception of the famine of 1348, due to bad crops, the Burgundian régime was free from the terrible calamities which had never ceased to devastate the country during the previous centuries.

POPULATION

Through the census made for Brabant in 1435 and for Flanders in 1469, it is possible to estimate the total population of the Burgundian States in the Netherlands at two millions, to which 700,000 ought to be added if we include Liége. This, considering the size of these States and the economic conditions of the period, is a very high figure, and implies an economic activity at least equal to that of modern Belgium. How far such a rise in the population was due to the wise administration of Philip the Good is shown by a closer inspection of the facts. The years from 1435 to 1464 are marked by a steady increase, while the period from 1464 to 1472, when Charles the Bold imperilled the prosperity of the country by his foreign wars, shows a slow decrease, which becomes far more accentuated after the death of the duke and during the troubled period which succeeded the Burgundian rule.

Emile Cammaerts

Chapter XI The Adoration Of The Lamb

The hôtels de ville built during the Burgundian period afford an excellent example of the new economic tendencies prevailing at the time, but they are by no means the greatest works of art illustrating this period of Belgian efflorescence. Neither in the Town Hall of Bruges, begun in 1376 by Jean de Valenciennes, nor in those of Brussels (1402 to 1444), built by Jacques van Thienen and Jean de Ruysbroeck, or of Louvain, completed in 1448 by Matthieu de Layens, still less in the pretty municipal buildings of Oudenarde or destroyed Arras, can we find any adequate representation of the wonderful intellectual and artistic movement which placed the Netherlands, during the fifteenth century, at the head of Northern European civilization. This can only be realized by a careful study of the pictures of the period, generally known as the works of the Early Flemish School.

INTELLECTUAL MOVEMENT

Before trying to determine the position of this school in the history of Art, it may be well to give a rapid survey of the intellectual movement under the Burgundian régime, and to show that in every department, literature, architecture and music, the civilization of the period produced some remarkable works. In this way, the Netherlands of the fifteenth century are comparable with the Italian republics and principalities which flourished at the same time. In Belgium, as in Tuscany and Umbria, all arts were cultivated at the same time and sometimes by the same man, and people and princes took an equal interest in all the manifestations of human genius. One would have to go back as far as ancient Greece to find such a harmonious development, and the world has never produced it since.

Literary activity was perhaps the least brilliant, owing mostly to the division of languages. Though the intercourse between the Flemish and the Walloon parts of the country was intimate and never constituted an obstacle in the work of unification, Belgium can scarcely boast of one common literature at the time when its nationality was founded.

As far as political and administrative activity was concerned, an almost exact balance was struck between the languages of the North and the South. In Flanders, from the beginning of the fourteenth century, French influence had considerably decreased, owing partly to the loss of Artois and Walloon Flanders and to the blow inflicted on French prestige by the reverses of the Hundred Years' War. The use of French was only maintained among the nobility and the rich bourgeoisie, and in all intercourse with other countries; Flemish made considerable progress and took the place of Latin in all acts of common administration. Its prestige as a literary language had been enhanced by the reputation of van Maerlant, and it served also in all relations with Lower Germany. By the end of the century, bilingualism was a consecrated institution both in Flanders and Brabant, the judges rendering their sentences in the tongue spoken by the parties and some officials using, according to circumstances, either French, Latin or Flemish. Under John the Fearless and Philip the Good, this situation, which favoured the centralizing influence of the dukes, remained unchanged. In Holland and Zeeland, where French was practically unknown, State officials only used Flemish. The dukes themselves knew both languages, included Flemish books in their libraries, and encouraged Flemish letters. Owing to the economic attraction of Antwerp, a great number of Walloon traders used both languages, and the number of those who understood Flemish and French was considerable enough to allow the production of Flemish plays to the south and of French plays to the north of the dividing language line. It is true that Charles the Bold attempted vainly to enforce French for administrative purposes in Flemish districts, but, owing to subsidiary evidence, this must be considered much more as an act of political absolutism than as a sign of hostility towards Flemish. As a matter of fact, we should seek vainly for proof of any attempt to frenchify the country at the time. In holding their courts in the Netherlands, the dukes of Burgundy had renounced their French origin.

Bilingualism must thus be considered as a solution of the language question in Belgium in the fifteenth century. But though the people remained united, the literatures of the two parts of the country followed different lines.

On the Flemish side, poetry had never ceased to decline since the death of van Maerlant, in spite of the numerous works produced by thedisciples of this master, especially in Brabant. Jean Boendaele (1280-1365) described in his remarkable *Brabantsche Yeesten* the struggle of the duke against his enemies. His attitude of mind is thoroughly typical of the time. Boendaele is a bourgeois poet, and distrusts equally the democracy of the towns and the nobility. He places his faith in the prince, the merchants and the peasants.

JAN RUYSBROECK

The mystic treatises of Jan Ruysbroeck (1292-1381), who may be considered as the founder of Flemish prose, just as van Maerlant is the founder of Flemish poetry, are far more important than the rhymed chronicles of Boendaele. Not only do they rank among the most inspired religious writings of the Middle Ages, but they are the expression of a deep-rooted religious movement which animated the Flemish bourgeoisie at the time, and which had its origin in the foundation of the institution of the Béguines and the Beggards, so active and so influential during the twelfth century. This movement aimed at bringing religion closer to the common people through the work of laymen who, though deeply attached to the Church, were conscious of its limitations and of the barrier which aristocracy and privilege had built around it. One of Ruysbroeck's disciples, Gérard de Groote (1340-84), founded the Order of the "Frères de la Vie Commune" (Brothers of the Common Life), and the "Sustershuysen," which contributed so much to the revival of religious studies and general education in the early days of the fifteenth century. Like the Beggards, the Brothers did not strictly constitute a religious order, they did not pronounce any binding vow and retained their lay character. Refusing any gift or endowment from outside, they had to provide for their own needs, but, while the Beggards devoted most of their time to the weaving industry, the Brothers gave themselves up to copying manuscripts, learning and teaching. Under Florent Radewyn, one of de Groote's early disciples, they acquired a very complete organization and founded numerous schools, specially in Brussels (1422) and in Ghent (1432), their influence spreading as far as Germany. Thierry Maertens, the first well-known Belgian printer, was one of their pupils. This educational and religious revival is closely connected with the foundation of the University of

Louvain in 1426. De Groote and his disciples were frequently attacked, chiefly by the monks, who became jealous of their success, but their strict orthodoxy and the unimpeachable character of their life made their position unassailable. De Groote was equally well known for his criticism of the abuses among the clergy, his denunciation of the luxury displayed by the rich and the mystic character of his preaching. He was equally severe against heretics, and was called by his contemporaries "malleus hereticorum." Another of his followers founded the celebrated monastery of Windesheim, where, half a century later, the *Imitation of Christ* was written.

While the Flemish writers of the fourteenth and fifteenth centuries wrote mostly for the bourgeoisie and the people and kept in close contact with the religious aspirations of the time, the authors belonging to the Walloon part of the country were nearly all attached to some court and confined themselves to the production of chronicles and mémoires destined for the aristocracy. Though extremely limited, this genre was cultivated with great success by the Walloon writers and is typical of the Belgian branch of the French letters of the period. As early as the fourteenth century, Jean Le Bel of Liége had related with extraordinary vividness his adventures at the court of Hainault and the part played by his master, Jean de Beaumont, in the expedition led by Edward III against the Scots. Le Bel writes in French, but as far as his political views are concerned remains impervious to French influence and chooses an English King, "le noble roi Edowart," for his hero, while he has nothing but harsh words for Philip de Valois.

JEAN FROISSART

Jean Froissart, of Valenciennes, who continued the work of Le Bel and served as a link between him and the Burgundian school of chroniclers, had a much wider field of vision. Attached successively to Albert of Bavaria, Queen Philippa of England and Wenceslas of Luxemburg, he had many opportunities to study European affairs, and, as a Belgian, was able to consider them from an independent and even a sceptical point of view. Though generally considered as a French writer, he remains independent of French influence. With Monstrelet, Chastellain, Jean Molinet and Jean Lemaire de Belges, who wrote for the dukes of Burgundy, this independent attitude is still further strengthened. All these writers extolled the Burgundian régime and supported the duke's policy, whether friendly or antagonistic to France. From a literary point of view, they are greatly inferior to their predecessors and often lapse into rhetorical eloquence. Their style, which appears to be overloaded with flowery images, excited great admiration at the time, especially in the case of Chastellain, who was hailed by his contemporaries as a "supreme rhetorician."

Music was not hampered, like literature, by the division of languages, and might, under different circumstances, have given a more accurate expression to the Belgian national spirit. Its style was, unhappily, still so formal that national characteristics cannot immediately be recognized in the works of Guillaume Dufay, of Chimay (1350-1432) and Giles de Binche, Chapelmasters to Philip the Good, and those of the Fleming Jean Ockeghem (dec. 1494-6) and of Josquin des Prés, of Hainault (c. 1450-1521). These musicians, who enjoyed European celebrity and exerted a widespread influence on the musical movement in France and Italy, are

Belgium

well known to musical historians as having largely contributed to the development of polyphonic music as opposed to the monody of the Gregorian chant. They were thus pioneers in the art of musical ornamentation, and their method may be associated with the flowery images of Chastellain's style, the architectural luxury of Burgundian Gothic and the display of colouring of the early Flemish painters. In all branches of intellectual activity, Belgium enters decidedly, from the beginning of the fifteenth century, into the Renaissance period. But, unlike the Italian, the Belgian Renaissance was at first only very slightly affected by the study of the classics. It was more realistic in its aims than the mediæval period. It revelled in the display of harmony, whether in sound, colour or form, and abundance of tracery, but as far as the subject was concerned it remained essentially and profoundly Christian.

SOCIAL LIFE

Though the works of Belgian writers and artists of the period are very remarkable, they are somewhat misleading if we want to form an accurate idea of social life in the fifteenth century. Neither the *Libri Teutonici*, published by Ruysbroeck's followers, nor the great paintings of the brothers Van Eyck, Van der Weyden and Memling, suggest for one moment the laxity of morals prevalent at the time and revealed by the writers of the Chronicles. The number of illegitimate births was extraordinarily high, the example being set by the dukes themselves, Philip the Good alone being responsible for eighteen bastards and Jean de Heinsberg, Bishop of Liége, for nearly as many. It must be pointed out, however, that the illegitimate character of their birth did not stand in the way of many prominent men of the time, such as the Chancellor Rolin, the Dean of St. Donatian of Bruges, the great financier Pierre Bladelin, the Bishop of Tournai and many high officials. All these had, of course, received their letters of legitimation. Numerous edicts made by the dukes were unable to check gambling, prostitution and prodigality. The scant effect of the regulations relating to the latter may be easily understood when we read that, on the occasion of the marriage of Margaret of York to Charles the Bold, Belgian artists and artisans were ordered to prepare and to decorate a large wooden house which was subsequently transported by water from Brussels to Bruges. In a tower 41 feet high attached to this house, the noble company invited to the ceremony witnessed the movements and heard the cries of a number of mechanical animals, monkeys, wolves and boars, while a whale 60 feet long moved around the hall together with elephants, amid thirty large trees, a fountain of crystal and a pelican "spouting hippocras from his beak." The fact is that the situation in the Netherlands, in the second half of the fifteenth century, was very much the same as that in Florence at the same time, the people being swayed between an exuberant enjoyment of life and a severe asceticism. There are many points of contact between Charles the Bold and Lorenzo the Magnificent, and no figure comes closer to Savonarola than that of the Carthusian, Thomas Conecte, who stirred public feeling to such a pitch that the people crowding to listen to his fiery speeches, in market-places, threw into the braziers burning before his platform all the instruments of their worldly life—chessboards, cards, dice, skittles, silks and jewels.

Strangely enough, no religious order benefited more from the sympathy and generosity of the people than the ascetic Carthusians. Philip the Bold erected in Dijon the famous Chartreuse of Champmol; Philip the Good and Margaret of York corresponded with the celebrated Carthusian Denys de Ryckel, the "doctor extaticus," and the Chartreuse of Louvain was endowed by rich bourgeois of the duke's entourage. Unless this apparent contradiction is fully realized, it is impossible to understand the spirit of an epoch which, though deeply absorbed by its worldly life, produced works almost wholly devoted to Faith, and in which luxurious garments and colours are only employed to enhance the glory of God.

THE BROTHERS VAN EYCK

Painting stands foremost among the achievements of the Burgundian period. Here again the difference of language does not hamper the genius of the nation. While in music the Walloon element dominates, the Flemish dominates in Art; but it must be clearly stated that, in this branch, as in all other branches of Burgundian civilization, the two parts of the country are strongly represented, and that the title of "Flemish School of Painting" is therefore misleading when referring to Belgian painting of the fifteenth century.

The greatest name associated with the period is that of the brothers Jan and Hubert Van Eyck, and the work which naturally comes to the mind, when thinking of them, is the monumental altarpiece which they painted for Jos. Vyt, lord of Pamele, to be placed in his chapel in the Cathedral of St. John in Ghent. This work, generally known as the "Mystic Lamb," is composed of ten smaller pictures, but the partitions separating the various divisions of the wings and the wings from the central piece scarcely detract from the majesty of the ensemble. The composition is well known: Above, God the Father, as Christ, enthroned, His hand raised in benediction, between St. John Baptist and the Virgin, with angels on both sides singing and playing on various instruments. On the extreme right and left of the upper panels, excluded, so to speak, from the company of heaven, stand Adam and Eve, in all the realistic weakness of their nakedness. Below, in the midst of a flowery meadow, behind the fountain of life, surrounded by groups of holy virgins, martyrs and saints, in the New Paradise, under the walls of the New Jerusalem, stands the Lamb, directly under the figure of Christ and the symbol of the Holy Ghost, the centre towards which every line, every attitude in the picture converges. Towards the holy spot walk, on the right, the pilgrims and the hermits, on the left, the good judges and the soldiers of Christ. The symbolism of the picture which enfolds the majestic plan of the redemption of man through Christ's sacrifice, of the second creation through the Spirit, as contrasted with the first creation through the flesh, is directly inspired by the mystic writings of the time, while the harmony and depth of colours, the gorgeous robes and jewels adorning the figures of God, the Virgin and the angels, the pompous cavalcade of knights and judges and the systematic grouping of the central scene, are an adequate expression of the love of ceremony and solemn luxury which characterized the Burgundian age. The whole picture appears as a sacred pageant in which the saints, the angels and the blessed take the place of nobles, ladies and clerics, as they were seen during the festivities and processions arranged at the ducal court.

Belgium

THE ADORATION OF THE LAMB (SAINT BAVON, GHENT).
Angels singing and playing.

THE MYSTIC LAMB

Considered as a purely religious picture, this work, like almost all the works of the school, stands in striking contrast to Italian fourteenth-century painting, especially as illustrated by the frescoes of Giotto. The latter are characterized by an extreme simplicity of outline and by vivid narrative power. In Padua, for instance, Giottotells us the story of Christ as he saw it in his mystical vision, without any concern for accessories or detail. He clings to essentials, to the figures of Christ and his apostles, while scorning any subordinate object, such as trees, architecture, costumes, etc., which are only represented in a rude fashion when necessary to the story. It is characteristic of Hubert Van Eyck's work (since, according to all evidence, Hubert must be considered as the author of the general outlines of the picture, which was finished by his brother Jan after his death) that perhaps the least satisfactory figure of the Adoration of the Lamb is the Deity, while our attention is immediately captured by the group of angels surrounding Him, and still more by the procession of worshippers at the bottom of the picture. To put it briefly, whereas Giotto's art is at its best when dealing with the *divine* side of the Christian drama, Van Eyck's genius stands foremost in the *human* interpretation of the subject. His greatest creations are not the figures of the worshipped but of the worshippers, and we must seek for religious inspiration not so much in the direct vision of the Divinity as in the expression of devotion reflected on the faces of the adoring crowds.

THE ADORATION OF THE LAMB (SAINT BAVON, GHENT).
The Annunciation (exterior of the shutters).
Hubert and Jan van Eyck.

It is true that we may find the same insistence on landscape, costume and the portraits of donors in the works of the Italian artists of the Early Renaissance, who painted at the same time as Van Eyck, and that the spirit of the period may, to a certain extent, account for it. But it would be difficult to discover in the pictures of Masaccio, Fra Filippo Lippi, Ghirlandajo, Botticelli and the other masters of the Italian fifteenth century, with the sole exception of Fra Angelico, the same depth of religious inspiration which pervades the works of the Van Eycks and of their disciples. If the Gospel story still provides most of the subjects of the Italian school, it is treated in a lighter vein, and pagan inspiration, prompted by the study of classics, is more and more conspicuous. Earthly loveliness is of greater importance than Christian teaching.

The virgins of Van Eyck, the Pietà of Van der Weyden and the saints of Memling occupy the intermediate position between the purely mediæval attitude of

Belgium

Giotto and of the sculptors of the French cathedrals and the worldly atmosphere of the Early Italian Renaissance. They preserve, to a great extent, the religious atmosphere of the former, and devote the same attention to technical skill and realistic representation as the second. The combination of these two elements is the chief source of originality of the Burgundian school of painters, and it is truly characteristic of the period, which, though strongly attached to the world and its pleasures, founded its greatest productions on the stern lessons of deep devotion and of a society in which the Beggards and the Brothers of the Common Life strove incessantly to bring religion closer to the heart of the people.

The Adoration of the Lamb is not only the most complete expression of the spirit of Belgium in the fifteenth century, it is also the first great work produced by Belgian painters. Art critics have been at great pains to explain the sudden appearance in history of such a highly skilled and complete production. But a closer study of Belgian civilization in the fourteenth century would show that it is merely the outcome of previous efforts and the blossoming of a great individual genius in an Art which had already found, in other departments, very remarkable means of expression.

SCULPTURE

From the end of the twelfth century, Belgian Art, as shown by the works of the goldsmiths, decorators, sculptors and miniaturists, had become independent of German and French influence. A highly trained class of artisans was formed, and, in the middle of the fourteenth century, was organized into regular corporations. Goldsmiths and decorators devoted their talent to the embellishment of churches and ecclesiastical treasures, as well as to decoration of secular buildings such as Cloth Halls or Town Halls and to the designing of banners for the guilds. We still possess a great number of engraved tombstones which reveal an extraordinary development of technique. Soon the figure of the deceased was raised in high relief, and even, as in the tomb of the Count of Artois in the cathedral of St. Denys, the work of Pepin of Huy, raised on the shoulders of standing figures. From the second half of the fourteenth century the most prominent sculptors ceased to be considered as mere artisans. Hennequin of Liége was attached to the court of the French king Charles V, while André Beauneveu (1364-90) remained in Flanders as the sculptor of Louis de Mâle. The striking sculptures of the pit of Moses, at Dijon, were executed by Claus Sluter of Zeeland. These statues, which bear comparison with those of Ghiberti and Donatello, Sluter's contemporaries, suffice to explain the sense of form and of line in the draperies revealed by the early Flemishmasters. In the North, as in the South, sculpture developed earlier than painting, and, just as Pisano precedes Giotto, Sluter precedes, and to a certain extent explains, the brothers Van Eyck. The influence of sculpture on painting is made evident from the fact that many statues of the time were gilded and coloured, painters being frequently called in to perform this part of the work. Besides, many sculptors such as Beauneveu and Hennequin were equally skilled in the art of painting. The result of these influences is shown in the *Book of Hours* of the Duke of Berry, the work of Pol de Limburg, and in the pictures painted in Dijon for Philip the Bold by Melchior Broederlam. The latter's Annunciation, Presentation in the Temple and Flight into Egypt prepare the way for the Adoration of the Lamb, though far from being equal to it. These pictures serve as a link between the Belgian Art of the fifteenth and the fourteenth centuries. The difference to be accounted for is certainly not larger than that separating, a century before, the frescoes of Giotto from the works of Cimabue and his school.

"PLOURANT".
Detail of the tomb of John the Fearless (Dijon Museum).
Netherlandish School of the fifteenth century.

FLEMISH SCHOOL

It would be impossible here to characterize the works of the various masters who followed in the wake of the brothers Van Eyck. Of the two brothers, hailing from Maeseyck, we know that Hubert settled in Ghent (c.1410) and Jan in Bruges in 1425. Roger de la Pasture, usually known as Van der Weyden, the foremost representative of the Walloon branch of the school, came from Tournai to Brussels in 1435. There were other Walloons, such as Robert Campin and Jacques Daret of Tournai, but the Flemish element, represented beside the brothers Van Eyck by the Brabançon Pieter Christus, Justus van Ghent, Hughes Van der Goes (of Ghent)

Belgium

and Thierry Bouts of Harlem, not to mention Memling (of Mayence), was manifestly prevalent. The renown enjoyed by these artists extended far beyond the limits of Belgium and France, and the influence exerted by their works in Italy can easily be traced. Strangely enough, while during the next century the Belgian painters were subjected so strongly to Italian influence, they were hailed, at this period, as pioneers by the Italians themselves. At home, the consideration which the great painters enjoyed is shown by the interest displayed in their work not only by the prince but also by his courtiers, among them Chancellor Rolin, and by rich foreigners, such as the Portinari and the Arnolfini established in Flanders. Philip the Good visited Jan Van Eyck frequently, was godfather to his daughter, and employed him on several occasions for secret missions. His position at the court of Burgundy was equal to that occupied later by Rubens at the court of Albert and Isabella.

Chapter XII Hapsburg And Burgundy

The disaster of Nancy naturally provoked a strong reaction in the Belgian provinces. We have seen that the large towns bore only with great reluctance the centralized rule of Philip the Good, in spite of the moderation and the diplomatic talents of this prince. In the latter part of his reign, Charles the Bold had completely disregarded local privileges and relentlessly crushed every attempt at rebellion. He raised taxes for his foreign expeditions which weighed heavily on the people. More and more absorbed by his struggle against Louis XI, he neglected internal affairs, and the Belgians were loath to support an expensive policy of foreign adventures which could only be detrimental to their own interests. Mary of Burgundy was thus left alone, in 1477, to confront, on one side the exigencies of the towns and States, and on the other the intrigues of Louis XI. The latter had not only confiscated the duke's French dominions, as soon as the news of his death reached him, but he proposed, with the support of the disaffected towns, to appropriate as well his Northern provinces. Fearing English interference, he thought of striking a bargain with the King of England and offered to conquer Brabant for him. Very wisely, Edward IV retorted that the province would be too difficult to hold and that "a war with the Netherlands would not be popular in England owing to the active trade between the two countries." Left to his own devices, Louis succeeded in persuading the Flemings that a marriage between Mary and the dauphin would be the most profitable solution of the crisis. On the refusal of the princess, who was already affianced to the Archduke Maximilian of Austria, the French king dropped the mask of friendship and invaded Hainault and Artois.

THE "GREAT PRIVILEGE"

By that time, Mary had given full satisfaction to the particularist demands by granting the "Great Privilege," which practically restored all provincial and urban liberties and brought to nought the patient work of centralization accomplished by the dukes. Under the threat of foreign invasion, the people rallied around her to the cry of "Vive Bourgogne!" and identified the cause of their national dynasty with that of their own independence. Arras was obliged to open its gates to the French armies, but Valenciennes and St. Omer made a desperate resistance. It was, however, evident that, under the circumstances, the Low Countries could not oppose the French advance without foreign help. The States therefore agreed to the marriage of Mary with Maximilian of Austria, who entered the country at the head of a small army.

This marriage proved fatal to the independence of the Low Countries, by bringing them more and more under the sway of the Hapsburg dynasty. In spite of their French possessions, the Burgundian princes had maintained a national policy, or, to speak more accurately, had, with the exception of Charles's last adventures, furthered their own interests to the greater benefit of the Belgian provinces. As far as foreign politics were concerned, they succeeded in remaining neutral between the three Powers surrounding them and in interfering in European affairs only when their possessions were directly threatened. There was no conflict between the economic and political interests of Belgium and those of the Burgundian dynasty. The dukes remained in the country and the welfare of the country was the essential condition of their own prosperity. Owing to the union of Maximilian with Mary of Burgundy, this situation was entirely altered. From the end of the fifteenth century to the time of the French Revolution, the Netherlands were more and more sacrificed to the interests of their masters, whether belonging to the Austrian or the Spanish branch of the Hapsburgs. They lost the benefit of the presence of their national and "natural" princes, who were absorbed in far more important affairs and spent most of their life out of the country. They were administered by regents or governors, who generally did not enjoy sufficient independence and authority to pursue a Netherlandish policy. They constituted a sort of outpost of the Power to which they were attached, and were, in consequence, first exposed to the attacks of the enemies of this Power. This is one of the main causes of the sixteenth-century revolution and the subsequent partition of the country, and of the decadence of the Southern provinces which became so evident during the seventeenth and eighteenth centuries.

For some time, however, the Hapsburg policy did not prevail, and it even appeared, at certain moments, as if a national dynasty might be restored. The Belgian States, and more especially the Belgian aristocracy, succeeded in influencing the princes and their governors, who, from time to time, reverted to a national policy. The story of the fifteenth and the sixteenth centuries in Belgium is composed of the struggle of the two opposing principles: the national Burgundian policy, based on peace and neutrality in European conflicts, and the Hapsburg policy, drawing the provinces in the wake of Hapsburg ambitions and rivalries.

Emile Cammaerts

MARY OF BURGUNDY.
From the mausoleum in the Church of Notre Dame, Bruges.

DEATH OF MARY

If Maximilian, after his victory at Guinegate, had limited his aims to the defence of the country and managed to conclude an early peace with Louis, the attitude of the people would no doubt have remained friendly. But, before being Mary's husband and the successor of the Burgundian dukes, he was an Austrian archduke, bound to pursue the policy of his House against France, whether it was to the interest of the Netherlands or not, and to oppose any local liberties which hampered his action. It is in this light that the intricate conflicts which arose between the archduke and the towns, more especially Ghent, must be viewed. The latter town rose against him, and even went as far as to re-enter into negotiations with France, far more to guard municipal liberties than from any friendly feeling towards that country. Mary died in 1482, leaving two children, Philip and Margaret, who had been entrusted to the care of Ghent. On the archduke's refusal to conclude peace, the Ghent deputies, reverting to the project of the French marriage, negotiated at Arras a treaty with Louis XI, according to which the young Princess Margaret was to marry the dauphin. Maximilian succeeded in defeating the Ghent militias, and transferred Philip from Ghent to Malines. But the Communes were not yet daunted. A rising occurred in Bruges and the citizens took Maximilian prisoner,

Belgium

obliging him, before restoring him to liberty, to abolish all the monarchical reforms which he had introduced since the granting of the Great Privilege. Bruges, however, was finally defeated, in 1490, and Ghent, which had allied itself with Charles VIII of France, in 1492. The next year peace was concluded at Senlis between Maximilian and Charles, who was compelled to restore Artois and Franche Comté. This date marks, for the time, the end of the stubborn fight waged by the towns against the central authority of the monarch and the triumph of the modern principle of the State against the mediæval principle of local privilege.

MAXIMILIAN I.
From a portrait by Ambrozio de Predis
(Imperial Museum, Vienna).

THE "JOYOUS ENTRY"

With the accession of Maximilian to the Empire (1493) and of his son Philip the Handsome, then sixteen years old, to the governance of Belgium, we witness a return to the traditional Burgundian policy on strictly national lines. The enthusiasm provoked by the change and the professions of loyalty made to Belgium's "natural prince" show how deep was the attachment for the Burgundian policy and how much Maximilian's foreign origin had counted against him. The new prince, who had never left his Belgian provinces and whose education had been entrusted to Belgian tutors, became the symbol of national independence, and all the restrictions which had been exacted from Mary of Burgundy and from Maximilian were allowed to lapse in his favour. He was not asked to ratify the Great Privilege nor the various promises made by Maximilian. His "Joyous Entry of Brabant" was very much on the same lines as those sworn previously by Philip the Good and Charles the Bold. The prince's commissaries were restored to their offices and had again the power to choose communal magistrates, thus removing them from the direct influence of the corporations. The Ducal Council was reappointed, and a special ordinance of 1495 provided for the reconstitution of the prince's estates. The Parliament of Malines was re-established under the name of "Grand Council." In fact, all the ground lost by centralization since the death of Charles the Bold was rapidly reconquered without any opposition, and the States General made no difficulty in granting the taxes. Such an extraordinary transformation can only be explained if we remember that almost all foreigners had been excluded from the Council of the prince. Out of fourteen councillors, two only were Germans and three of Burgundian origin. Philip himself did not even know German and had become estranged from his father. The readiness with which he accepted the counsels of his Belgian advisers, the Princes of Croy and the Counts of Berg and Lalaing, had gained for him the nickname of "Take-advice" (Croit-conseil).

Needless to say his foreign policy was entirely directed towards peace. In vain did Maximilian endeavour to lure him into his intrigues against France. Philip established the most cordial relations with Charles VIII. Henry VII of England, who had alienated Maximilian's sympathies since his reconciliation with France (the archduke having even encouraged the pretender Perkin Warbeck against him), and who had retaliated by transferring the staple of English cloth from Antwerp to Calais and by forbidding all trade with the Low Countries, was also pacified by Philip after some negotiations. In 1496, the two sovereigns signed the "Intercursus Magnus," which re-established commercial relations between the two countries. It is characteristic of the intimate economic connection between England and Belgium that they were the first to sign the most liberal treaty of commerce of the time.

In 1498, after a new attempt by Maximilian to enlist his support against Louis XII, Philip appealed to the States General, which strongly supported his pacific attitude. By the treaty of Paris, concluded in the same year, the Belgian prince went as far as renouncing his rights on Burgundy in order to maintain friendly relations and to keep the advantages granted by the treaty of Senlis. Philip the Handsome, in so doing, went farther than the dukes themselves: he deliberately sacrificed his dynastic interests to the welfare of the Northern provinces.

Belgium

PHILIP THE FAIR. JUANA OF CASTILE.
Portraits by an unknown Flemish painter of the sixteenth century.

PHILIP THE HANDSOME

This uncompromising attitude with regard to Belgian interests was unhappily not destined to be adhered to much longer by Philip. In 1495 he had been married to Juana of Castille, daughter of his father's allies, Ferdinand and Isabella. Through a series of deaths in the family, Juana became, in 1500, heiress to the throne of Spain. From this moment Philip's line of conduct changed, and the interests of the Low Countries were sacrificed to his dynastic ambitions. This brought about a reconciliation with Maximilian, who had at last succeeded in enlisting his son's support. On the death of Isabella, in 1504, Philip took the title of King of Castille in order to forestall the intrigues of his father-in-law, Ferdinand. With a view of securing the support of England, which had been somewhat estranged owing to the new policy followed by Philip, the latter concluded in 1506 a new treaty of commerce, very unsatisfactory from the Belgian point of view, and which was therefore called by the people the "Intercursus Malus." The new King of Spain died the same year, in Burgos, having lost a great deal of the popularity which he had so largely enjoyed during the first part of his reign.

The crisis which followed was not so severe as that of 1477, but was very similar to it. While protesting his friendship for the young Prince Charles of Luxemburg, then only six years old, Louis XII won the support of Erard de la Marck, Bishop of Liége, and endeavoured to influence the towns in order to exclude Maximilian from the Regency. Under the threat of French ambition, the States General, however, took the same line as after the death of Charles the Bold and sent a deputation to Germany. The Emperor chose his daughter, Margaret of Austria, aunt of Charles, to govern the Low Countries. This princess had not forgotten the affront she had suffered during her youth: when first affianced to Charles VIII she had been abducted by the French and subsequently restored to her father. Her hostility was, however, directed far more against the Valois than against France. Widow of Philibert of Savoy, she was the type of the great princess of the Renaissance, and combined an intense interest in Art and Letters with great diplomatic acumen. During the twenty-three years that she governed Belgium, she remained a foreigner to the people. She did not know either Flemish or German, and her culture as well as her surroundings remained entirely French. Devoted to her nephew, her first aim was to further his dynastic interests, but, being very independent of her father, whose Austrian policy she succeeded in checking several times, she was intelligent enough to realize that Charles's interests were also, at the time, those of the Netherlands. Her rule therefore struck a balance between the Hapsburg and the dynastic tendencies. Living a secluded life in her palace of Malines, and taking no part in the festivities so dear to the heart of the people, she governed the Netherlands without sympathy, but with enough wisdom for her ability to be recognized, on several occasions, both by the people and the nobility.

This was soon made apparent during the first year of her governance. She had to contend with the suspicions of the Belgian nobles, headed by Guillaume de Croy, Lord of Chièvres, whom Philip had appointed governor on leaving the country. The people of Ghent again became restive, while, owing to the intrigues of Louis XII, Robert de la Marck and the Duke of Gelder caused serious trouble in Luxemburg and in the North. The States General, on their side, clamoured for peace. While ordering the tax to be levied for war, in spite of the opposition of the States, Margaret managed to conclude with France the treaty of Cambrai. This caused great satisfaction all over the country. Chièvres was recalled to the court, where he acted as tutor to the prince. Again, in 1513, Margaret, who had been one of the principal agents in the League against France, which, besides the Emperor, included the Pope, the King of Aragon and the King of England, succeeded in maintaining the neutrality of the Low Countries, which, though benefiting from the allies' victory at Guinegate and from the taking of Tournai, had not to suffer from the military operations.

The opposition between Chièvres and the gouvernante was nevertheless constant. It had been embittered by a project of marriage between Charles and Princess Mary of England, which Margaret furthered for dynastic reasons, and which Chièvres opposed for fear of alienating France. The reconciliation which took place in 1514 between Louis XII and Henry VIII, and the marriage which followed between the French king and the English king's sister, Mary, were therefore a great disappointment to Margaret. Chièvres followed his advantage by estranging Maximilian from his daughter and by urging the States General to demand the emancipation of Charles, which was finally granted by the Emperor for a money consideration. Margaret, who had been kept in ignorance of these intrigues, though deeply hurt in her pride, could do nothing but accept the accomplished fact.

ACCESSION OF CHARLES V

The accession of Charles, which took place on January 5, 1515, was a triumph for Chièvres. The situation was exactly similar to that which prevailed when Philip the Handsome came into power. The youth of the prince, who, like his father, had received a Belgian education and was ignorant of German and Spanish, his veneration for Chièvres and his friendship for his Belgian counsellors, brought about a return to a purely national policy, to the exclusion of any dynastic tendencies. All foreigners were excluded from the Council, the confidants of Margaret and Maximilian became suspect, and a rapprochement was brought about with Francis I of France. A new commercial treaty was signed with Henry VIII, favouring, at the same time, relations with England.

This policy was not altered when, in 1516, through the death of Ferdinand and owing to the disability of Juana to succeed him, Charles took the title of King of Spain. Instead of countering Francis I's intrigues and his claims to the kingdom of Naples by military measures, Charles, still bent on maintaining peace with France, negotiated the treaty of Noyon, and succeeded in persuading Maximilian to agree to this treaty, in spite of the opposition of England. A few months later, the young king and his Belgian courtiers left for Spain (1517), Charles having meanwhile consented to become a candidate for the Empire.

CHARLES V.
From a contemporary engraving.
MARGARET OF AUSTRIA.
From a picture by Van Orley (1493-1542).

Emile Cammaerts

These events were bound to cause the same reaction towards a dynastic policy which had been provoked by the accession of Philip the Handsome to the throne of Spain. Once more Belgium lost her national prince and her interests were sacrificed to foreign ambitions. But Charles was so thoroughly Belgian in his sympathies and tastes that he succeeded, nevertheless, in retaining the friendship of the Belgian nobles. Spanish honours and titles were showered on Chièvres, Lalaing, Croy, Nassau and others, to the great annoyance of the Spanish, who had nothing but scorn for the boisterous manners of the Belgian nobility. A reconciliation was brought about between Chièvres and Margaret, who, after the death of Maximilian (1519), worked hard for the nomination of Charles as emperor. His election was loudly celebrated in Brussels and all over the country, for the people, delighted at the honour conferred on their prince, did not realize that henceforth their country was bound to be lost and neglected among Charles's huge possessions. It is true that the suzerainty of the Empire was purely nominal, but the bonds linking Belgium's destiny to Spain were far stronger, and the country acquired gradually the situation described above: she became an advance post, in the North, of the Spanish power, which was about the worst position she could occupy on the map of Europe, being cut off from Spain and isolated among her adversaries.

TREATY OF MADRID

This, however, was not yet apparent, and the protestations of friendship of the young emperor, who declared, in 1520, to the States General, that his heart had always been "par deça" (in the Netherlands), together with his military successes, which resulted in the signature of the treaty of Madrid (1525), were considered as a happy omen for the future. By this treaty, Francis I renounced all sovereignty over Artois and Flanders and all rights over Tournai.

It seemed as if, in his sympathy for his Belgian provinces, the emperor had been more clear-sighted than his subjects, for we know that he entertained, in 1527, the idea of forming the Low Countries into a separate kingdom. If this project had been realized, Belgian independence might have been maintained. But the very prosperity of the Low Countries made such realization impossible. In urgent need of money for his military expeditions, the emperor could not deliberately sacrifice his principal source of revenue—the taxes provided by the States General and the loans raised in Antwerp.

Since 1522, Margaret had again taken up the governorship, this time in full accord with the Belgian nobility. From that date till the end of the eighteenth century, with the sole exception of the short reign of Albert and Isabella, Belgium was administered, not by its natural princes, but by governors, most of them without power or initiative and obeying orders received from headquarters. Charles spent only ten years in the country until his abdication in 1555. Philip II made only a short appearance, and until Joseph II none of the rulers who had the responsibility of the government took enough interest in the welfare of their Belgian subjects to visit the provinces.

Margaret, however, preserved a great deal of independence, and succeeded in curbing the will of her nephew in the greater interests of the Netherlands, as she had curbed the will of her father. When, in 1528, war broke out again between the emperor and an Anglo-French coalition, she succeeded in maintaining the trade with England. In the same way she constantly opposed Charles's project to help his relative, Christian II of Denmark, to reconquer his throne, since such a policy would have ruined Belgian trade with Denmark and the Hanseatic towns. Finally, in 1529, she succeeded in negotiating the peace of Cambrai, whose clauses bear the mark of a truly national policy. Charles renounced all pretensions to Burgundy, while Francis gave up all claims on the Netherlands and recognized Charles's sovereignty over Artois, Flanders, Cambrai and Tournaisis. By inducing the two rivals to recognize the established position and to renounce ancient dynastic claims on each other's domains, Margaret hoped to ensure a long peace for the greater benefit of the Netherlands. The final renunciation of France of her rights over her old fiefs was bound also to consolidate Belgian unity, the link binding the provinces to the Empire being purely nominal. Thus, after a struggle of seven hundred years, the Western Netherlands were finally detached from France. In order to celebrate the event, Lancelot Blondeel designed the monumental mantelpiece in carved wood which may still be admired, in the Palace of Justice of Bruges, and where the victorious emperor is represented having, on one side, Ferdinand and Isabella, and on the other, Maximilian and Mary of Burgundy, his maternal and paternal ancestors.

DEATH OF MARGARET OF AUSTRIA

Margaret of Austria died in 1530, at her palace of Malines, "without any regret save for the privation of her nephew's presence." In her last letter to Charles, she claims that under her rule the Low Countries were considerably enlarged, and she expresses a wish to obtain for her work divine reward, the commendation of her sovereign and the good will of his subjects. She utters a last recommendation which shows how far the Burgundian tradition had been preserved by the Belgian People. She urges Charles not to abolish the name of Burgundy, and to leave the title to his successor in the Low Countries.

Emile Cammaerts

Chapter XIII The Last Stage Of Centralization

From the death of Margaret, the emperor's policy became entirely independent. Though absorbed by the affairs of the Empire, distant military expeditions and a recurrent war with France, he managed to devote a great deal of attention to the Netherlands, and during the last years of his reign, from 1544 to 1555, scarcely left the country. The Netherlands were far more important to the ruler of Germany, Spain and half of the New World than their actual size might suggest. Not only did they provide one of the main sources of his revenue, but their central position allowed him to reach comparatively easily the various parts of his Empire where his presence might become necessary. The scattered possessions of Charles V cannot very well be compared with the homogeneous domains of Charlemagne, which stretched all across Western Europe, but we may nevertheless notice that, in both Empires, the Netherlands were allowed to play a part disproportionate to their size and population. Though France remained in the hands of his rival, the great emperor of the Renaissance, just as the great emperor of the Middle Ages, was obliged to divide his attention between East and West, and Brussels was allowed to play a part similar to that of Aix-la-Chapelle. It is significant that, at the time of Charles V's abdication, this town was selected, in preference to Madrid or Vienna, as the stage for the ceremony.

The second part of the reign of Charles V is characterized by the completion of the work of the Burgundian dukes, the seventeen provinces being finally brought under one rule. At the same time, the last local resistance was mercilessly crushed and political centralization completely established.

MARGARET OF HUNGARY

Mary of Hungary, Charles V's sister, who was chosen by him to succeed Margaret of Austria, did not enjoy the independence of her predecessor. She confined herself to executing faithfully the instructions she received, even at the cost of her popularity. The emperor installed her at Brussels in 1531. He had been previously absolved by the pope from his oath at the time of the Joyous Entry of Brabant, and proceeded to strengthen the Central Government by the creation of three collateral Councils and the proclamation of a Perpetual Edict giving a common constitution to all the provinces of the Netherlands. After his departure, Mary was at once confronted with military difficulties. Christian II, no longer restrained by Margaret, had concentrated troops in Holland in order to attack Frederick of Holstein. His violation of the neutrality of the Netherlands caused reprisals against the Dutch merchant fleet, but Antwerp and Brussels refused to wage war in its defence. Thanks to the death of Holstein, Mary succeeded in negotiating a satisfactory treaty with Denmark at Ghent (1533). The resistance of the States General and the towns to the warlike policy of Charles caused further trouble when, in 1536, hostilities between the two rivals were resumed. In vain did Mary endeavour to obtain the neutralization of the Low Countries, in vain did she offer her resignation. In spite of serious reverses, the emperor maintained his attitude, while the States General declared "that they were not rich enough to help him to conquer France and Italy." Their resistance was only overborne when, in 1537, the French armies invaded the Low Countries. Under this threat, they voted the taxes and organized resistance. The French king, disappointed in his hopes, signed the truce of Nice, 1538.

The revolt of Ghent, which broke out the next year, must be considered as the last attempt made by the towns to save their old privileges. For the last time, a Commune raised its head to challenge central power. In spite of the peace of Cadzand, Ghent had succeeded in preserving a privileged situation in the State, and many popular leaders had witnessed with dismay the progress made in 1531 by centralizing tendencies. Beside the defence of local liberties, the aim of the revolutionaries was to restore the situation of the old corporations, which was directly threatened by the economic transformation of the modern régime. Under the new conditions, the "masters" had succeeded in enriching themselves, but the "companions" and prentices had lost all the advantages of the old corporation system. Riots caused by unstable labour conditions had already taken place in Bois-le-Duc (1525) and Brussels (1532). In Ghent, however, the movement acquired more threatening proportions, the magistrates being overwhelmed by the crowd and the workmen seizing the direction of affairs. Charles, who had obtained from Francis I permission to cross France with an army, condemned to torture most of the leaders of the movement, suppressed all the town's privileges by the "Caroline concession" (1540), and even ordered that the well-known bell "Roland" should be unhung. This last punishment remained in the memory of the people as a symbol of the deepest humiliation which might be inflicted on any town.

TREATY OF VENLOO

As soon as Charles departed for his expedition to Algiers, the Netherlands were again exposed to the attacks of his enemies, including Francis I, the King of Denmark and the Duke of Cleves, who had inherited the county of Gelder. This time Mary was strongly supported by the States General, and succeeded in facing the attacks on both sides pending the return of the emperor (1543). The latter took the opportunity given him by a prompt victory to settle once for all the Gelder question by the treaty of Venloo. The Duke of Cleves was obliged to renounce all rights over Gelder and Zutphen, which became integral parts of the Netherlands. This was the last act of the work of territorial unification pursued by the dukes of Burgundy. At the same time, in order to protect the Low Countries from French attacks, Charles V fortified the three towns of Marienbourg, Charlemont and Philippeville, called after Mary of Hungary, Charles himself and his son Philip.

Thus, at last, the Low Countries reaped some advantage from the constant expenses which they had to sustain owing to incessant European wars. They were no longer able to pursue an independent policy, and, if the States preserved a certain liberty, it was mainly because they could be induced to vote war-taxes, these being, so to speak, the ransom which the so-called "free" Netherlands paid to their ruler. During Charles's youth, almost all the revenues of the State had been drawn from the prince's domain, but towards the end of his reign the levies extorted from the people became more and more heavy and frequent. The annual budget rose from one million pounds in 1541 to two and a half millions in 1542 and six and a half millions in 1555. To these annual contributions we must add the numerous loans raised by the Government on the security of the provinces. The interest on these loans weighed heavily on the budget. It was £141,300 in 1552, £424,765 in 1555, and rose to £1,357,287 in 1556. As a matter of fact, the States General could grant taxes but not control expenditure, so that most of the money raised in the Netherlands was spent on foreign expeditions from which the country could reap no benefit. Up to 1552, when gold from Mexico and Peru arrived in Spain, the Low Countries remained the main source of the income of the emperor.

With the annexation of Tournaisis, Friesland, Utrecht, Gelder and Zutphen and the protectorate over the prince-bishopric of Liége, which, under Erard de la Marck (1506-38), had finally accepted Hapsburgian control, the unification of the Low Countries was completed. It still remained to give the country its definite status. Thanks to the treaties of Madrid and Cambrai, all connection with France had been severed, but the Reichstag endeavoured, on several occasions, to revive the nominal rights of the Empire on the Low Countries and to compel the provinces to pay the imperial tax. The emperor, foreseeing that his son might not succeed him in Germany, was not at all keen to encourage such claims. On the contrary, he exempted, by his own free will, the Low Countries from the imperial tax, and he endeavoured to make it a sovereign country attached to Spain, which should remain, with it, the heritage of the Hapsburg family. We are far from the time when he entertained the suggestion of creating a separate kingdom in the Low Countries, under the inspiration of his Burgundian advisers, and though this suggestion recurred in 1539 and 1544, connected with the project of the marriage of the emperor's daughter with the French prince, the sincerity of the emperor's proposals, at that time, may certainly be questioned.

TRANSACTION OF AUGSBURG

The victory of Muhlberg (1547) provided Charles with an excellent opportunity to settle definitely the situation of the Netherlands towards the Empire. Cowed into submission, the Reichstag readily admitted the Transaction of Augsburg (1548), by which the Netherlands became the "circle of Burgundy," under the protection of the Empire, and whose sovereign was represented on the Reichstag. The circle undertook to pay a small subsidy, but was entirely independent of imperial jurisdiction and imperial laws. In fact, it constituted an independent sovereign State, which benefited from the Empire's military protection without any obligation on its side, since the emperor had no means to enforce the payment of the tax in case it should be refused.

The Augsburg Transaction was completed in 1549 by the Pragmatic Sanction, which unified the successorial rights of all the provinces. This new edict marked a new stage in the work of centralization by securing the inheritance of all the provinces to the same prince. Thus, of the two essential characteristics of modern States, unity and independence, the first was practically achieved; the second, however, was not yet within sight. It is characteristic of the status of Belgium, as established by Charles V, that this period of consolidation marks the final break up of the Burgundian tradition. The principle of nationality, which had asserted itself so clearly under Philip the Handsome and at the beginning of the reign of Charles V, was finally defeated, and, for two centuries and a half, the dynastic principle of the Hapsburgs was destined to dominate the fate of the country.

In the same year that the Pragmatic Sanction was signed, Prince Philip visited the Netherlands. The appearance of the young prince and his education were in complete contrast to those of his father and grandfather. His name only was Burgundian. He did not know a word of Flemish and only spoke French with great difficulty. All his manners, all his views, were those of a Spanish aristocrat, and it did not take long for the Belgian nobles and notables who were brought into contact with him to realize that their future ruler would always remain a foreigner in the country.

The failure of Philip to secure the title of King of the Romans strengthened still more the links which bound Belgium to Spain. His marriage with Queen Mary of England might have re-established a healthier balance between South and North, to the greater benefit of the Low Countries, but this union was only an episode in Philip's life, and he was perhaps more foreign to England than he was to Belgium, since he did not benefit in the former country from any sentimental attachment to his family.

ABDICATION OF CHARLES V

On October 25, 1555, the emperor, who suffered from ill-health and desired to spend his last years in retreat, called together the States General in Brussels and solemnly abdicated his power in favour of his son. He recalled in his speech the ceremony of his accession, which had taken place forty years before in the same hall, and, after surveying rapidly the wars and struggles of his reign and the perils to which he had been exposed, he recommended his son to the affection of his subjects, exhorting them to remain united, to uphold justice and to fight heresy. At the end of his speech, he asked forgiveness for the wrongs he had committed and was unable to control his feelings. "If I weep, gentlemen," he concluded, "do not think that it is because I regret the sovereign power which I abandon; it is because I am compelled to leave the country of my birth and to part from such vassals as I had here." His emotion was shared by the Belgian representatives, who realized that, whatever harm the great emperor had inflicted upon his favourite provinces, Belgium had nevertheless found in him, on several occasions, some sympathy and understanding. Parting from him, they may have foreseen that they were parting from their last natural and national prince. This feeling was only increased when Charles, turning towards his son, addressed him in Spanish, and when the latter, in his answer to the address of the States General, excused himself for not being able to speak to them in French.

The Burgundian dukes had endeavoured to convert Belgium into a modern centralized State, with common institutions, a permanent army, a loyal nobility and docile States General. This part of their work was crowned with success, and it is significant that the word "patrie" comes to be used by Belgian writers towards the middle of the sixteenth century. But the dukes had also pursued an independent policy, free from any foreign influence and inspired by the country's interests, since the country's prosperity was a condition of their own welfare and of the stability of their dynasty. This part of their work had been progressively destroyed. Belgium was hereafter ruled neither from Bruges nor from Brussels, but from distant capitals and by ministers and councillors entirely unacquainted with and indifferent to its economic interests and social aspirations.

Emile Cammaerts

Chapter XIV Antwerp

The economic and social development, accompanying the political transformation which we have just witnessed, was entirely dominated by the amazing prosperity of the city of Antwerp. The latter became, during the first part of the sixteenth century, the first market and the first banking centre in the world. For trade, limited during the two former centuries to Europe, now extended to the New World, and the Atlantic route hereafter played a more and more important part. The same causes which brought about the decadence of Venice were the direct causes of the growth of Antwerp. It is true that Bruges occupied a similar position on the map, and from being a purely European market might have become a world-metropolis. We have seen that the silting up of the Zwyn did not account alone for the rapid decadence of the Flemish city, and that the conservatism of the Guilds and Corporations, their attachment to their old privileges and their disregard of modern tendencies, were the main reasons of its downfall. In 1513, Damme and Sluis were partly in ruins, and in the middle of the century, whole quarters of Bruges were emptied of their inhabitants, while over seven thousand destitute depended on charity. Unhampered by mediæval traditions and enjoying the advantages of a deeper and more accessible harbour, Antwerp was bound to secure the heritage of its former rival and to add to it the prosperity derived from the opening of new markets and the rapid widening of the circle of trade activity during the Renaissance.

As opposed to Bruges, Antwerp characterizes modern capitalist tendencies resting on the freedom of trade and on individual initiative. The advantages enjoyed by foreigners in the new metropolis drew gradually towards it the powerful companies of Spanish, English and German merchants, whose presence was so essential in a market where most of the imported goods were re-exported to distant countries. The Florentine Guicciardini, who resided in the Low Countries from 1542 to 1589, describes Antwerp as "an excellent and famous city," where 30,000,000 florins' worth of merchandise arrives every year, and in whose Exchange transactions of 40,000,000 ducats take place. Out of its 100,000 inhabitants, 10,000 to 15,000 were foreigners. There were 13,500 "beautiful, agreeable and spacious" houses, and the rents varied from 200 to 500 écus yearly. The inhabitants "are well and gaily clothed; their houses are well kept, well ordered and furnished with all sorts of household objects. The air of the country is thick and damp, but it is healthy and encourages the appetite and the fecundity of the people." He insists, in his description, on the abundant life led by the rich bourgeois of the great city.

The decadence of the cloth industry, caused by the development of English weaving, did not greatly affect the prosperity of Antwerp, since it benefited from the import of English cloth, which arrived at its docks in a rough state and was dyed and prepared by local artisans. Besides, urban industry in Flanders and Brabant had to a great extent been replaced by rural industry. Employers found in the country districts the cheap labour that was needed, owing to foreign competition, and, for a hundred workers who lost their employment in the towns, thousands of weavers were only too ready to work up the raw material provided for them by the merchants. The linen industry, which more and more took the lead, recruited its labour in the same way, not only in Flanders but also in Brabant, Holland and Hainault. The flax of the country provided excellent raw material, notably in the region of the Lys, whose water was specially suitable for retting. In 1530, England bought from Flanders 100,000 marks' worth of linen in the course of the year. It was soon found necessary to import flax from Russia.

INDUSTRIAL PROSPERITY

The development of tapestry contributed also to fill up the gap caused by the decadence of clothmaking. From Arras, where it had flourished since the eleventh century, it extended, in the fifteenth century, to the regions of Alost, Oudenarde, Enghien, Tournai and Brussels, and, in the sixteenth, to those of Binche, Ath, Lille, Louvain and Ghent. The Low Countries were especially suited to this branch of industry, owing to the perfection of dyeing methods and to the great number of painters and draughtsmen able to provide the workers with beautiful designs. Here, again, most of the artisans were villagers, in spite of the resistance of the old corporations. Around Oudenarde, in 1539, about fourteen thousand men, women and children were engaged in this work.

Even the region of the Meuse was affected. It possessed mineral resources besides great hydraulic power in its rapid streams. At the beginning of the reign of Charles V, a great number of forges and blast furnaces heated with wood were installed in Namurois. According to Guicciardini "there was a constant hammering, forging, smelting and tempering in so many furnaces, among so many flames, sparks and so much smoke, that it seemed as if one were in the glowing forges of Vulcan." Such a description must not be taken too literally, and the beginnings of the metal industry in the Southern provinces were very modest indeed, compared with present conditions. But, even then, a sharp distinction was drawn between the employers, usually some rich bourgeois of the town, who had the means to set up these embryo factories, and the rural population employed to work them. While these new conditions were developing, the corporations of Dinant, which had for a long time monopolized the copper industry, were fast disappearing, partly owing to the difficulty of obtaining the raw material from the mines of Moresnet, but chiefly owing to the protectionist spirit of the Guilds, which would not adapt themselves to modern needs. At the same period, the coal industry was growing in importance in the Liége district, the use of coal being extended from domestic consumption to the metal industry. By the end of the sixteenth century, all the superficial seams which could be worked by means of inclined planes were practically exhausted, and it was found necessary to resort to blasting and to sink pits, in order to reach the lower strata. The bourgeois of Liége furnished the necessary funds for this innovation, which they were the first in Europe to undertake, so that the new industry soon acquired the same capitalistic character which we have noticed in the metal industry, tapestry and textiles.

RURAL CONDITIONS

Though the condition of the peasantry was very prosperous and agricultural methods had improved, the increase of large properties, due to the investment in land of the money acquired by trade and industry, favoured the development of a large class of agricultural labourers, whose situation contrasted unfavourably with that of the large tenant and the smaller farmer.

In every branch of economic activity, modern methods rapidly supplanted mediæval conditions. From the general point of view of the country's prosperity, the change was beneficial and the princes showed wisdom in supporting it. A return to the narrow regulations and guild monopolies of the fourteenth century would have proved as fatal, in the fifteenth, as a return to the feudal system in the thirteenth. The princes supported the rich merchants and employers in the Renaissance, as they supported the Communes in the twelfth century. The corporation system, which had proved a boon at that time, had become an obstacle to free activity and initiative and had therefore to be sacrificed. But, at the same time, the formation of a large class of unorganized rural workers, who had no means of defending themselves against the ruthless exploitation of their employers, was bound to prove a cause of social unrest. It was among these uneducated masses that the Anabaptists recruited most of their followers, and the industrial population around Hondschoote and Armentières provided the first bands of iconoclasts whose excesses contributed so much to confuse the issue of the revolution against Spain. Modern monarchy, which had upheld the new order of things, became the scapegoat of the discontented, and the suffering and exasperated people were no longer able to distinguish between the evil brought about by unrestrained capitalism and the good resulting from the organization of a strongly centralized State.

HUMANISM

Antwerp was not only the centre of economic activity for the Low Countries, it became, as early as 1518, the cradle of Lutheranism. It is needless to recall here how the doctrines of Martin Luther, born in the German Empire, had gradually spread through Northern Europe, and how his criticism of the morals of the clergy had originated a criticism of the dogmas of the Roman Catholic religion. Hitherto similar movements, such as those started in the Low Countries by Gérard de Brogne and the Beggards during the Middle Ages, and, during the last century, by Gérard de Groote, the founder of the Brothers of the Common Life, had confined themselves to fighting the excesses of the Church, remaining throughout orthodox, as far as the dogmas were concerned. Now the principle of free individualism was transplanted from the economic to the religious domain, and capitalistic initiative and freedom of trade found corresponding expression in free interpretation of the Bible. The movement had been prepared and, to a certain extent, favoured by the educative action of the Brothers of the Common Life, who, though remaining strictly faithful to the Church, had nevertheless substituted, in their schools, lay for clerical teaching. It is interesting to remark that both Humanism, as represented by its greatest master, Erasmus, and the art of printing, represented by Thierry Maertens and Jean Veldener, who were its originators at Alost and Louvain, were closely connected with the educational movement promoted by the Brothers. Erasmus had first studied at Deventer. The extraordinary success of his *Adagia*, published in 1500, and of his early works, influenced by Thomas More (with whom he had been brought into contact during his stay in England as a protégé of Lord Mountjoy), seems certainly strange in view of the unbending attitude taken by Charles V towards Lutheranism. But Humanism had become the fashion in high aristocratic and ecclesiastical circles, and neither the young emperor nor his gouvernante, Mary of Hungary, disguised their interest in the movement. It is true that Erasmus endeavoured to reconcile Christian dogmas with the new philosophy inspired by the Classics, but his attacks against asceticism, the celibacy of the priests and the superstition and ignorance of the monks would certainly not have been tolerated if they had influenced social life at large. The situation, at the beginning of the fifteenth century, among intellectuals and aristocrats was very much the same as that which prevailed at the courts of France, Prussia and Russia at the end of the eighteenth century. Princes and nobles extended to Voltaire similar favours, and for the same reasons. As long as their situation in the State was not threatened, they encouraged doctrines and intellectual pursuits which, besides providing them with fresh interests and distractions, justified to a certain extent the laxity of their morals. But, whatever their personal convictions might have been, their attitude had to change entirely as soon as the doctrine was adopted by the common people and when the privileges of Church and State, so closely bound together, began to be questioned by the masses. That Charles V's policy was not prompted only by his affection for the Church is shown by the fact that, a few years before, he had subjected the pope's Bull to his "placet," taken measures to restrict mortmain (which exempted Church property from taxation), and had obtained the right to designate bishops.

ANABAPTISTS

It must be acknowledged that, as the new doctrines spread from the aristocracy to the people, they assumed a more extreme character. The first step in this direction was taken by Lutheranism, whose attacks against dogmas were far more precise and categoric than those of the Humanists. In the Low Countries, however, Lutheranism, at the beginning of the sixteenth century, was still tolerant. It mainly affected a few nobles and a number of rich bourgeois. Church and State, according to them, were separate entities, and one could remain perfectly loyal to the prince while denying the authority of the pope. They professed, in other words, the principle of liberty of conscience, and, while preserving the right to separate themselves from the dominant Church, they did not make any attempt to enforce their theories on any unwilling converts. The first "placard" issued against them by the emperor was extremely severe in terms, since it condemned all heretics to death, but was very lightly applied. The men were to perish by the sword, the women to be buried alive and recanters to be burnt. But the Belgian bishops were unwilling to denounce the Lutherans and to deliver them to the secular arm. Influenced by his Spanish advisers, some of whom had initiated the Spanish Inquisition, Charles, in 1523, transferred the right of prosecution from the bishops to three special inquisitors enjoying full powers. The first executions were too rare to impress the public mind in an age when such spectacles were so frequent for other reasons, and the "placards," which had received the sanction of the States General, did not provoke much opposition. A new stage was reached in 1530 by the appearance of Anabaptism, which had spread from Münster into Holland and Gelder. Melchior Hoffmann, the leader of this movement, claimed to found the kingdom of heaven by the sword. He incensed the poor people by inflammatory speeches in which he invited them to install the new régime of brotherhood on the ruins of the old world. Their triumph would be the "day of vengeance." His success among the sailors and the agricultural labourers of the North, who endured great sufferings under the new economic conditions and owing to the war with Denmark, was very rapid, and ought to have been a warning to the governing classes. The Anabaptists did not make any distinction between Church and State, like the Lutherans, neither did they entertain the idea of freedom of conscience. They were as extremist in their views as the Spanish inquisitors. They intended to enforce their social and mystic doctrines on a reluctant population and appealed to open revolution. In fighting them, the Government was backed by the immense majority of the population, and, after the fall of Münster, this danger was for the time averted.

CALVINISTS

A few years later, however, Calvinism, spread by Swiss and French disguised predicants, began to make considerable progress among the rural population of the Western and Northern provinces. The Calvinists, like the Anabaptists, did not believe in freedom of conscience. They opposed the fanaticism of the Spanish inquisition with the fanaticism of the Reformers and opened the fight without any idea of conciliation. They distributed satiric pamphlets, secretly printed, in which the Church and the court were grossly caricatured, and their loathing for the worship of the Virgin and the Saints degenerated into blasphemy and sacrilege. They found very little favour among the educated classes, but made a number of converts among the discontented proletarians, who led a very miserable life in the neighbourhood of the most important industrial centres. To counteract this propaganda, Charles issued a new "placard," in 1550, which forbade the printing, selling or buying of reformist pamphlets, together with any public or private discussion on religious matters. Even to ask forgiveness for a heretic or to abstain from denouncing him was considered as a crime punishable by death and confiscation of property. Half of the fortune of the condemned went to the denunciator, the other half to the State. Only in one quarter, in the nominally independent bishopric of Liége, where Erard de la Marck issued similar decrees, was the repression successful. Everywhere else, the number of new proselytes increased with that of the executions, and when the emperor abdicated, it seemed evident that a war of religion could not be averted. This war was destined to break up Belgian unity, which had only just been entirely achieved. This might have been averted if Belgium had been allowed to cope with the Reformation crisis in all independence, according to the social conditions of the time, like other European States. A truly national prince and Government would, no doubt, have succeeded in keeping the country together, but Belgium no longer enjoyed the advantage of being ruled by national princes. Hapsburgian dynastic principles had conquered Burgundian traditions. Orders no longer emanated from Brussels but from Madrid, so that to the obstacles created by religious differences and class hatred was added the bitter conflict between patriots and foreign rulers.

Chapter XV The Beggars

Through a most unhappy coincidence, the prince on whose shoulders the fate of the country was to rest during the critical times to come was the first, since the beginning of unification, to be entirely unpopular in the Low Countries. Even Maximilian, who could not adapt himself to Belgian manners, found some moral support in the presence of his wife, and, later on, of his son and heir. But no link of sympathy and understanding could exist between the haughty and taciturn Spaniard and his genial subjects, between the bigoted incarnation of autocracy and the liberty-loving population of the Netherlands, so that even the personal element contributed to render the task of government more difficult.

Philip's first visit, in 1549, had hardly been a success. His second stay in the country did not improve the impression he had produced on those who had approached him. In 1557 Henry II of France had resumed hostilities. The campaign which followed was signalled by the brilliant operations of the Count of Egmont, who, first before St. Quentin and the next year at Gravelines, inflicted severe reverses on the enemy. But, in spite of the satisfactory treaties of Cateau-Cambraisis and the marriage of Philip with the French Princess Elisabeth, which was a good omen for peace, the people of the Netherlands remained discontented. They had again been called upon to pay the cost of a war which did not concern them directly, and they were deeply incensed by the continued presence of Spanish troops, who, irregularly paid, committed incessant excesses. Several Belgian deputies vented their grievances rather freely, urging the king to deliver them from these "destructive brigands." Philip, hurt in his pride, left the Low Countries for Spain, on August 25, 1559, without any intention of ever returning.

MARGUERITE OF PARMA

He had left behind him as gouvernante Marguerite of Parma, a natural daughter of Charles, who lacked neither education nor intelligence, but whose initiative was paralysed by the detailed secret instructions she had received. She had been told not to make any important decision without the advice of a secret council called the "Consulta," formed by three courtiers who were merely creatures of the king: Granvelle, Bishop of Arras, the jurist Viglius d'Ayetta and Charles de Berlaymont. It was, however, impossible to keep such an institution secret, and the Council of State, whose functions were unconstitutionally superseded by the action of the Consulta, naturally resented such interference. Among the most prominent members of the opposition were William of Nassau, Prince of Orange, governor of Holland, Zeeland and Utrecht; Lamoral, Count of Egmont, governor of Flanders and Artois; and Philippe de Montmorency, Count of Horn, grand admiral of the Flemish seas. These three nobles were moderate Catholics, the two first being strongly influenced by the tolerant spirit of Humanism, especially Orange, who, though brought up as a Catholic, had had a Lutheran father.

The clergy had been also aggravated by Philip owing to the creation, in 1559, of fourteen new dioceses, added to the four ancient bishoprics of Arras, Cambrai, Tournai and Utrecht. Such a reform had already been contemplated by Philip the

Emile Cammaerts

Good, and it would have caused no opposition if the bishops had been nominated by the pope, as in mediæval times. But, owing to Charles V's religious policy, they were now selected by the king, and his choice, which included several inquisitors, was much criticized by the Belgian clergy and the abbots. The promotion of the parvenu Granvelle to the supreme dignity of Archbishop of Malines, in 1561, added still more to the discontent.

The same year, ceding to the entreaties of Marguerite, Philip consented to withdraw the Spanish troops. This measure gave satisfaction to the people, but did not placate the grievances of the nobles and of the clergy. At the instigation of William of Orange, the States of Brabant openly supported the Council of State in its opposition to Granvelle and the Consulta. This was brought to a climax by the refusal of Orange, Egmont and Horn to sit on the Council as long as Granvelle remained in the country. Again, Marguerite supported the attitude of her Council and, reluctantly, Philip resigned himself to recall his minister (1564).

THE PLACARDS

These first incidents were insignificant compared with the crisis confronting the Government owing to the rigorous application of Charles V's "placards." Philip had issued no new edicts, deeming, no doubt, that his father's were sufficiently comprehensive, but these were to be rigorously enforced. In his farewell message to the States General, he had declared that "a change of religion cannot occur without at the same time changing the republic," and it was a subject on which he was not prepared to compromise. The increasing number of Protestants, owing to the continued Calvinistic propaganda, rendered the placards more and more odious and their application almost impossible. Marguerite herself declared that "continual executions strained public opinion more than the country could stand." In 1565 the Council of State deputed Egmont to go to Spain in order to entreat Philip to moderate his instructions, but, in spite of the courteous reception given to him, the journey of the count remained without result. The horror inspired by the Inquisition to Catholics and Protestants alike increased every day, and the constant emigration of intellectuals and skilled workers to England caused considerable uneasiness.

Queen Elizabeth was ready to welcome Belgian Calvinists. She assigned the town of Norwich as the principal centre for their settlement. Quite apart from her sympathy for the followers of the Reform, she realized that the introduction of the refugees' various industries into England—including tapestry—was likely to prove invaluable to this country. She resented the economic rivalry of the Low Countries, and, on several occasions, disregarded commercial treaties, levying taxes on imports, from the Netherlands and ignoring the raids of English privateers in the North Sea. It was high time to find means of checking emigration.

THE BEGGARS

A few Calvinist notables, Jean de Marnix and Louis of Nassau, William's brother, among them, conceived the plan of linking together all the nobles opposed to Philip's policy. They drew up a compromise acceptable to both parties in which the signatories swore to "defend the privileges of the country and prevent the maintenance of the Inquisition," without undertaking anything "which would be to the dishonour of God and the king." Over two thousand adherents, nobles, bourgeois and ecclesiastics, signed this document, and on April 5, 1556, three hundred nobles presented a petition to Marguerite. The regent having assured them that she would apply the placards with moderation while awaiting the king's orders, they promised, on their side, to do their utmost to maintain public order. Two days later, the delegates were invited to a banquet by the Calvinist Count of Keulenburg. They appeared at this function dressed as beggars in rough gowns, carrying wallets and bowls, and when Bréderode, emptying his bowl, toasted them, the cry of "Long live the Beggars!" was repeated with enthusiasm by the whole assembly. Tradition has it that the reason for this disguise was a disparaging reflection made by Count Berlaymont when the nobles appeared before the regent in simple dress as a sign of protest against the reckless expenditure which was ruining the provinces. But the medals struck at the time and worn by nobles and bourgeois suffice to explain the incident. These medals bore, on one side, the effigy of the king, and on the other, two hands joined over a wallet, with the inscription: "Faithful to the king even to beggary."

The "Compromise" implied liberty of conscience, but this remained open to interpretation. Most of the signatories considered that the followers of the Reform would merely be tolerated, Catholicism remaining the only State and public worship. These were the "Beggars of State." The Calvinists, on the other hand, the "Beggars of Religion," claimed full liberty to proclaim their faith, to "fight Roman idolatry" through their propaganda and to transform the institutions of the country. In order to keep the two parties together, in their struggle against foreign interference, it would have been necessary to persuade both sides to adopt a more moderate attitude and entirely to dissociate the affairs of State from religious convictions. Orange tried to obtain this result. At the time, he drew his main support from the German Lutherans, who had accepted the "Religions Friede." But the Lutherans were only a small minority in the Low Countries compared to the Calvinists, who were in close touch with the French Huguenots. In order to conciliate Catholics and Protestants, the prince endeavoured to bring the Lutherans and Calvinists together, and even entered into negotiations with the Calvinist leader, Gui de Bray. His efforts failed completely, the Calvinists declaring that "they would rather die than become Lutherans." From that time, owing partly to Philip's policy in exasperating the people by the application of the placards and partly also to the fanatic attitude adopted by the new sect, the Reform entered on a new phase in the Low Countries. No concessions on the part of the Government would satisfy the extremists, bent on complete victory or separation.

These tendencies were soon made apparent by the return of many emigrants and the number of open air "predicants" who held meetings where the people flocked, armed with sticks and weapons. The moderation shown by Marguerite came too late. It was merely considered as a proof of weakness and emboldened the Reformers to redouble their attacks.

Their task was considerably facilitated by the misery prevalent in the country, due to the bad harvest of the year and to the increased cost of living brought about by the paralysis of many branches of trade. A great many merchants had left Antwerp, and in the region of Oudenarde alone eight thousand weavers were unemployed. The Church was held responsible for the misery endured by the people; class hatred and fanaticism combined to make it the scapegoat for all grievances. In Flanders, some agitators produced letters, supposed to have been sealed by the king, by which the pillage of the churches was ordered.

Emile Cammaerts

Suddenly, on August 11th, armed bands invaded the churches, convents and monasteries of the region of Hondschoote and Armentières, breaking all statues, tearing pictures and manuscripts, and destroying church treasures and ornaments. The movement spread to Ypres and Ghent, ravaged the cathedral of Antwerp and passed like a hurricane over Holland and Zeeland only to stop in Friesland, on September 6th. During nearly a month the authorities of the Western and Northern provinces allowed the destruction to continue without daring or trying to stop it. Under the impression caused by the rising of the "Iconoclasts," the Council of State obtained from Marguerite the abolition of the Inquisition and the authorization for the Protestants to hold their meetings publicly, but unarmed and only in such places where similar meetings had already been organized. In return for these last concessions, the nobles dissolved their confederation and applied themselves to the re-establishment of order.

THE INQUISITION

Just as the Inquisition had deepened the gulf between the two parties and stiffened the resistance of the followers of the Reform, the excesses of the Iconoclasts exasperated the moderate Catholics and rendered union more and more difficult. The Count of Mansfeld, a Belgian Catholic, was made governor of Brussels by Marguerite, who placed herself under his protection. A great many moderate nobles, who had taken part in the Compromise, rallied round the Government, and it was suggested that, in order to counteract the revolutionary movement, it would be wise to obtain from all the nobles of the kingdom a new oath of fealty to the king. This measure was bound to cause a split. The small group of Calvinist nobles, headed by the brothers Marnix, Louis of Nassau and Bréderode, abstained from taking the oath. Orange himself was led by his followers into adopting an intransigent attitude, though he had not yet given up the hope of realizing union.

Chapter XVI Separation

The year 1567 marks the beginning of civil war in the Low Countries. Up till then, the nobility and the States General had worked more or less together, acting as intermediaries between the Government and the people. The sovereign rights of the king had never been questioned. Henceforth, the Low Countries were to be divided into two parties, having their headquarters in the South and in the North. Both aimed at preserving their national liberties and equally resented foreign oppression, but, while the people of the Northern provinces decided to sever all connection with Spain, the people of the South were loath to part from their national dynasty and were easily conciliated as soon as the Government adopted a moderate attitude; while the people of the North adopted Calvinism as their only public religion, the people of the South remained attached to the Roman Church.

NORTH AND SOUTH

The story of the sixteenth-century revolution in the Low Countries is so well known that it is scarcely necessary to recall again here the details of events. From the point of view of the formation of Belgian nationality, the revolution has an extraordinary importance, since it engendered the separation of the Low Countries into two distinct nationalities, which were later to be known as Belgian and Dutch. Most English readers who remember their Motley, or any of the less valuable writings he inspired, are under the impression that if the Belgians did not adopt the same attitude as the Dutch all through the struggle against Spain, it was either because they were blinded by their religious prejudices or because their patriotism did not rise to the same exalted height. Such an opinion is perfectly plausible, but it does not sufficiently take into account the intransigent and selfish attitude adopted by the Northern provinces, the political mistakes committed by their leader, and the difference between the strategical position and the economic interests of the revolutionaries in the North and in the South of the country. It may therefore be useful to examine the efforts made towards unity during the struggle and the causes of their failure.

The steps taken by the Calvinist nobles which resulted in the failure of de Marnix to seize Antwerp (March 13th) and the taking of Valenciennes by Government troops (March 24th) were followed by a strong reaction. The placards were again enforced, and a rumour began to spread that the Duke of Alba was being sent by Philip to the Netherlands at the head of a strong army. At this news over a hundred thousand Protestants emigrated to England or to the North.

Many people in Southern Belgium were, however, unable to believe in the possibility of ruthless repression, and even some of those who had taken an active part in recent events remained in the country. They did not know the intentions of the Duke of Alba and the instructions he had received from his master. "I will try to arrange the affairs of religion in the Low Countries," wrote Philip at the time, "if possible without having recourse to force, because this means would imply the total destruction of the country, but I am determined to use it nevertheless, if I cannot otherwise arrange everything as I wish." When, after a fortnight of festivities, the duke suddenly ordered the arrest of the Counts of Egmont and Horn (September 9th), the people were taken entirely by surprise. In spite of the protests of Marguerite and the counsels of moderation of the pope and the Emperor Maximilian, repression was systematically organized by the Council of Troubles, soon called the "Council of Blood." Egmont and Horn were executed on June 5th, and all those who had participated in the agitation of the Compromise and the Iconoclast movement were arrested. During the three years which followed, from six to eight thousand people perished. All resistance was impossible. Only a few bands of Beggars kept to the woods ("Boschgeuzen") and a few privateers operated in the North Sea ("Zeegeuzen"). Alba repulsed with equal success the attacks of Louis of Nassau and of the Prince of Orange. "The people are very pleased," he declared; "there is no people in the world more easy to govern when one knows how to manage them." The new taxes he raised in 1569 to pay for the cost of the war rendered his régime still more odious. These taxes of 1 per cent. on all property, 5 per cent. on the sale of real estate and 10 per cent. on the sale of all goods, were of course unconstitutional, and for a long time Brussels and Louvain refused to pay them. When at last they came into force, in 1571, all trade stopped and the people opposed passive resistance amid great privations and sufferings. The situation was at last relieved by the bold coup de main of the Sea Beggars on the port of La Brielle, in Zeeland. Up till then, they had sought refuge in the English ports, but in 1572 Queen Elizabeth closed her ports to them, and the seizure of a naval base in the Low Countries became imperative. The taking of La Brielle, coming as it did in the worst time of Spanish oppression, provoked unbounded enthusiasm. Successively Flushing, Rotterdam, Schiedam, and soon all Zeeland and Holland, with the exception of a few towns, revolted against the duke. The Huguenots were no less active in the South, where La Noue seized Valenciennes and Louis of Nassau Mons (May 25th). Orange himself advanced victoriously through Gelder towards Brabant. These successes roused great hopes in the Southern provinces, but were unhappily marred by the massacre of the monks at Gorcum and other excesses. They were abruptly stopped by the news of the massacre of St. Bartholomew, Orange's French allies being obliged to leave his army.

PROTESTANT SUCCESSES

Holland and Zeeland became henceforth the centre of resistance. These provinces had not taken an important share in the life of the Low Countries during the Middle Ages. Their prosperity was of comparatively recent date and mainly due to their merchant fleet, which brought to Antwerp wood and corn from the Baltic and wine from Bordeaux. Their sailors had ventured as far as Madeira and the Azores, and, on being stopped by Charles V from reaching America by the Southern route, had endeavoured to find a route to India by the North. From the beginning of the sixteenth century, Amsterdam had become the great corn market, Middleburg the centre of the French wine trade, and the shipyards of Vere, Goes and Arnemuyden were among the most active in Northern Europe. The influx of capital resulting from trade and shipping was used to reclaim marshes, to build fresh dikes and to increase considerably the cultivated area. Nowhere else, according to Guicciardini, was prosperity so general or did the traveller meet such "clean and agreeable houses and such smiling and well cared for country." Economically speaking, the Northern provinces were only beginning to feel the benefit of the advantages of their position, already so manifest in Antwerp. They were, so to speak, in a stage of formation, and far more ready to cut loose the links of tradition with an obscure past and to throw themselves into some great adventure in which they might try their strength.

They occupied, besides, a safer situation than the South, controlling the outlets of three great streams and the adjoining seas, among low-lying lands which, as a last resort, could be flooded in order to stop the advance of an enemy or cut off his retreat. This situation adapted itself remarkably well to a defensive strategy by land and an aggressive strategy by sea. The small number of inhabitants and the small forces available rendered any offensive by land against the Spanish armies extremely dangerous, so that the Southern provinces, exposed on all sides to invasion, were left to shift for themselves. It so happened that the Prince of Orange, the principal leader of the opposition, had, as governor of Holland and Zeeland, acquired a great popularity in the country, which was considerably increased by his conversion to Calvinism. He had been made "Stadhouder" of his provinces and had found great resources in the confiscation of ecclesiastical property.

The next campaign (1572-73) affords an excellent example of the strength of Orange's position. He was finally able to compel the duke to raise the siege of Alkmaar, in spite of his overwhelming superiority in numbers and of the striking successes which had marked his progress from Malines to Zutphen, to Naarden and to Harlem. The Spanish retreat, in October 1573, coincided with a naval defeat off Enkhuizen. Alba, discouraged, left the Low Countries in December and was replaced by a Spanish aristocrat, Louis de Zuniga y Requesens.

REQUESENS

Philip was at last resigned to make some concessions, but remained adamant with regard to religion. Thanks to the victory won by the Spaniards at Mook, where Louis of Nassau lost his life, Requesens was able to grant some of the claims of the States General without losing prestige. He proclaimed a general amnesty, suppressed the taxes of 10 per cent. and 5 per cent., and induced the Council of Troubles not to pronounce any more death sentences. He would not, however, dismiss the Spanish troops, and the North having refused to negotiate, the Spaniards laid siege to Leyden. In 1575 Maximilian offered his mediation, and a congress was held at Breda between the representatives of Philip and of the Prince of Orange. The religiousquestion, however, proved a stumbling-block, Philip maintaining Catholicism as the only State religion and the prince asking for a guarantee with regard to the preservation of liberty of conscience.

After the death of Requesens, on March 15, 1576, the administration was taken over by the Council of State, including the moderate Catholics, Mansfeld, Berlaymont and Viglius. They hastened to suppress the Council of Troubles, but were unable to disband the Spanish army, in spite of the insistence of the provincial States, owing to the lack of funds for their arrears of pay. At the beginning of July some Spanish units took Alost, which became the centre of pillaging expeditions. These excesses and the increasing danger of the situation brought about a reconciliation between Orange and the Belgian nobles, and once more the dream of a common country came within reach of realization. The States of Brabant proscribed the Spanish soldiers and called the citizens to arms. The members of the Council of State were arrested and the States General assembled. In spite of the irregularity of such procedure, all the provinces sent their representatives with the sole exception of Luxemburg. Philip was still proclaimed "sovereign lord and natural prince," but the command of the national troops was given to the Belgian nobles, and Orange was asked to help in reducing the rebellious soldiery and in besieging the citadels of Ghent and Antwerp. While the delegates of the Stadhouder and of the States conferred in Ghent, news reached them of the terrible excesses committed, on November 4th, by the Spanish soldiers in Antwerp, during the course of which seven thousand people lost their lives. These riots are remembered as the "Spanish Fury."

PACIFICATION OF GHENT

Deplorable though they were, they would not have been too heavy a price to pay if national unity could have been maintained. Never did it seem nearer at hand. With fresh memories of Alba's régime and the wholesale executions of the Council of Blood, under the direct influence of the terrible news from Antwerp, the Belgian Catholics were never more ready to wipe off old grievances, to forget the sacrileges of the Iconoclasts, the massacre of Gorcum and the persecution of those of their faith in the North. The Pacification of Ghent was signed on November 8th. The seventeen provinces allied themselves into a confederation, promised to render each other mutual help, to expel the Spanish armies, to suppress the placards and the ordinances of the Duke of Alba and to proclaim a general amnesty. Liberty of conscience, however, was only proclaimed in fifteen provinces. Calvinism remained the only religion permitted in Holland and Zeeland. It is true that the pre-eminent situation of Catholicism was recognized and that the Protestants were not allowed any public manifestations outside Holland and Zeeland, but if we take into account the fact that, all over the country, the Catholics were far more numerous than their rivals, this last clause of the Pacification of Ghent shows that the Calvinists were bent on exacting all the advantages of the situation they had so heroically conquered and that the moderates of the Southern provinces still found themselves placed between the hammer of Spanish domination and the anvil of Calvinist sectarianism.

The Prince of Orange cannot be held entirely responsible for missing this unique opportunity of concluding with his compatriots a fair and liberal compact. His correspondence shows that he had hard work to reconcile his partisans even to such one-sided religious conclusions as those expressed in the Pacification of Ghent, and that in many instances he had to resign himself to being led in order to be allowed to lead.

DON JUAN

This mistake was bound to bear fruit, when the new Governor, Don Juan of Austria, a natural son of Charles V who had covered himself with glory at the battle of Lepanto, reached the country, in November 1576. Philip, aware that the Netherlands would escape him if he did not make some sacrifices, had given Don Juan still freer instructions than those given to Requesens. The religious question only was excluded from concessions. Besides, the king hoped that the Belgians would be flattered by the choice of a prince of the blood and would be captivated by the romantic reputation of this striking representative of Renaissance nobility. Negotiations between Don Juan and the States General were rendered difficult by the opposition of the partisans of Orange and by the want of good faith on the part of the new Governor, who, while promising to recall the Spanish troops, was discovered secretly negotiating with them. The first Union of Brussels was, however, concluded on January 9, 1577. The States promised to obey the king and to maintain the Catholic religion as the only State religion all through the country. On the other hand, Don Juan, by the Edict of Marche, known as "Edit Perpétuel," undertook to convoke the States General, to recall the Spanish troops and not to persecute the partisans of the Reform. Orange and his partisans in Holland and Zeeland naturally refused to ratify such an arrangement, which violated the articles of the Pacification of Ghent.

Don Juan entered Brussels in May, after dismissing the Spanish troops, but, in spite of all his efforts, was unable to ingratiate himself in the eyes of the population. Most of the people had resented the signature of the Union of Brussels, and when the negotiations with the Northerners broke off and Don Juan asked for troops to fight them, he met with a curt refusal. Alarmed by this veiled hostility and exasperated by his protracted negotiations with Orange, Don Juan shut himself up in the fortress of Namur and recalled the Spanish troops. Nothing better could have happened from the point of view of the patriots, and the differences which had begun to undermine the work of the Pacification of Ghent, during the last months, were promptly forgotten. William of Orange made a triumphal entry into Brussels on September 23rd. He was greeted as the liberator of his country, amid scenes of unbounded enthusiasm. He was proclaimed "Ruwaert" of Brabant and his authority did not meet with any further open opposition.

Faithful to his principles, Orange endeavoured to establish liberty of conscience in the Low Countries. His ideas, however, were only shared by a few friends whose rather elastic religious principles allowed them to sacrifice sectarianism to the higher interests of the State. They did not suit the Catholic aristocracy, who, though strongly opposed to Spain, remained attached to legitimist principles. They did not suit Calvinist democrats, who, though in a minority, intended to overwhelm all opposition. The intellectuals among them propounded the idea of the "Monarchomaques" that "the prince existed for the people, not the people for the prince," while the uneducated classes already proclaimed the principle of modern democracy and universal suffrage and questioned the right of the States to represent the people. Since August 1577 Brussels had been practically in the hands of the Commune, represented by a Council of Eighteen. Similar Councils had seized power in some provincial towns, and at Ghent, where the Calvinists dominated the Commune, the articles of the Pacification were entirely disregarded, the churches being plundered and the priests persecuted. Holland and Zeeland maintained an expectant and somewhat moody attitude. They resented their leader's concessions to the Catholics and were not over-enthusiastic towards unification. They felt themselves stronger than the rest of the country and had largely benefited from the closing of the Scheldt and the momentary stoppage of Antwerp's trade. They were loath to sacrifice such advantages for the sake of joining hands with "Papists and monarchists."

POLICY OF ORANGE

As the democratic tendencies and Calvinist excesses were more and more apparent, following the return of Orange to Brussels, the Catholic aristocracy of the Southern provinces became alarmed. The nobles were afraid of the attitude adopted by the people concerning their privileges and of the personal prestige of Orange.

They endeavoured to check his power by inviting foreign princes to take the leadership of the country. The Duke of Aerschot induced Archduke Matthias, brother of the Emperor, to come to the Low Countries, but Orange easily countered this manœuvre by arresting the duke and opening negotiations with Matthias, who signed the second Union of Brussels, on December 10, 1577, and guaranteed liberty of conscience. The young archduke was henceforth a mere figurehead and Orange remained the real ruler of the country.

To add to the confusion, Don Juan opened an offensive, a few days later, and easily defeated the national troops which opposed his progress in Luxemburg, Namur and Hainault, forcing the Government to take refuge in Antwerp. It became more and more apparent that the provinces could not rid themselves of the Spaniards without appealing to foreign help. The Emperor Rudolph being unwilling to support Matthias, the latter had become practically useless. In spite of repeated entreaties, Queen Elizabeth would not consent to give military help. She encouraged the revolution, since it proved a drain on Philip's resources and an efficient protection from Spanish enterprise against England, but she would not openly break with Spain. Only France remained. As early as July 1578, Count de Lalaing endeavoured to repeat with the Duke of Anjou, Henry III's brother, the manœuvre of Aerschot. He sought, at the same time, to deliver the country from Spain with foreign help and to check the increasing power of Orange and all he stood for in his eyes. Anjou had no respect for the liberties and aspirations of the provinces, neither did his rather tepid religious convictions, as a Catholic prince, stand in his way. He hoped to obtain the title of sovereign of the Netherlands and thus to increase his chances of succeeding in his suit for the hand of Queen Elizabeth.

Once more Orange took for himself the plans propounded by his enemies. He negotiated with Anjou, who received the title of "Defender of the Liberties of the Low Countries" in exchange for some military help. Don Juan was obliged to retreat on Namur, where he died, completely disheartened, on October 1, 1578, leaving his lieutenant, Alexander Farnese, Duke of Parma, to continue the struggle.

THE MALCONTENTS

The situation, during the last months of 1578, had become extremely intricate. The Spanish troops, commanded by Farnese, held the Southern provinces as far as the Sambre and the Meuse. Holland and Zeeland maintained their powerful position in the North, but, between Spanish and Dutch headquarters, the country was thrown into a state of complete anarchy, and the power of the Stadhouder, who, from Antwerp, tried vainly to maintain unity, was more and more disregarded. The Act of Religious Peace, which he had issued in June and which placed the two confessions on a footing of equality, though endeavouring to conciliate everybody, only increased the discontent. Its clauses were entirely ignored by the Calvinist Republic of Ghent, which pursued its own ruthless policy under the leadership of Ryhove and terrorized the Catholics. On the other hand, the Catholic nobles, who commanded some units of the national army, formed themselves into a new party, the "Malcontents," and occupied Menin on October 1st. Civil war became more and more inevitable. Ryhove called the Prince Palatine, John Casimir, a protégé of Queen Elizabeth, to his help, while Anjou, alarmed by the apparition of this unexpected rival, helped the Malcontents to reduce the Calvinist Communes in Arras, Lille and Valenciennes.

Belgium

William of Orange, who had displayed such extraordinary political aptitudes during the first years of the revolution, seemed, since his entry into Brussels, to have disregarded some essential conditions of success. Though imbued by the principle of national unity, he never threw himself wholeheartedly into the struggle and never gave the country the leadership it so badly needed. He first seemed to ignore the difficulties ahead, owing to the rivalry of religious factions, and, when these were made clear to him, he did not take any strong measure to enforce on the people the principle of liberty of conscience which he so loudly proclaimed. The recurrence of excesses and cruelties committed by the fanatic leaders of the Communes contributed to create a widespread impression, among the Catholics, that he was merely paying lip-service to them, while determined to tolerate any disobedience among his own followers. His retirement to Antwerp, in close contact with Holland and Zeeland, but far removed from the Southern provinces, was also unfavourable to the maintenance of the Union under his leadership. Finally, the interference in national affairs of such disreputable adventurers as John Casimir and Anjou diminished, to a certain degree, the reluctance with which the Catholics envisaged the possibility of treating with Spain.

UNION OF ARRAS

On January 6, 1579, Artois, Hainault and Walloon Flanders formed the "Confederation of Arras," which sanctioned the first Union of Brussels—that is to say, the maintenance of Catholicism all over the country; and from that time negotiations began between the Catholic bourgeoisie and nobility and Farnese. Had Orange proved more active or Farnese less diplomatic, the Union might still have been maintained even at the eleventh hour. For nothing but religious passion, and perhaps, to a certain extent, the fear of mob rule, prompted the Southern provinces to accept the Spanish offers. The States of Hainault had declared that they would not undertake anything contrary to the common cause, but wanted only to preserve their existence, to "maintain the Pacification of Ghent against an insolent and barbarian tyranny worse than the Spanish" and "to prevent the extinction of their holy faith and religion, of the nobility and of all order and state." They did not abandon any of their old claims against Spain, but they refused to acknowledge the social and religious transformation which had taken place in the country since the signature of the Pacification. The defenders of the new confederation expressed the hope that in all towns the oppressed Catholics would join hands with them. The Union of Arras ought to be considered therefore, not as a Walloon, but as a purely Catholic League. It confirms the first Union of Brussels, including all its anti-Spanish stipulations concerning the restoration of the old privileges, the voting of taxes by the States, the defence of the country by native troops, the maintenance of the Catholic religion in all the provinces being the only common ground on which Spaniards and Belgians could meet. It was, nevertheless, a breach of the Pacification of Ghent, and was destined to link Belgium with Spain for many years to come. It was also a definite and irretrievable step towards separation.

It has been suggested that the difference of race and languages might have influenced the fateful decision of the Walloon provinces. Such an interpretation does not take into account the language situation in the Low Countries at the time. One seeks vainly for any grievance which the Southern provinces might have entertained on that ground. French was used in all the acts of the central

Government and in the deliberations of the States General. Even the Prince of Orange had kept the Burgundian tradition and considered French as his mother-tongue. He was surrounded and supported by a great number of French Huguenots and Walloon Calvinists. Owing to their smaller population the Southern provinces were rather over-represented in the States General, where the vote went by province and not by numbers. Besides, we must not overlook the fact that the confederates represented themselves not as dissenters, but as the true supporters of the Act of Union, which had been violated by the Calvinists. They did not show any separatist tendencies like Holland and Zeeland, but opposed their policy of Union to the policy of the Prince of Orange. One of their most urgent demands was that the Prince of the Netherlands should henceforth be of royal and legitimate blood, in order to restore a national policy, similar to that followed during the early years of the reigns of Philip the Handsome and Charles V. All through the troubled period of the last twenty years, Walloons and Flemings never ceased to emphasize their will to live together. Their mottoes are, "Viribus unitis"; "Belgium fœderatum"; "Concordia res parvæ crescunt"; and almost every speech and public manifestation insists on the necessity of protecting a common "patrie" against a common enemy through a common defence. As a matter of fact, the principle of unity was so popular at the time in the Southern provinces that the confederates would have made themselves thoroughly unpopular if they had dared to preach separation, and, on both sides, it was only by pretending to defend the Union that the extremists, moved by class hatred and religious passion, succeeded in destroying it.

The centre of Catholic reaction might have been formed in any other part of the Southern provinces under similar circumstances. The region of Armentières and Valenciennes had been the cradle of the Iconoclast rebellion, but repression in that quarter was far more effective than in any other. A great proportion of the Walloon workers who did not perish under Alba's rule emigrated to England. The Southern cities were thus considerably depleted of their Calvinist element, and the peasants and the bourgeois outnumbered them far more than in any other part of the country. Even under ordinary circumstances the workers of the towns exercised very little influence on the States of Hainault and Artois. In Hainault (Valenciennes and Tournai forming special circumscriptions), Mons remained alone to represent their interests. In Artois, Arras, St. Omer and Béthune were the only important centres whose representatives could oppose those of the far more important agricultural districts. The question of race and language had no more influence on the attitude of the Walloon provinces than on that of Holland, Zeeland and Utrecht. Both were determined by economic, social and religious conditions as well as by their strategic situation.

UNION OF UTRECHT

The Confederation of Arras was proclaimed on January 6, 1579. On the 23rd the Union of Utrecht was constituted, under the same claim of defending the Pacification of Ghent. It grouped around Holland and Zeeland the provinces of Utrecht, Gelder, Friesland, Over-Yssel and Groningen, together with the most important towns of Flanders and Brabant: Ghent, Ypres, Bruges, Antwerp, Brussels, etc. They undertook to act jointly in reference to peace, war, alliances and all external matters, while retaining their local autonomy. The exercise of religion remained free, with the exception of Holland and Zeeland, from which Catholicism was excluded. The Union of Utrecht was the origin of the Republic of the Seven United Provinces. It was entirely dominated by the particularist policy of Holland and Zeeland, which, as events developed more and more in favour of Farnese in the South, took less and less interest in their Southern confederates. The small forces at their disposal rendered any offensive towards Flanders and Brabant, which would have provided the beleaguered cities with food and arms, very difficult, and the reopening of the Scheldt, which must have taken place in the event of the integral preservation of the Union of Utrecht, would have reacted unfavourably on the trade of the Northern ports.

ALEXANDER FARNESE

Owing to the defensive attitude of the North, events moved rather slowly during the following years. After the fall of Maestricht, which was marked by further massacres of the people by the Spanish soldiery, Farnese, who had staked all on a policy of conciliation, gradually dismissed the Spanish troops and organized native units with the help of the Malcontents. Now that all bonds were severed between the Union of Utrecht and the crown of Spain, Philip II endeavoured to revenge himself on his opponent by putting a price on his head (1580). The apology written by the Prince of Orange in answer to Philip's accusations, in the shape of a letter addressed to the States General, is one of the most dignified pleas of such a kind in history. Orange had no difficulty in showing the sincerity of his motives and his devotion to the common weal. The reader of this eloquent document will, however, realize that its author lacked the energy and self-reliance necessary to deal with the desperate situation in which the country was placed. In his eagerness to save the Belgian towns and to safeguard unity, in spite of the unwillingness of Holland and Zeeland to depart from their expectant attitude, he concluded with the Duke of Anjou, on September 29th, the treaty of Plessis-lez-Tours, by which, in exchange for military help, the duke was to receive the title of hereditary sovereign of the United Provinces, undertook to respect the rights of the States General and maintain the representatives of the House of Orange-Nassau as hereditary Stadhouders of Holland, Zeeland and Utrecht. This last clause was introduced far more to pacify the Northerners, who strongly objected to these negotiations, than to further Orange's personal ambition. It shows once more the privileged situation occupied by the three provinces and their strong particularist tendencies. The treaty of Plessis-lez-Tours, which was supposed to save the Union, was destined to give it its death-blow and to strengthen the alliance between the Southern provinces and Farnese. By that time, the central Government in Antwerp had become purely nominal. The Northern provinces had ceased to send their representatives and the delegates from the South could not claim to represent the people, who were more and more unfavourable to their attitude. The States General was only used to register and sanction Orange's decisions. In spite of some opposition, it finally proclaimed, on July 26, 1581, the deposition of the king.

Hostilities were at once resumed, Farnese besieging Cambrai and Tournai, which had not yet joined the Confederation. The first town was saved by the intervention of the French troops of Anjou, but the second capitulated on November 3rd. From that time, Farnese endeavoured to treat his enemies with the greatest clemency. He suppressed severely all acts of terrorism or pillage and offered honourable conditions to any city willing to surrender, the Protestants being free to leave the town after settling their affairs and the local liberties remaining intact. By these moderate conditions and by the loyalty with which he kept to them, he gradually earned the respect, if not the sympathy, of a great number of his former opponents, and his attitude contrasted favourably with the vagaries of Anjou, whose rule was, after all, the only alternative offered to the Southern provinces at the time. After a journey to England, where he received a rebuff from Queen Elizabeth, Anjou was greeted with great honours at Antwerp (February 19, 1582). During the year which followed, he grew more and more impatient of the obstacles placed in his way and the restrictions imposed on his authority. He finally decided to make a bid for power, and, on the night of January 16-17, 1583, his soldiers endeavoured to seize the gates of Antwerp and occupy the public buildings. They were, however, defeated by the armed citizens, and the duke, entirely discredited, was obliged to leave the country. This episode is remembered as the "French Fury."

The last hopes of reconstituting the unity of the Netherlands were ruined by the murder, on July 10, 1584, at Delft, of the Prince of Orange, the only statesman who had pursued this aim with some consistency, in spite of all his mistakes. This action was as criminal as it was senseless. The prince had failed in his great enterprise of uniting the Netherlands against Spain, and no efforts on his part could have restored the situation. Thanks to the Spanish reinforcements the Confederation had allowed him to receive, Farnese was systematically blockading and besieging every important Flemish town. Already Dunkirk, Ypres and Bruges had opened their gates to him and obtained very favourable conditions. Ghent itself, the stronghold of Calvinism in Flanders, whose population had distinguished itself by so many cruelties and excesses and which was considered as the arch-enemy of the Malcontents, benefited from the same policy when obliged to surrender, on September 17th. All the old customs were restored, the town was obliged to pay 200,000 golden écus, its hostages were pardoned, and, though the Protestants were not allowed to celebrate their worship in public, they obtained a delay of two years before leaving the city.

FALL OF ANTWERP

At the beginning of 1585 almost every town had been reduced as far as Malines. Brussels, which had vainly expected some help from the North, opened its gates to Farnese on March 10th, and the taking of Antwerp, on August 16th, closed the series of operations which definitely separated Belgium from Holland and again placed the Southern provinces under the subjection of Spain. Antwerp had been defended obstinately by its burgomaster, the Calvinist pamphleteer, Marnix de St. Aldegonde, who confidently hoped that his Northern allies would create a diversion and at least prevent the Spanish from cutting off the great port from the sea. In the case of Antwerp, Holland and Zeeland might have interfered without so much danger, but Orange was no longer there to plead for unity and the great port of the Southern provinces was abandoned to its fate.

Chapter XVII Dream Of Independence

The fall of Antwerp had doomed all projects of anti-Spanish unity. It had settled for centuries to come the fate of the Southern provinces, which were henceforth attached to a foreign dynasty and administered as foreign possessions. This ultimate result was not, however, apparent at once, and for some years the people entertained a hope of a return to the Burgundian tradition and to a national policy. This period of transition is covered by the reign of Albert and Isabella, who were, nominally at least, the sovereigns of the Low Countries.

BELGIUM UNDER THE RULE OF THE KINGS OF SPAIN.

Before giving the Low Countries as a dowry to his daughter Isabella, Philip II made several attempts to break the resistance of Holland and Zeeland. Had Farnese been left to deal with the situation after the fall of Antwerp, he might have succeeded in this difficult enterprise. But all the successes he had obtained against Maurice of Nassau in Zeeland Flanders, Brabant and Gelder were jeopardized by the European policy of the Spanish king. From August 20, 1585, Queen Elizabeth had at last openly allied herself with the United Provinces, and the whole attention of Philip was now centred upon England and upon the bold project of forcing the entry of the Thames with a powerful fleet. Farnese was therefore obliged to concentrate most of his troops near Dunkirk, in view of the projected landing. The complete failure of the expedition released these forces, but their absence from the Northern provinces had already given Maurice of Nassau the opportunity of restoring the situation (1588). The next year, instead of resuming the campaign against the United Provinces, Farnese was obliged to fight in France to support the Catholic League. It was in the course of one of these expeditions that he died in Arras, on December 3, 1593.

THE INFANTA ISABELLA.
From a picture by Rubens (Brussels Museum).
ARCHDUKE ALBERT.
From a picture by Rubens (Brussels Museum).

ALBERT AND ISABELLA

Philip was bound by his promises to send to Belgium a prince of the blood. His choice of Archduke Ernest, son of Maximilian II, was, however, an unhappy one, as the weak prince was entirely dominated by his Spanish general, Fuentès, brother-in-law of the Duke of Alba. The country suffered, at the time, from the combined attacks of Maurice of Nassau and of Henry IV of France. After the death of Archduke Ernest, Philip chose as governor-general the former's younger brother, Archduke Albert, who had distinguished himself as Viceroy of Portugal. He arrived just in time, in 1596, to relieve the situation by the taking of Calais. This success was short-lived, and by the treaty of Vervins (May 2, 1597) Philip was obliged to restore Calais to France, together with the Vermandois and part of Picardy. The next year the king negotiated the marriage of his daughter Isabella with Archduke Albert. He died on September 13, 1598, before the marriage could be celebrated. Had Philip II come to this last determination willingly, the future of the Low Countries, at least of the Southern provinces, might still have been saved. But this last act of the sovereign whose rule had been so fatal to the Netherlands proved as disappointing as the others. While he wrote in the act of cession that "the greatest happiness which might occur to a country is to be governed under the eyes and in the presence of its natural prince and lord," he almost annihilated this very wise concession to Belgian aspirations by adding stringent restrictions. The inhabitants of the Low Countries were not allowed to trade with the Indies; in the eventuality of the Infanta Isabella having no children, the provinces would return to the crown. Besides, the act contained some secret clauses according to which the new sovereigns undertook to obey all orders received from Madrid and to maintain Spanish garrisons in the principal towns. The Spanish king reserved to himself the right to re-annex the Low Countries in any case, under certain circumstances.

This half-hearted arrangement, besides placing the archduke in a false position in his relations with his subjects, deprived him of all initiative in foreign matters. In fact, in spite of his sincere attempts to shake off Spanish influence, he enjoyed less independence than some former governors, like Margaret of Austria.

These secret clauses were not known to the Belgian people, and they greeted their new sovereigns with unbounded enthusiasm. Their journey from Luxemburg to Brussels, where they made their entry on September 15, 1599, was a triumphal progress. After so many years of war and foreign subjection, the Belgians believed that Albert and Isabella would bring them a much needed peace and an independence similar to that which they enjoyed under Charles V and Philip the Handsome. They considered their accession to the throne as a return to the Burgundian policy to which they had been so consistently loyal all through their struggle against Spain, and whose remembrance had done so much to separate them from the Northern provinces. On several occasions, and more especially at the time of the peace of Arras, they had expressed a wish to be governed by a prince of the blood who would be allowed to act as their independent sovereign, and they confidently imagined that this wish was going to be realized and that, under her new rulers, the country would be at last able to repair the damage caused by the war and to restore her economic prosperity.

CATHOLIC REACTION

They knew that the new régime implied the exclusion of the Protestants from the Southern provinces, but this did not cause much discontent at the time. All through the struggle the Catholics had been in great majority not only in the country but also in the principal towns, with the sole exception of Antwerp, which was the meeting-place of many refugees. Though at the time of the Pacification of Ghent a great number of citizens had adopted the new faith in order to avoid Calvinistic persecutions, they had given it up as soon as the armies of Farnese entered their towns. The sincere Protestants had been obliged to emigrate to the Northern provinces. Though the number of these emigrants has been somewhat exaggerated, they included a great many intellectuals, big traders and skilful artisans, whose loss was bound to affect the Southern provinces, as their presence was destined to benefit Holland, where the names of the Bruxellois Hans van Aerssen, the Gantois Heinsius and the Tournaisiens Jacques and Issac Lemaire are still remembered.

At the time of the arrival of Albert and Isabella in Belgium, Protestantism had practically disappeared from the towns and maintained itself only in a few remote villages, much as Dour (Hainault), Horebeke, Estaires (Flanders) and Hodimont (Limburg), where Protestant communities still exist to-day. Though the placards had not been abolished, they were no longer applied, and all executions had ceased. Except in case of a public manifestation causing scandal, the judges did not interfere, and even then, penalties were limited to castigation or fine.

Contrary to some popular conceptions, Protestantism was not uprooted by the violence and cruelties of the Inquisition in the Southern provinces. On the contrary, these violences, under the Duke of Alba, only contributed to extend its influence. The Calvinist excesses of 1577-79 and the leniency of Farnese did more to counteract Calvinist propaganda than the wholesale massacres organized by the Council of Blood. It was against these persecutions, not against the Catholic religion, that the Southern provinces fought throughout the period of revolution, and the breaking off of all relations with the North automatically brought to an end the influence of Calvinism.

The rapid success obtained by Farnese's policy, and the fact that his successors had no need to have recourse to violent measures, shows that Protestantism was not deeply rooted in the South and that the people would have been only too pleased to agree to its exclusion if they had obtained in exchange peace and independence. But the war went on and the archduke was compelled to remain governor for Philip III.

SIEGE OF OSTEND

This became apparent immediately when, in 1600, the States General claimed a voice in the administration of the country and in the control of expenditure. They met with a curt refusal and were obliged to agree to pay a regular subsidy in place of the old "special grants." The same year, Maurice of Nassau invaded Northern Flanders in the hope of provoking a rising, but the people did not answer to his call. The Spanish, however, were defeated at the battle of Nieuport, where the archduke was severely wounded. The next year began the siege of Ostend, which had remained faithful to the United Provinces and which was easily able to receive provisions by sea. After three years of struggle, the town was obliged to surrender, thanks to the skilful operations of Ambrose Spinola, who was placed at the head of the Spanish army. After further indecisive operations, a twelve years' truce was finally declared, on April 9, 1609, between the United Provinces and Spain. Philip III virtually recognized the independence of the Republic and even allowed the Dutch merchants to trade with the West Indies, a privilege which he had refused to his own subjects in Belgium. The Southern provinces were further sacrificed by the recognition of the blockade of the Scheldt, which remained closed to all ships wishing to enter Antwerp, to the greater benefit of Dutch ports.

As soon as hostilities were resumed, in 1621, it became apparent that Philip IV would not support Belgium any more energetically than his father had done. Spinola, who had the whole responsibility of the defence of the country after the death of Archduke Albert (1621), succeeded in taking Breda (1625). With the Spanish general's disgrace, owing to a court intrigue, the armies of the United Provinces were once more successful in consolidating their situation in Northern

Brabant and Limburg, which they considered as the bulwarks of their independence. Frederick Henry of Nassau, who had succeeded his brother in the command of the Republic's armies, took Bois-le-Duc in 1629, and Venloo, Ruremonde and Maestricht in 1632. He was supported, in these last operations, by Louis XIII, who, prompted by Richelieu, took this opportunity of humiliating the Hapsburg dynasty. The Spanish commander, the Marquis of Santa Cruz, proved so inefficient that some Belgian patriots tried to take matters into their own hands and to deliver their country from a foreign domination which was so fatal to its interests. It soon became clear, however, that any step taken against Spain would deliver Belgium into the hands of either the French or the Dutch. A first ill-considered and hasty attempt was made by Henry, Count of Bergh, and René de Renesse, who opened secret negotiations at The Hague with some Dutch statesmen and the French ambassador. On June 18th they attempted a rising at Liége, but were obliged to take refuge in the United Provinces. A more serious conspiracy was entered into, almost at the same time, by Count Egmont and Prince d'Epinoy, who, with some followers, formed a Walloon League. Their aim was to drive the Spaniards out of the country with the help of the French and to found a "Belgian Federative and Independent State." On being denounced to the Government, the conspirators were obliged to take flight before their plans had matured.

THE STATES GENERAL

The fall of Maestricht had induced Isabella to assemble once more the States General. After thirty-two years' silence, the latter put forward the same grievances concerning the restoration of old privileges and the defence of the country by native troops, together with new complaints referring to the recent Spanish administration. The people had become so restless that the Marquis of Santa Cruz and Cardinal de La Cueva, the representative of Philip IV in the Low Countries, were obliged to fly from Brussels. Under pressure of public opinion, Isabella allowed the States General to send a deputation to The Hague to negotiate peace (September 17, 1632). The deputies left the town amid great rejoicings. With undaunted optimism, the Belgians hoped that where the Spanish armies had failed their representatives would be successful, and that the new negotiations would bring them at last peace and independence, for they realized that they could not obtain one without the other. According to a contemporary, they believed that they saw "the dawn of the day of peace and tranquillity after such a long and black night of evil war." But they had reckoned without the exigencies of the Dutch, whose policy was even then to secure their own safety, independence and prosperity by drastically sacrificing the interests of the Southern provinces. The delegates were met with the proposal of establishing in Belgium a Catholic Federative Republic at the price of heavy territorial concessions both to Holland and to the French. They could obtain independence, but on such conditions that they would never have been able to defend it.

The following year (1633), after the death of Isabella, Philip IV recalled the Belgian delegates. He dissolved the States General a few months later (1634). From this time to the end of the eighteenth century, during the Brabançonne revolution, the representatives of the Belgian people were no longer consulted and had no share in the central Government of Belgium.

Emile Cammaerts

Chapter XVIII The Twelve Years' Truce

The truce of 1609-21 was used by the Government and the people to restore as far as possible the economic prosperity of the Catholic Netherlands. The relative success with which these efforts were crowned shows that some energy was left in the country, in spite of the blockade imposed on her trade and of the emigration of some of her most prominent sons to the United Provinces. It is a common mistake to presume that, from the beginning of the seventeenth century, all economic and intellectual life left the Southern provinces and was absorbed by the Northern. The contrast was indeed striking between the young republic which was becoming the first maritime Power in Europe and the mother-country from which it had been torn, and which had ceased to occupy a prominent rank in European affairs. A medal was struck, in 1587, showing, on one side, symbols of want and misery, applied to the Catholic Netherlands, and, on the other, symbols of riches and prosperity, applied to the Northern Netherlands, whilst the inscriptions made it clear that these were the punishment of the impious and the reward of the faithful. But a careful study of the period would show that her most valuable treasure, the stubborn energy of her people, did not desert Belgium during this critical period, and that in a remarkably short time she succeeded in rebuilding her home, or at least those parts of it which she was allowed to repair.

At the end of the sixteenth century the situation, especially in Flanders and Brabant, was pitiful. The dikes were pierced, the polders were flooded and by far the greater part of the cultivated area left fallow. The amount of unclaimed land was so large in Flanders that the first new-comer was allowed to till it. Wild beasts had invaded the country, and only a mile from Ghent travellers were attacked by wolves. Bands of robbers infested the land, and in 1599 an order was issued to fell all the woods along roads and canals, in order to render travelling more secure. In Brabant, many villages had lost more than half their houses, the mills were destroyed and the flocks scattered. The conditions in several of the towns were still worse. At Ghent the famine was so acute among the poor that they even ate the garbage thrown in the streets. The population of Antwerp, from 100,000 in the fifteenth century, had fallen to 56,948 in 1645. Lille, on account of its industry, and Brussels, owing to the presence of the court, were the only centres which succeeded in maintaining their prosperity. The excesses of the foreign garrisons, often ill-paid and living on the population, added still further to the misery. The English traveller Overbury, who visited the seventeen provinces at the beginning of the truce, declared that, as soon as he had passed the frontier, he found "a Province distressed with Warre; the people heartlesse, and rather repining against their Governours, then revengefull against the Enemies, the bravery of that Gentriewhich was left, and the Industry of the Merchant quite decayed; the Husbandman labouring only to live, without desire to be rich to another's use; the Townes (whatsoever concerned not the strength of them) ruinous; And to conclude, the people here growing poore with lesse taxes, then they flourish with on the States side."

BLOCKADE

Belgium

The truce had declared the re-establishment of commercial liberty, but the blockade of the coast remained as stringent as ever. Flushing, Middleburg and Amsterdam had inherited the transit trade of Antwerp, now completely abandoned by foreign merchants. In 1609 only two Genoese and one merchant from Lucca remained in the place, while the last Portuguese and English were taking their departure. The Exchange was now so completely deserted that, in 1648, it was used as a library. The docks were only frequented by a few Dutch boats which brought their cargo of corn and took away manufactured articles. Any foreign boat laden for Antwerp was obliged to discharge its cargo in Zeeland, the Dutch merchant fleet monopolizing the trade of the Scheldt.

The Belgians could not alter this situation themselves. They could only appeal to Spanish help, and Spain was neither in a situation nor in a mood to help them. Most of its naval forces had been destroyed during the Armada adventure, and neither the few galleys brought by Spinola to Sluis, before the taking of this town by Maurice of Nassau (1604), nor the privateers from Dunkirk were able to do more than harass Dutch trade. With the defeat of the reorganized Spanish fleet at the Battle of the Downs, the last hope of seeing the Dutch blockade raised vanished. Not only was the Lower Scheldt firmly held, but enemy ships cruised permanently outside Ostend, Nieuport and Dunkirk. The attempts made by the Government to counter these measures by the closing of the land frontier were equally doomed to failure, since the Dutch did not depend in any way on their Belgian market, while the Belgians needed the corn imported from the Northern provinces. The extraordinary indifference of the Spanish kings to the trade of their Northern possessions is made evident by the fact that, while the treaty of 1609 allowed the Dutch to trade with the Indies, it was only thirty-one years later that the Belgians received the same permission.

Thwarted in this direction, the activity of the people and of the Government concentrated on industry and agriculture. Dikes were rebuilt, marshes drained and cattle brought into the country. Though trade had been ruined, the raw material remained. The region of Valenciennes, Tournai and Lille was the first to recover. The wool which could no longer come through Antwerp was imported from Rouen, a staple being fixed at St. Omer. In 1597 an enthusiastic contemporary compared Lille to a small Antwerp. The Walloon provinces had been less severely tried, and the coal industry, as well as the foundries, in the Meuse valley soon recovered their former activity. Tapestry-making was also resumed in Oudenarde and Brussels, copper-working in Malines, dyeing in Antwerp and linen-weaving in the Flemish country districts. But the economic upheaval caused by the civil wars had given the death-blow to the decaying town industries, paralysed by the régime of the corporations. The coppersmiths of Dinant and Namur were now completely ruined, and the cloth industry in Ghent had become so insignificant that, in 1613, the cloth hall of the town was ceded to the society of the "Fencers of St. Michael." Rural industry and capitalist organization, which had made such strides at the beginning of the sixteenth century, had now definitely superseded mediæval institutions.

It was on the same lines that the new industries which developed in the country at the time were organized by their promoters. The manufacture of silk stuffs started in Antwerp, while the State attempted the cultivation of mulberry-trees to provide raw material. Similar attention was devoted by Albert and Isabella to lace-making, which produced one of the most important articles of export. Glass furnaces were established in Ghent, Liége and Hainault, paper-works in Huy, the manufacture of iron cauldrons began in Liége, and soap factories and distilleries were set up in other places.

NEW CANALS

The solicitude of the central Government was not limited to industry. Roads and canals were repaired all over the country and new important public works were undertaken. Though the project of a Rhine-Scheldt Canal, favoured by Isabella, had to be given up owing to Dutch opposition, the canals from Bruges to Ghent (1614), from Bruges to Ostend (1624-66) and from Bruges to Ypres (1635-39) were completed at this time. Navigation on the Dendre was also improved, and it was in 1656 that the project was made to connect Brussels with the province of Hainault by a waterway. This plan was only realized a century later.

The conditions prevailing in the Catholic Low Countries during the first part of the seventeenth century were, therefore, on the whole, favourable. With regard to world trade and foreign politics the country was entirely paralysed, but the activity of the people and the solicitude of the sovereigns succeeded in realizing the economic restoration of the country as far as this restoration depended upon them. The real economic decadence of Belgium did not occur on the date of the separation, but fifty years later, during the second half of the seventeenth century, when its exports were reduced by the protective tariffs of France, when the Thirty Years' War ruined the German market and when Spain remained the only country open for its produce.

SOCIAL LIFE

This relative prosperity extended beyond the twelve years of the truce. For, even when hostilities were resumed, they did not deeply affect the life of the nation, most of the operations being limited to the frontier. Some Belgian historians have drawn a very flattering picture of this period and extolled the personal qualities of Albert and Isabella. We must, however, realize that, in spite of the archduke's good intentions, the promises made at the peace of Arras were not kept, that the States General were only twice assembled and that all the political guarantees obtained by the patriots from Farnese were disregarded. Spanish garrisons remained in the country and the representatives of the people had no control over the expenditure. In fact, Belgium was nearer to having an absolutist monarchical régime than it had ever been before. The Council of State was only assembled to conciliate the nobility, whose loyalty was still further encouraged by the granting of honours, such as that of the Order of the Golden Fleece, and entrusting to them missions to foreign countries. The upper bourgeoisie, on the other hand, were largely permitted to enter the ranks of the nobility by receiving titles. From 1602 to 1638 no less than forty-one estates were raised to the rank of counties, marquisates and principalities, and a contemporary writer complains that "as many nobles are made now in one year as formerly in a hundred." It was among these new nobles, or would-be nobles, who constituted a class very similar to that of the English gentry of the same period, that the State recruited the officers of its army and many officials, whose loyalty was, of course, ensured.

No opposition was likely from the ranks of the clergy. The new bishoprics founded by Philip II had been reconstituted and the bishops selected by the king exercised strict discipline in their dioceses. Besides, all religious orders were now united by the necessity of opposing a common front to the attacks of the Protestants, and they felt that the fate of the religion was intimately bound up with that of the dynasty. The principle of the Divine right of Kings was opposed to the doctrine of the right of the people to choose their monarch propounded by the Monarchomaques, and Roman Catholics were, by then, attached to the monarchy just as Calvinists were attached to the Republic. The experiences of the last century prevented any return to the situation existing under Charles V, when, on certain questions, the clergy were inclined to side with the people against the prince. The close alliance of Church and State had now become an accomplished fact, and was destined to influence Belgian politics right up to modern times. The loyalty of the people was even stimulated by this alliance, the work of public charity being more and more taken from the communal authorities to be monopolized by the clergy. Attendance at church and, for children, at catechism and Sunday school was encouraged by benevolence, the distribution of prizes and small favours, while religious slackness or any revolutionary tendency implied a loss of all similar advantages. Here, again, the skilful propaganda against heresy constituted a powerful weapon in the hands of the State. It must, in all fairness, be added that charity contributed greatly to relieve the misery so widespread during the first years of the century, and that the people were genuinely grateful to such orders as the Récollets and the Capuchins, who resumed the work undertaken with such enthusiasm by the Minor Orders in the previous centuries. They visited the prisoners and the sick, sheltered the insane and the destitute, and even undertook such public duties as those of firemen. These efforts soon succeeded in obliterating the last traces of Calvinist and republican tendencies, which had never succeeded in affecting the bulk of the population.

As a modern sovereign, bent on increasing the power of the State, Archduke Albert resented the encroachments of the clergy, as Charles V had done before him. But he was as powerless to extricate himself from the circumstances which identified the interests of his internal policy with those of the Church, as to liberate himself from the severe restrictions with which the Spanish régime paralysed his initiative in foreign matters.

Emile Cammaerts

Chapter XIX Rubens

If it be true that the spirit of a period can best be judged by its intellectual and artistic achievements, we ought certainly to find in the pictures of Rubens (1577-1640) an adequate expression of the tendencies and aspirations of the Counter Reformation in Belgium. Compared with the religious pictures of the Van Eycks and of Van der Weyden, such works as the "Spear Thrust" (Antwerp Museum), "The Erection of the Cross" and the "Descent from the Cross" (Antwerp Cathedral) form a complete contrast. There is no trace left in them of the mystic atmosphere, the sense of repose and of the intense inner tragedy which pervade the works of the primitives. Within a century, Flemish art is completely transformed. It appeals to the senses more than to the soul, and finds greatness in the display of physical effort and majestic lines more than in any spiritual fervour. Two predominant influences contributed to bring about this extraordinary transformation—the influence of Italy and that of the Catholic Restoration, specially as expressed by the Jesuits.

While, in the fifteenth century, Art, in the Low Countries, had remained purely Flemish, or, to speak more accurately, faithful to native tendencies, all through the sixteenth century the attraction of the Italian Renaissance became more and more apparent. We know that Van der Weyden, in 1450, and Josse van Ghent, in 1468, visited Italy, but they went there more as teachers than as students. Their works were appreciated by the Italian patrons for their intense originality and for their technical perfection. Jean Gossaert, better known as Mabuse on account of his being born in Maubeuge (*c.* 1472), was the first of a numerous series of artists who, all through the sixteenth century, considered the imitation of the Italian art of the period as an essential condition of success. Just as the primitive National school had been patronized by the dukes of Burgundy, the Italianizants were patronized by Charles V, Margaret of Austria and Mary of Hungary. The worship of Raphael and Michael Angelo, so apparent in the paintings of Van Orley, Peter Pourbus, J. Massys and many others, marks the transition between the primitive tendencies of Van Eyck and the modern tendencies of Rubens. Both tendencies are sometimes aptly combined in their works, and their portraits, especially those of Antoine Moro, still place the Antwerp school of the sixteenth century in the forefront of European Art, but the general decadence of native inspiration is nevertheless plainly apparent. The favour shown to these painters by the governors under Charles V and Philip II is significant. Whatever their personal opinions may have been, the Italianizants adapted themselves to the pomp displayed by the Monarchists and to the modern spirit of Catholicism, as opposed to the Reformation, whose critical and satiric tendencies were expressed, to a certain extent, by realists like Jérôme Bosch (1460-1516) and Peter Breughel (*c.* 1525-69) who painted, at the same time, genre pictures of a popular character and who remained absolutely free from Italian influence. The same opposition which divided society and religion reflected itself in Art.

RUBENS

Though he succeeded in transforming their methods, Rubens is nevertheless the spiritual descendant of the Italianizants. It is from them and from his direct contact with the works of Michael Angelo and Titian that he inherits his association of spiritual sublimity with physical strength. Adopting without reserve Michael Angelo's pagan vision of Christianity, he transformed his saints and apostles into powerful heroes and endeavoured to convey the awe and majesty inspired by the Christian drama through an imposing combination of forceful lines and striking colouring.

Rubens was chosen by the Jesuits to decorate the great church they had erected in Antwerp in 1620. Such a choice at first appears strange, considering that, on several occasions, Rubens does not seem to conform to the strict rule which the powerful brotherhood succeeded in imposing on other intellectual activities. Translated into poetry, such works as the "Rape of the Daughters of Lucippus," "The Judgment of Paris," "The Progress of Silenus," would suggest a style very much akin to that of Shakespeare's *Venus and Adonis*, and, needless to say, would never have passed the Church's censor. For the reaction against the moral license and the intellectual liberty of the previous century was by now completed. Higher education was monopolized by the reformed University of Louvain and the new University of Douai, and no Belgian was allowed to study abroad. All traces of Humanism had disappeared from Louvain, where Justus Lipsius remained as the last representative of Renaissance tendencies strongly tempered by orthodoxy. Scientific novelties were so much distrusted that when, in 1621, Van Helmont dared to make public his observations on animal magnetism, he was denounced as a heretic and obliged to recant. For fear of exposing themselves to similar persecutions, the historians of the time confined themselves to the study of national antiquities. The theatre was confined to the representation of conventional Passions and Mysteries and to the plays produced every year by the Jesuits in their schools.

PULPIT OF SAINTE GUDULE, BRUSSELS.
(Eighteenth century). *Ph. B.*

As a matter of fact, the tolerance and even the encouragement granted, at the time, to an exuberant display of forms and colours and to an overloaded ornamental architecture, were not opposed to the Jesuit methods. They were determined, by all means at their disposal, to transform the Low Countries into an advance citadel of Roman Catholicism. Their policy was far more positive than negative. They were far more bent on bringing to the Church new converts and stimulating the zeal of their flock than on eradicating Protestantism. They thought that the only means to obtain such a result was to attract the people by pleasant surroundings and not to rebuke them by morose asceticism. They were the first to introduce dancing, music and games into their colleges. They organized processions and sacred pageants. They surrounded the first solemn communion with a new ceremonial. They stimulated emulation and showered prizes on all those who distinguished themselves.

THE JESUITS

Society was merely for them a larger school in which they used the same means in order to consolidate their position. During the first years of the seventeenth century, an enormous number of new churches were built. Never had architects been so busy since the time of Philip the Good. The church of Douai, erected in 1583, was a replica of the Gésù in Rome, and the general adoption of the Italian "barocco" by the Jesuits has encouraged the idea, in modern times, that there really existed a Jesuit type of architecture. The flowery ornaments on the façades of these churches, their columns, gilded torches, elaborate and heavy designs, cannot be compared to Rubens's masterpieces, but, from the point of view of propaganda, which was the only point of view that mattered, the glorious paintings of the Antwerp master fulfilled the same purpose. They rendered religion attractive to the masses, they combined with music and incense to fill the congregation with a sacred awe conducive to faith.

It ought not to be assumed, however, that the painters of the period enjoyed complete liberty of expression. If the Church showed great tolerance with regard to the choice of certain profane subjects, Christian art was directly influenced by the reforms promulgated by the Council of Trent. In a pamphlet published in 1570 by Jean Molanus, *De Picturis et Imaginibus sacris*, the new rules are strictly set forth. All subjects inspired by the apocryphal books and popular legends are proscribed, and even such details of treatment as the representation of St. Joseph as an old man and the removal of the lily from the hand of the Angel of the Annunciation to a vase are severely criticized. The censors of the period would have given short shrift to Memling's interpretation of St. Ursula's story and all similar legends which could not be upheld by the authority of the *Acta Sanctorum*. This remarkable historical work, initiated by Bollandus at the time, endeavoured to weed out from the lives of the saints most of the popular anecdotes which had inspired mediæval artists. All episodes connected with the birth and marriage of the Virgin disappeared, at the same time, from the churches. The Jesuits were stern rationalists, and, considering themselves as the defenders of a besieged fortress, were determined not to lay the Church open to attack and to remove any cause for criticism. Their point of view was entirely contrary to that of the mediæval artists. For the latter, Art sprang naturally from a fervent mysticism, just as flowers spring from the soil. Its intimate faith does not need any effort, any artifices, to make itself apparent; even secondary works retain a religious value. The sacred pictures of the seventeenth century appear, in contrast, as a gigantic and wonderful piece of religious advertisement. Based on purely pagan motives, they succeed in capturing the wandering attention on some sacred subject, by overloading it with a luxury of ornament and an exuberance of gesture unknown to the primitives. The treatment may be free, it is even necessary that it should be so in order to flatter the taste of the period, but the repertory of subjects becomes more and more limited. Brilliant colours, floating draperies, powerful draughtsmanship, become the obedient servants of a stern and dogmatic mind. The pagans exalted sensuousness, the mediæval artists magnified faith, the artists of the Counter-Reformation used all the means of the former to reach the aim of the latter "ad majorem Dei gloriam."

INTELLECTUAL LIFE

The result of this intellectual and artistic movement was stupendous. While the Récollets and Capuchins, Carmelites, Brigittines, Ursulines and Clarisses worked among the poor, the Jesuits succeeded in capturing the upper classes. All the children of the rich bourgeoisie and the nobility attended their schools and colleges, and, in 1626, the number of pupils with their parents who had entered the Congregation of the Virgin reached 13,727. One might say that the Jesuits had taken intellectual power from the hands of the laity in order to wield it for the benefit of the Church. From their ranks rose all the most prominent men of the period, philosophers like Lessius, economists like Scribani, historians like the Bollandists, physicians, mathematicians, architects and painters.

The direct result of this clericalization of Art and Letters was to thwart the progress realized during the last century by the vulgar tongue. Latin replaced French in philosophy, history and science, and even in literature the elite preferred to express themselves in the classic tongue. Flemish was completely disdained. According to Geulinx, "it ought not to have been heard outside the kitchen or the inn." This period, which from the artistic point of view was marked by such bold innovations, favoured a reaction towards the mediæval use of Latin in preference to the vulgar tongue. But Latin was not read by the people.

Rubens was not only the most successful religious painter of his time, he was also the favourite and ambassador of Albert and Isabella, the great courtier and portrait painter and the decorator of the Luxemburg Palace in Paris. He not only paid court to the Church, he also placed his talent at the service of the sovereigns and nobles of his day, and certainly the encouragement given by the latter to pagan subjects may account for the leniency of the Church towards them. In 1636 the King of Spain ordered from the Antwerp master fifty-six pictures illustrating the *Metamorphoses* of Ovid, destined for his hunting lodge near Madrid. Rubens's pupil, Van Dyck, was the accomplished type of the court painter of the period. His portraits of Charles I and of his children and of Lord John and Lord Bernard Stewart are among the best-known examples of the work he accomplished in England.

BREUGHEL AND JORDAENS

There is a third aspect of Rubens which cannot be ignored and through which he may be associated with the realist artists of the seventeenth century, who succeeded in preserving a purely Flemish and popular tradition in spite of Italian and monarchist influences. The "Kermesse" of the Louvre and the wonderful landscapes disseminated in so many European museums are the best proofs that the master did not lose touch with his native land and with the people who tilled it. This special aspect of his art is even more prominent in the works of his follower, Jacques Jordaens (1593-1678). It is significant that the latter became a Calvinist in 1655. While Rubens and Van Dyck represent mostly the aristocratic and clerical side of the Flemish art of the period, Jordaens appears as the direct descendant of Jérôme Bosch and Peter Breughel. Breughel's satires, such as the "Fight between the

Lean and the Fat" and the "Triumph of Death," show plainly that his sympathies were certainly not on the side of Spanish oppression. His interpretation of the "Massacre of the Innocents" (Imperial Museum, Vienna) is nothing but a tragic description of a raid of Spanish soldiery on a Flemish village. Quite apart from their extraordinary suggestiveness, these works, like most of Breughel's drawings and paintings, constitute admirable illustrations of the popular life of the Low Countries during the religious wars. It must never be forgotten that all through the sixteenth century, starting from Quentin Matsys, the founder of the Antwerp school, the popular and Flemish tradition remains distinct from the flowery style of the Italianizants. Though it is impossible to divide the two groups of artists among the two political and religious tendencies in conflict, the works of Breughel and Jordaens may be considered as a necessary counterpart to those of Frans Floris and Rubens if we wish to form a complete idea of the civilization of the period.

THE MASSACRE OF THE INNOCENTS (SIXTEENTH CENTURY).
(Imperial Museum, Vienna.) P. Breugghel

Chapter XX Political Decadence Under Spain

Though the seven Northern provinces could be considered as definitely lost after the failure of Farnese's last attempt to reconquer them, the Spanish Netherlands still included, at the beginning of the seventeenth century, the three duchies of Brabant, Limburg (with its dependencies beyond the Meuse, Daelhem, Fauquemont and Rolduc), Luxemburg and a small part of Gelder with Ruremonde; four counties, Flanders, Artois, Hainault and Namur, and the two seigneuries of Malines and Tournai. When, in 1715, the Southern Netherlands passed under Austrian sovereignty, they had lost Maestricht and part of Northern Limburg, Northern Brabant, Zeeland Flanders, Walloon Flanders and Artois, and various small enclaves, most of their fortified towns being further obliged to receive foreign garrisons, maintained at the expense of the State. Antwerp remained closed, and the efforts made during the first years of the seventeenth century to restore the economic situation through industrial and agricultural activity were practically annihilated by incessant wars.

This situation was evidently caused by the weakness of Spain, which, though clinging to its Northern possessions, did not possess the means to defend them against the ambition of European Powers, more especially France. It was due also to the policy of the United Provinces, who considered Belgium as a mere buffer State which they could use for their own protection and whose ruin, through the closing of Antwerp, was one of the conditions of their own prosperity. Up to the War of the Spanish Succession, England played a less prominent part in the various conflicts affecting the Southern Netherlands, but she succeeded, on several occasions, in checking the annexationist projects of France, whose presence along the Belgian coast was a far greater danger than that of a weak and impoverished Spain.

WEAKNESS OF BELGIUM

There is no better illustration of the paramount importance of a strong and independent Belgium to the peace of Europe than the series of wars which followed each other in such rapid succession during the seventeenth century. It is true that, in nearly every instance, the new situation created in the Netherlands cannot be given as the direct cause of these various conflicts, resulting from territorial ambitions, dynastic susceptibilities and even, as in the case of the Thirty Years' War, from circumstances quite independent of those prevalent on the Meuse and the Scheldt. But, whatever the nominal cause of these wars may have been, they certainly acquired a more widespread character from the fact that the Spanish Netherlands lay as an easy prey at the mercy of the invader and constituted a kind of open arena where European armies could meet and carry on their contests on enemy ground. It is not a mere chance that the separation of the Southern and Northern provinces coincided with a remarkable recrudescence of the warlike spirit all over Europe. The contrast between the fifteenth century, when the Seventeen Provinces constituted a powerful State under the dukes of Burgundy, and the seventeenth, when the greater part of it was ruined and undefended, at the mercy of foreign invasion, is particularly enlightening. All through the Middle Ages first Flanders, later the Burgundian Netherlands, had exerted their sobering and regulating influence between France, on one side, and England or Germany on the other. The Belgian princes were directly interested in maintaining peace, and, in most cases, only went to war when their independence, and incidentally the peace of Europe, was threatened by the increasing ambition of one of their neighbours. The system of alliances concluded with this object could not possibly prevent conflicts, but it certainly limited their scope and preserved Europe from general conflagration, the combination of the Netherlands with one Power being usually enough to keep a third Power in order. The weakening of the Southern provinces under Spanish rule thus caused an irreparable gap in the most sensitive and dangerous spot on the political map of Europe. Triple and Quadruple Alliances were entered into and inaugurated the system of Grand Alliances which was henceforth to characterize almost every European conflict and increase on such a large scale the numbers of opposed forces and the devastations accompanying their warlike operations.

DUTCH POLICY

It may be said that the United Provinces might have played the part formerly filled by the Burgundian Netherlands and the county of Flanders, but, in spite of their amazing maritime expansion and of the prosperity of their trade, they did not enjoy the same military prestige on land. Besides, they did not care to undertake such a heavy responsibility, and pursued most of the time a narrowly self-centred policy. Though they had some excellent opportunities of reconstituting the unity of the Low Countries, and though some of their statesmen contemplated such a step, the United Provinces never embarked upon a definite policy of reconstitution. They played for safety first and were far too wary to sacrifice solid material advantages for a problematic European prestige. Unification would have meant the reopening of the Scheldt and the resurrection of Antwerp, whose rivalry was always dreaded by the Northern ports. It would have meant the admission of a far more numerous population on an equal footing, with religious freedom, to the privileges of the Republic. It would have implied the sacrifice of an extraordinarily strong strategic situation and the risks involved by the defence of weak and extended frontiers. The maintenance of a weak buffer State, as a glacis against any attacks from the South, seemed far more advantageous, especially if its fortified positions were garrisoned with Dutch forces. It gave all the same strategic advantages which unification might have given, without any of its risks and inconveniences. "It is far better," wrote a Dutch Grand Pensioner, at the time, "to defend oneself in Brussels or Antwerp than in Breda or Dordrecht." Such an attitude was perfectly justified as long as Holland did not claim the advantages attached to the position of a moderating central Power and ask for the reward without having taken the risks.

We have seen how, in 1632, the delegates of the States General were met at The Hague with the proposal of the creation of a Federative Catholic Republic under the tutelage of France and Holland. This project, already entertained in 1602 by the Grand Pensioner Oldenbarneveldt, was very much favoured by Cardinal Richelieu, who, in 1634, signed a secret convention with the United Provinces, according to which such a proposal would be made to the people of the Southern Netherlands. In the event of their refusing this arrangement, the country would be divided among the two allies, following a line running from Blankenberghe to Luxemburg. If we remember the attitude of the Belgians at the time of the

Conspiracy of the Nobles, led by the Count of Bergh (1632), such a refusal must have been anticipated, so that the proposal amounted really to a project of partition. This project would anyhow have been opposed by England, since, according to the Dutch diplomat Grotius, Charles I "would not admit" the presence of France on the Flemish coast.

In 1635 a formal and public alliance was declared between the United Provinces and France, and war broke out once more between Spain and the confederates. The operations which followed form part of the fourth phase of the Thirty Years' War, but we are only concerned here with their result with regard to the Netherlands. While the Dutch took Breda and concentrated near Maestricht, the French advanced through the Southern provinces towards Limburg, where they made their junction with their allies to proceed against Brussels. The Belgians had not answered the Franco-Batavian manifesto, inviting them to rebel, and gave whatever help they could to their Spanish governor, the Cardinal Infant Ferdinand. Students co-operated in the defence of Louvain, and the people showed the greatest loyalty during the campaign. They knew by now that they had very little good to expect from a Franco-Dutch protectorate and that even the shadow of independence they were allowed to preserve under the Spanish régime would be taken from them. Powerless to reconquer full independence, they preferred a weak rule which secured for them at least religious liberty to the strong rule of those whom they considered as foreigners and as enemies to their country.

RICHELIEU AND MAZARIN

Operations were pursued with alternating success until 1642, when Mazarin succeeded Richelieu as French Prime Minister. Mazarin favoured a more radical solution of the Netherlands difficulty. He persuaded Louis XIV that the possession of the left bank of the Rhine was essential to the safety of the kingdom, and aimed at the total annexation of the Belgian Provinces. The negotiations begun in that direction met with Dutch and English opposition and the curt refusal of Spain to renounce her rights on her Northern possessions. This new attitude of France brought about a rapprochement between Spain and the United Provinces, who began to fear Louis XIV's ambitious schemes. The two countries settled their difficulties by the treaty of Münster (1648), while, after a new series of defeats, culminating, in 1658, in the Battle of the Dunes, won by Turenne against Don Juan, Philip IV was finally obliged to submit to the treaty of the Pyrenees (1659).

The Dutch plenipotentiaries had practically a free hand in the settling of the Münster treaty. They acquired all the territories they claimed, and they only claimed the territories they wanted and which they already held. Their choice was dictated neither by territorial ambition nor by the desire to realize the unity of the Netherlands. They obtained, of course, the official recognition of their full independence and the maintenance of the closing of the Scheldt and of its dependencies. The annexation of Zeeland Flanders, henceforth known as Flanders of the States, ensured their position on the left bank of the stream, that of North Brabant with Bergen-op-Zoom, Breda and Bois-le-Duc, ensured the protection of their central provinces, while Maestricht, together with Fauquemont, Daelhem and Rolduc, secured their position on the Meuse. These were purely strategic annexations, prompted by strategic motives and by the desire to keep a firm hold on some key positions from which the United Provinces could check any attack, either from Spain or from France, with the least effort.

By the treaty of the Pyrenees Philip IV abandoned to France the whole of Artois and a series of fortified positions in Southern Flanders, Hainault, Namur and Luxemburg. These latter demands were prompted by an evident desire to extend French territory towards the Netherlands and to obtain a position which should afford a good starting-point for such extension.

The treaties of Münster and of the Pyrenees had, broadly speaking, determined the new status of the Southern provinces, considerably diminished to comply with the wishes and the interests of the United Provinces and of France. This status was not considerably altered by the succession of wars which took place during the second half of the seventeenth century and the early years of the eighteenth, and which ended by the substitution of Austrian for Spanish rule. It was, however, considered as provisional by Louis XIV, whose territorial ambitions extended far beyond Walloon Flanders, and, before obtaining the right to live within her new frontiers, Belgium had still to undergo the ordeal of five devastating wars.

PROCLAMATION OF THE PEACE OF MÜNSTER IN FRONT OF THE ANTWERP TOWN HALL.
From an old print (1648).

PROJECTS OF PARTITION

At the time of the death of Philip IV (1665), the Southern provinces, impoverished and inadequately defended, were an easy prey to foreign territorial greed. The Dutch Grand Pensioner De Witt returned to the old plan of 1634, whereby Holland and France should agree to the constitution of a protected buffer State, and, in case this proposal should not meet with the support of the States, to a partition along a line extending from Ostend to Maestricht. Holland and England, however, were soon to realize that no compromise was possible with France and that their safety required prompt joint action.

Emile Cammaerts

The Roi-Soleil would not agree to recognize the right of the new King of Spain, Charles II, to the Southern Netherlands. A few years before, King Louis had married Maria Theresa, the eldest daughter of Philip IV, and his legal advisors made a pretext of the non-payment of her dowry and of a custom prevalent in some parts of Brabant, according to which the children of a first marriage were favoured ("dévolution"), to claim this part of the Spanish succession. The King's troops entered the Netherlands in 1667, without meeting with any serious opposition, and hostilities only came to an end when, after concluding a hasty peace and enlisting the support of Sweden, the United Provinces and England concluded the Triple Alliance (1668). By the treaty of Aix-la-Chapelle, France nevertheless obtained the fortified towns of Bergues, Furnes, Armentières, Courtrai, Lille, Oudenarde, Tournai, Ath, Douai, Binche and Charleroi, strengthening her position still further on the borders of Walloon Flanders and in Hainault. The allies understood by then that Louis's ambitions threatened their very existence. When the French resumed hostilities, four years later, a revolution took place in Holland which overthrew De Witt in favour of William III of Orange, who was hereafter the strongest opponent of French policy. Charles II of England took an equally strong attitude, following the traditional English policy of not allowing the French to obtain a hold on the Flemish coast. Addressing Parliament, a few years later, he declared that England could not admit "that even one town like Ostend should fall into French hands, and could not tolerate that even only forty French soldiers should occupy such a position, just opposite the mouth of the Thames." William had therefore no difficulty in constituting a powerful alliance, including, besides the United Provinces and England, Spain, Germany and Denmark. In face of such opposition, Louis was finally compelled to sign the treaty of Nymegen, which restored to Spain some of the advanced positions obtained by the treaty of Aix-la-Chapelle, but confirmed the loss of Walloon Flanders and Southern Hainault.

After a few years, however, seeing the alliance broken off and his enemies otherwise engaged, the King of France assumed a more and more aggressive attitude and encroached so much on the rights of Spain that Charles II was finally compelled to resist his pretensions. Luxemburg was the only town which offered any serious resistance; everywhere else French armies pursued their methods of terrorism, bombarded the towns and ravaged the country. The Truce of Ratisbon, concluded in 1684 for twenty years, added Chimay, Beaumont and Luxemburg to the French spoils.

THE AUGSBURG LEAGUE

William III, alarmed by this progress, succeeded in enlisting the support of the Emperor Leopold I, the King of Spain, the King of Sweden and the Duke of Savoy. A new League against France was founded in Augsburg (1686). When, two years later, William succeeded in supplanting James II on the throne of England, this country entered the League and a new conflict became inevitable. Belgium was not directly interested in it, and, as on former occasions, served as the battleground of foreign armies. In spite of the series of victories won by the French general, the Marshal of Luxemburg, at Fleurus (1690), Steenkerque (1692) and Neerwinden (1693), William III always succeeded in reconstituting his army. Two years later, he retook Namur, in spite of Marshal de Villeroi's attack on Brussels, during which the capital was bombarded for two days (August 13th to 15th) with red-hot bullets, over four thousand houses, including those of the Grand' Place, being destroyed by fire. The peace of Ryswyck, September 20, 1697, gave back to Spain the advanced fortresses annexed by the two previous treaties, William being definitely recognized as King of England.

The personal union between the two countries reacted somewhat on British policy in the Netherlands, this country taking a far more important share in the last period of the struggle against Louis XIV. Up till then, England had been content with checking France's encroachments in Flanders and maintaining the balance of power in Europe. The closer relationships with the United Provinces, during the reigns of William and Mary and of Queen Anne, involved England in further responsibilities and even induced her to impose, for a short time, an Anglo-Dutch protectorate on the Belgian provinces. This attitude was made more apparent by Marlborough's personal ambitions concerning the governorship of the Southern provinces, but the failure of these projects and the prompt return to traditional policy, after the treaty of Utrecht, only makes more apparent the general territorial disinterestedness of this country concerning the Netherlands.

MARLBOROUGH'S CAMPAIGNS

Charles II of Spain had died in 1700, leaving all his possessions and the crown of Spain to Philip, Duke of Anjou, the second grandson of Louis XIV, thus depriving of his hopes of the succession Archduke Charles, son of the Emperor Leopold I, who stood in exactly the same relation to the deceased monarch. The emperor at once sought the support of the United Provinces, which, however, hesitated to reopen hostilities. The Spanish governor in Belgium was then Maximilian Emmanuel of Bavaria, who harboured the project of restoring the Southern provinces to their former prosperity and of becoming the sovereign of the new State, with or without a Spanish protectorate. French agents at his court encouraged his plan and so lured him by false promises that, in 1701, he allowed French troops to enter Belgium unopposed and to establish themselves in the principal towns. The Grand Alliance, including the same partners as the Augsburg League, was at once re-formed, in spite of the death, in 1702, of William, and the Duke of Marlborough was placed at the head of the allied troops. During the first years of the War of the Spanish Succession, operations were purely defensive in the Netherlands, owing specially to the anxiety of the Dutch not to risk any offensive which might have left a gap for the enemy's attacks. It was not until 1706 that Marlborough was able to break through the enemy's defences at Ramillies, near Tirlemont. This victory was followed by a French retreat, and the Belgians expected to be placed at once under the rule of Charles III, the other claimant of the Spanish crown, instead of which the Council of State, summoned in Brussels, was subjected to the orders of an Anglo-Batavian Conference, which had no legitimate right to rule the country. The Council protested, upon several occasions, and the exactions of the allies, who had been first hailed as deliverers, caused such indignation in the provinces that some towns, such as Ghent, opened their gates to the French. The defeat of Louis XIV was, however, consummated at Oudenarde (1708) and Malplaquet (1709). The French forces had been so considerably reduced that, had Louis's openings for peace been met at the time, the integrity of the Southern provinces might have been restored. The Allies were, however, rather indifferent to such advantages, since it became more and more evident that, owing to Anglo-

Dutch rivalries, they could not reap any direct benefit from them, and the Netherlands would finally have to be restored to Charles III, who, at the death of the emperor, in 1710, succeeded his brother under the name of Charles VI. The Whig Party had fallen from power in England in the previous year, and Marlborough, no longer supported at home, could not undertake any further operations. Under these conditions negotiations became possible, and the result was not so damaging to the prestige of France as might have been expected. By the treaty of Utrecht (1713) the Southern Netherlands were transferred to the Austrian branch of the Hapsburgs as a compensation for its loss of the Spanish crown. Louis restored Tournai, and a portion of West Flanders beyond the Yser including Furnes and Ypres, but Artois, Walloon Flanders, the south of Hainault and of Luxemburg remained French.

TREATY OF UTRECHT

From the point of view of the Netherlands, the treaties of Rastadt and of Baden (1714) were merely the ratification, by the emperor and by the Holy Roman Empire, of the clauses of the treaty of Utrecht. But the treaty of Antwerp, or of the Barriers, concluded the next year, between Austria and the United Provinces, included new stipulations practically placing the new Austrian Netherlands under the tutelage of Holland and still increasing her territorial encroachments. This was the outcome of previous conventions concluded between England and the United Provinces and according to which the latter were promised, beside some territorial advantages, the possession of a certain number of fortified towns "in order that they should serve as a barrier of safety to the States General" (1705). If, at Utrecht, the British had obtained new possessions in Canada, at Antwerp the Dutch claimed their share of advantages and exacted from Charles VI the price of their services. Namur, Tournai, Menin, Ypres, Warneton, Furnes, Knocke and Termonde were to be the fixed points of the Barrier where the United Provinces might keep their troops at the expense of the Belgian provinces. Further advantages were obtained in Zeeland Flanders and on the Meuse by the annexation of Venloo, Stevensweert and Montfort. The fortifications of Liége, Huy and Ghent were to be razed and the Dutch had further the right to flood certain parts of the country if they considered it necessary for defence. The Scheldt, of course, remained closed, since, according to Article XXVI, "the trade of the Austrian Netherlands and everything depending on it would be on the same footing as that established by the treaty of Münster, which was confirmed."

The treaty of the Barriers marked the lowest ebb of Belgian nationality. During the protracted war which preceded it, complete anarchy reigned, imperialists, the allied conference, Maximilian Emmanuel and the French administering various parts of the country. The great nation raised in the heart of Europe by the dukes of Burgundy seemed practically annihilated, but the people had retained, in spite of all reverses and tribulations, the memory of their past, and, from the very depth of their misery, evolved a new strength and reasserted their right to live, in spite of the attitude of all European Powers, which seemed, at the time, to consider their nationality as non-existent.

"We are reduced to the last extremity," wrote the States of Brabant to Charles II in 1691, "we are exhausted to the last substance by long and costly wars, and we can only present your Majesty with our infirmities, our wounds and our cries of sorrow."

BELGIUM UNDER THE RULE OF THE EMPERORS OF AUSTRIA.

Chapter XXI The Ostend Company

The Austrian régime is characterized by a return to more peaceful conditions, since, with the exception of the period of 1740 to 1748, the country was not directly affected by European conflicts. Under any rule, this period of peace must have been marked by an economic renaissance in a country disposing of such natural riches as the Southern provinces. The Austrian governors encouraged this movement, as the archdukes had encouraged it before, but, like them, they were unable to deliver the country from its economic bondage, as far as foreign trade was concerned. The maritime countries had made stringent conditions on the cession of the Southern Netherlands to the Austrian dynasty. The treaties stipulated that "the loyal subjects of his Imperial Majesty could neither buy nor sell without the consent of their neighbours." During the last years of the Spanish régime, a small group of Ostend merchants had chartered a ship, the *Prince Eugène*, and founded factories near Canton. This was the origin of the "General Company of the Indies to trade in Bengal and the extreme East," usually known as the "Ostend Company," founded in 1723. Within seven hours' time, the capital of 6,000,000 florins was subscribed, and soon eleven ships plied between Ostend and a series of factories established on the coast of Bengal and Southern China. This success was looked at askance by the maritime Powers, which, basing their claim on a clause in the treaty of Münster forbidding the Spanish to trade in the East Indies, made the suppression of the new company a condition to the acceptance of the Pragmatic Sanction. By this act, Charles VI endeavoured to ensure the succession of Maria Theresa to the Austrian throne. Once more, Belgium was sacrificed to dynastic interests, and on May 31, 1727, the concession of the Company of Ostend was suspended, to be finally suppressed in 1731. A similar attempt was made, later in the century, by the Company of Asia and Africa, whose seat was at Trieste, with a branch at Ostend. This company chose for its ventures the deserted group of islands surrounding Tristan d'Acunha, with the idea that such a modest enterprise could not possibly awake the jealousy of the Powers. But, in the same way, in 1785, Holland, England and France brought about the failure of the new company. Ostend had to be satisfied with the transit of Spanish wool towards the Empire and with the temporary activity brought to her port by the American War of Independence.

INDUSTRIAL PROGRESS

In spite of their apparent insignificance and of their total failure, these attempts to reopen communication with the outer world, notwithstanding the closing of the Scheldt, are symptomatic of a remarkable economic revival. The population had risen from two to three millions, during the first half of the eighteenth century, and Brussels, with 70,000 inhabitants, Ghent and Antwerp, with 50,000 each, had regained a certain part of their former prosperity. Native industry, strongly encouraged by protective measures, made a wonderful recovery. In the small towns and the country-side, the linen industry benefited largely from the invention of the fly shuttle, over two hundred thousand weavers and spinners being employed in 1765. Lace-making had made further progress, specially in Brussels, where fifteen thousand women followed this trade. In 1750 Tournai became an important centre for the china industry, its wares acquiring great renown. The extraction of coal in the deeper seams had been facilitated by the use of recently invented steam-pumps, and the woollen industry around Verviers was producing, in 1757, 70,000 pieces of material a year. Such progress largely compensated for the decadence of tapestry, which had been ruined by the rivalry of printed stuffs.

The Government intervened also actively in agricultural matters by encouraging small ownership, at the expense of great estates, and the breaking up of new ground. The land tax was more evenly distributed and the great work of draining the Moeres (flooded land between Furnes and Dunkirk), which had been begun by the archdukes, was successfully completed (1780). The peasants also benefited from the cultivation of potatoes, which were becoming more and more popular.

The only severe check to economic activity was caused by the War of the Austrian Succession, which opened at the accession of Maria Theresa (1740), and which opposed the forces of Austria, England and Holland against the coalition of Prussia, France, Spain and Poland. A British landing in Ostend prevented an early invasion of the Southern Netherlands by France during the first year of the struggle, but in 1744 French troops appeared in West Flanders, and Belgium became once more the "Cockpit of Europe."

The victory of Maurice de Saxe at Fontenoy against the allied armies commanded by the Duke of Cumberland placed the Southern Netherlands under French occupation. After a month's siege, Brussels was obliged to capitulate, and was soon followed by Antwerp and the principal towns of the country. The Marshal de Saxe treated the Belgian provinces as conquered territory, and the exactions of his intendant, Moreau de Seychelles, provoked some protests, which were abruptly silenced. After two years' operations, during which the allies sustained some reverses on land but obtained some victories at sea, peace was finally signed at Aix-la-Chapelle (1748). The Belgian provinces came again under Austrian rule, and Maestricht and Bergen-op-Zoom, which had been conquered by the French, were given back to Holland, together with the fortresses of the Barrier, which were again occupied by Dutch troops.

Dutch occupation had, from the beginning, been strongly resented by the Belgian people, who felt the humiliation of entertaining foreign garrisons in their own towns. Now that the Dutch had proved unable to defend the Barrier, its re-establishment was still less justified and was considered as a gratuitous insult. Nothing did more to deepen the gulf between the Southern and Northern Netherlands than the maintenance of the Barrier system, combined with the repeated actions taken by the Dutch to ruin the trade of Ostend and to enforce the free import of certain goods. The popularity enjoyed by Charles de Lorraine, the brother in-law of Maria Theresa, who governed the Belgian provinces from 1744 to 1780, was partly due to the resentment provoked by Dutch supremacy.

AUSTRIAN SUCCESSION

On the whole, the Austrian régime was not very different from the Spanish. The provinces were governed from Vienna, where the Council of the Low Countries invariably adopted the Government's decision. The States General were never summoned and no affair of importance was submitted to the Council of State in

Brussels. Charles de Lorraine, however, showed a greater respect for local privileges than his predecessors and gained the sympathy of the nobles by his genial manners. He held court either in Brussels or in his castles of Mariemont and Tervueren, where French fashions were introduced and which recalled, on a modest scale, the glories of Versailles. Some members of the aristocracy, like Charles Joseph de Ligne, who was, besides, a remarkable writer, were in close relations with the French philosophers, but they were only a small minority and most of the Belgian nobles were decidedly hostile to the new ideas. Voltaire, who visited Brussels in 1738, did not appreciate this provincial atmosphere: "The Arts do not dwell in Brussels, neither do the Pleasures; a retired and quiet life is here the lot of nearly all, but this quiet life is so much like tedium that one may easily be mistaken for the other."

As a matter of fact, though the eighteenth century contrasted favourably with the seventeenth, in the Southern provinces, from the economic point of view, its intellectual life was extraordinarily poor. There is no name to mention among the Flemish writers. Indeed, one might even say that Flemish had practically ceased to be written and had become a mere dialect. The Prince de Ligne remained isolated in his castle of Belœil, designed by Lenôtre, and was merely a French intellectual in exile. A Royal Academy of Drawing had been founded, but the period hardly produced any painter worthy of note. An Imperial and Royal Academy of Science and Letters had been inaugurated in 1772, but the only members were scholars and antiquaries without any originality. Maria Theresa tried to react against this intellectual apathy. She substituted civil for ecclesiastical censorship, she commissioned Count de Nény, the famous jurist, to reform the University of Louvain. When the order of the Jesuits was suppressed by the pope in 1773, she founded fifteen new lay colleges, known as Collèges Thérésiens, and took a personal interest in the framing of the programme of studies and in the least detail of organization. She favoured the teaching of Flemish as well as French in the secondary schools and the two languages were placed on exactly the same footing. In the judicial domain she succeeded in abolishing torture as a means of inquiry. She also attempted to relieve pauperism by the foundation of orphanages and almshouses.

MARIA THERESA

In spite of the fact that neither Charles VI nor Maria Theresa ever visited Belgium, the people felt a genuine attachment to the monarchy. They lived with the memory of such severe trials that they were grateful for the scant attention they received. Besides, the Hapsburg dynasty remained one of their links with the past, and it is significant that, at a time when all eyes were turned towards the future, the Belgians, and especially the popular classes, were more and more thrown back on their own traditions. No doubt the economic restrictions to which they were subjected and the fact that they were practically isolated must have conduced to this state of mind, but the lack of political independence is mainly responsible for it. Unable to take their fate in their own hands, obliged to submit to the greatest calamities without being allowed to avoid or to prevent them, the Belgians clung to the last vestige of their past privileges as if their salvation could only be found among the ruins of their bygone glory.

POPULAR RESTLESSNESS

Belgium

The only serious civil trouble which occurred under Spanish and Austrian rule was caused by trivial infringements by the Government of some of the old privileges of the corporations. For such reasons, riots broke out in Brussels (1619), Antwerp (1659) and Louvain (1684). The people did not rise against foreign domination or in order to obtain their share in the administration of the country, but because they thought, rightly or wrongly, that some mediæval custom, which they considered as their sacred privilege, had not been observed. During the last years of the Spanish régime, frequent riots broke out in Brussels because, after the accidental collapse of a tower containing old documents, the people had been able to read again the Grand Privilege of Mary of Burgundy, granted two centuries before. They had reprints made of it under the name *Luyster van Brabant* (Ornament of Brabant) and wanted to persuade Maximilian Emmanuel to apply the old charter. After long delays, the governor had finally to enforce severe regulations, known as "réglements additionnels." This incident was the origin of further trouble at the beginning of the Austrian régime, when Prince Eugène, being engaged in the war against the Turks, delegated the Marquis de Prié to represent him in the Low Countries. Unwilling to comply with the new regulations, the Brussels artisans refused to pay the taxes. They were led by a chair-maker, François Anneessens. Riots broke out in 1718 in Brussels and Malines, and Prié was obliged to let the local militia restore order. He had meanwhile sent for troops, and in October 1719 Brussels was militarily occupied. Anneessens was executed, and the bitterness provoked by this tyrannical measure obliged the Government to recall Prié a few years later (1724). These popular movements were only the first signs of the increasing restlessness of the people which caused the Brabançonne revolution of 1789. While the conservative and even reactionary character of these civil troubles must be made clear, in order to avoid any confusion between the Belgian and the French revolutions, it must at the same time be admitted that both movements started from the same desire for change and from the same confused feeling that, under a new régime, life would become more tolerable. The social conditions caused by the "ancien régime" were not nearly so oppressive in the Belgian provinces as in France, and, under the enlightened rule of Maria Theresa and Joseph II, some amelioration was certainly to be expected. But the people suffered from the artificial conditions under which they lived economically, and though they did not see clearly the cause of their trouble, they were inclined to seize upon any pretext to manifest their discontent. In spite of all appearances, one could suggest that the closing of the Scheldt may have had something to do with the overthrow of the Austrian régime.

Chapter XXII The Brabançonne Revolution

Philip II's policy ruined the Southern Netherlands at the end of the sixteenth century. Two hundred years later, Joseph II's methods of government provoked a popular reaction which practically brought to an end the Hapsburg régime. The contrast between the two sovereigns is striking. Philip II is the type of the monarchic tyrant basing his claim to sovereignty on the Divine Right of Kings and pursuing these principles to their extreme conclusions. Not only did he consider his mission to govern his people's bodies, but he also felt bound to govern their souls, and sincerely believed that, by persecuting heresy by the most cruel means, he was in reality working for their good. Opposed to this clerical fanatic, issuing decrees from a monastery cell, Joseph II stands as the type of the modern monarch, brought up on eighteenth-century enlightened philosophy, for whom the State was not to serve the Church but to be served by it. For this young philosopher, who affected the greatest simplicity in manners and habits, the sovereign himself was the first servant of the State, and his autocratic rule was only justified by his belief that a reasonable and wise government could not be subjected to the peoples' control.

JOSEPH II

But, in spite of this contrast in education, external appearance and outlook, Philip II and Joseph II had certain points in common. They were both conscientious workers, over-anxious to control every act of their representatives, and they had both the greatest contempt for the feelings of the people they governed. Having come to certain conclusions, they applied them mechanically, scornful of all resistance. They held the secret of their people's happiness or salvation in their hands and they were resolved to enforce this happiness and this salvation on them whether they agreed or not. They both possessed the hard, intolerant and virtuous mind which makes the worst autocrats. The only striking difference between the wishes of the two monarchs was that the fanatic of eighteenth-century philosophy was determined that his people should find happiness in this life, while the fanatic of the Catholic Renaissance was determined that they should find this happiness in the next.

JOSEPH II.
From a contemporary engraving.

JOSEPH'S VISIT TO BELGIUM

Such appreciation may seem strange if one considers that one of Joseph II's cardinal principles of government was precisely religious and philosophic tolerance and the complete dissociation of State politics from personal belief. But we are not concerned at present with the personal philosophy of the two kings, but with the way it affected their people. This people, as far as the Netherlands were concerned, were the last in Europe to tolerate such hard and abstract methods of government, and nothing perhaps is more enlightening, if we try to form an adequate opinion of Belgian temperament, than the upheaval caused by the reforms proclaimed by the "benighted" and by the "enlightened" monarch. It was not so much that the Belgians rebelled against Inquisition, in one case, and against secularization in the other. We have seen that, in the sixteenth century, the great majority had remained Catholic, in spite of Calvinistic propaganda, and, though the Church had obtained still greater authority during the seventeenth century, the minority influenced by the ideas of the French Revolution was by no means to be disregarded. The principle to which the Belgians most objected was State worship, because it broke up all the traditions of the Burgundian and post-Burgundian periods. As long as these traditions and local privileges, giving them still a shadow of provincial independence, were respected, they submitted without too much difficulty to the imposition of centralized institutions and to foreign rule. They were even ready, when this rule proved at all congenial, to give solid proofs of their loyalty. They were very sensible of any mark of sympathy and showed an almost exaggerated gratitude to any prince who condescended to preside over their festivals and share in their pleasures. This had been the secret of Charles V's popularity, and the successful governorship of Charles de Lorraine had no other cause. But Charles de Lorraine was just the type of man whom a puritan dogmatist like Joseph II could not stand. Though he had visited most of his estates, as heir apparent, he had always refrained from going to Belgium, owing to his antipathy for his uncle, whose popularity he envied. When Charles died, he changed the name of the regiment which had been called after him. His visit to Belgium, in 1781, was a great disappointment to the people—as great a disappointment as the first appearance of Philip II in Brussels. He started with the intention of "undertaking a serious and thorough study" of the Southern Netherlands. When asked to preside over a festivity, in Luxemburg, he answered that he had not come "to eat, drink and dance, but on serious business." When shown, at Ghent, the glorious masterpiece of Flemish art, the crowning glory of the Burgundian time, Van Eyck's Adoration of the Lamb, he objected to the nude figures of Adam and Eve and had them removed. He appeared in simple uniform, accompanied by one servant, stayed at the public inn and travelled in public coaches. He spent most of his time in government offices, taking no opportunity to mix with the people and visiting in a hurried way schools, barracks and workshops. Such were his serious studies. How could the people understand a prince who understood them so little? Perceiving this lack of sympathy, he had already judged them; they were, for him, "frenchified heads who cared for nothing but beer."

Maria Theresa, though her policy had remained strictly dynastic, involving even the possible exchange of her Belgian provinces against other States, had acquired a certain knowledge of the people and realized that their prejudices, though absurd according to her own lights, had to be indulged. She had urged her son to be patient with regard to such prejudices, "of which too many had already been scraped away." She realized that the acceptance by the Government of local customs and privileges was an essential condition to the continuance of Austrian rule, that the people, unable to defend themselves, centred all their affection and their pride on these last remnants of their former glory, and that religious ceremonies and popular feasts were a healthy overflow for popular energy which might otherwise become dangerous. Choosing her opportunities, she had gradually worked towards the secularization of education and the limitation of the privileges of the clergy, but she had not attempted wholesale reforms.

Belgium

Joseph II, on the contrary, worked according to plan, and was bent on destroying whatever seemed to him absurd in the customs and institutions of the country. Practically everything seemed so to him: the anachronism of the Joyous Entry, the mediævalism of the Grand Privilege of Mary of Burgundy, the regionalism of provincial States, the prestige of the Church, the pilgrimages, the intolerance, down to the popular festivities, the drinking bouts of the "kermesses" and the mad craving of the people for good cheer. This last trait was as characteristic of the Belgian people in those days as in mediæval and modern times. All the realist painters, from Breughel to Jordaens and from Jordaens to Teniers, had exalted the joys of popular holidays, and it is remarkable that, during a century when there was so little to eat in the country and so little cause for merrymaking, the works of art which are the truest expression of the people's aspirations dwell on no other subject with so much relish and insistence. The tragic side of life was not represented, and one might venture to say that the admirers of such merry kermesses must often have taken their wish for the reality. Like Breughel's "Pays de Cocagne," they described an earthly paradise far more distant than the heavenly one.

WAR OF THE CAULDRON

In one way only the emperor understood the aspirations of his people and supported them up to a certain point. Before organizing his possessions according to the ideal project he had already sketched, he intended to consolidate their political situation. The Barrier system was as distasteful to him as to the population of Flanders and Hainault, and he shared the grievances of the merchants of Antwerp with regard to the closing of the Scheldt. As early as 1756 Maria Theresa had refused to pay the annual tribute for the upkeep of the Dutch garrisons, which had done so little to defend Belgium during the previous war, but she had been unable to prevent the Prince of Brunswick from rebuilding the destroyed fortresses and from reinstating the garrisons. After the break up of the Dutch-British alliance, owing to the American War, Joseph II did not hesitate to demolish the fortresses, and the Dutch garrisons were obliged to depart (1782). Encouraged by this first success and finding England eager to reopen the Scheldt, owing to the blockade of the Dutch coast, the emperor announced the liberty of the river, and followed this announcement by sending, rather rashly, a small brig, the *Louis*, flying his flag, from Antwerp down to the sea. A shot, fired from a Dutch cutter, hit a cauldron which happened to be on deck and Europe was faced with the prospect of a new war. The "War of the Cauldron" was, however, prevented by the mediation of Louis XVI, and the treaty of Fontainebleau (1785), while recognizing the suppression of the Barrier, maintained the closing of the Scheldt.

This check in his foreign policy further increased the unpopularity of Joseph II in Belgium. Jealous of the authority of Duke Albert Casimir of Saxe-Teschen and of his sister, Marie Christine, his representatives in the country, the emperor deprived them of all initiative and acted directly through his minister plenipotentiary, the Count of Belgiojioso. In order to restrict the influence of the clergy and to bring Belgian institutions into complete harmony with the organization of his other States, Joseph II issued, from 1781 to 1786, a series of edicts which could not fail to cause great indignation among the Catholics: all public functions were rendered accessible to Catholics and non-Catholics alike, complete liberty of worship was proclaimed, mixed marriages (between Catholics and Protestants) were authorized, the keeping of the parish registers was taken from the ecclesiastical authorities, all "useless" convents and monasteries were suppressed, all episcopal charges were subjected to imperial sanction, all episcopal seminaries were suppressed, to be replaced by controlled seminaries at Louvain and Luxemburg. The parish limits were altered and strong regulations were made with regard to processions, pilgrimages and even sacerdotal costume, while burying in consecrated ground was forbidden, in order that all dead, whatever their creed, should be equally honoured.

INTERNAL REFORMS

Some of these measures might have been quite justified, and the example of Maria Theresa shows that they might have been taken progressively, under favourable circumstances, without causing trouble. What hurt the people most was their sweeping character, their frequency and the petty tyranny with which they were applied. It was not without reason that Frederick II of Prussia nicknamed Joseph "my brother the sacristan." The emperor had gone as far as replacing the Catholic brotherhoods by the "Brotherhood of the Active Love of My Neighbour." All protests remained without the least result. They were merely, according to Joseph II, "the effect of delirium." Within five years, this too sensible sovereign, by calling all those who did not agree with him "madmen," had succeeded in undoing all the good work undertaken by Charles de Lorraine and in ruining Austrian authority in the Netherlands. In 1786 Joseph II undertook to regulate the people's pleasures. In order to prevent the inhabitants of neighbouring villages and towns from taking part in each other's kermesses, he fixed one day in the year for the celebration of all these festivities. No wonder that his good intentions were not appreciated and that this constant interference of the State in the people's most intimate and cherished traditions was met with growing dislike.

The emperor, nevertheless, did not slacken his activity, and the next year issued a decree which completely upset the administrative and judicial organization of the provinces. A "General Council of the Low Countries" replaced the three collateral Councils. The country was divided into nine circles, under the authority of intendants, each of which was subdivided into districts under the authority of commissaries. All supreme courts, provincial, municipal, ecclesiastical, university and corporation courts were replaced, from one day to another, by sixty-four ordinary tribunals, two courts of appeal and one court of revision.

This last measure, which really meant the final break up of all the privileges and institutions so anxiously defended and preserved through centuries of foreign oppression, provoked a unanimous protest. The Catholics, headed by the popular tribune Van der Noot, were joined by the minority of nobles and bourgeois influenced by the ideas of the French Revolution, whose principal representative was François Vonck. The States of Brabant refused to pay the taxes, as long as the 1787 decrees were not repealed, and the few partisans of Belgiojioso, or "Figs," were persecuted by the populace. On May 18, 1787, Duke Albert Casimir wrote to Joseph II: "Convinced that it is attacked in its most sacred rights and its very liberty, the whole nation, from the first to the last citizen, is permeated with a patriotic enthusiasm which would cause them to shed the last drop of their blood rather than obey laws which the authorities would endeavour to impose and which appear contrary to the Constitution."

Belgium

VAN DER NOOT.
From a contemporary engraving.

Meanwhile Van der Noot and Vonck had founded a Patriotic Committee, heavily subsidized by the clergy, which enlisted volunteers and circulated anti-imperial pamphlets. In August 1787 Joseph II was at last persuaded to suspend his last decrees, on the condition that the Committee should be dissolved and the volunteers disbanded. He sent to Brussels, as plenipotentiary, Count Trautmansdorff, with dictatorial powers, and General d'Alton as commander of the imperial forces. Under the threat of the military, the Council of Brabant was obliged to submit.

The religious reforms, however, were still provoking strong opposition. The Seminary General remained without pupils. The University of Louvain, having rebelled against the new regulations, was closed. Riots broke out in Louvain, Malines and Antwerp which were sternly repressed. The States of Hainault, having refused subsidies, were dissolved. When the States of Brabant adopted a similar attitude, the emperor had guns trained on the Grand' Place of Brussels and threatened "to turn the capital into a desert where grass would grow in the streets." The autocrat was now showing under the dogmatist. Exasperated by resistance, Joseph II asked from the States of Brabant a perpetual subsidy, declared his intention of revising the Joyous Entry, which he had sworn to maintain, and of taking up his plans of judiciary reorganization. The States, having refused their support, were dissolved and the Joyous Entry annulled.

It so happened that public opinion was stirred most acutely in the provinces at the time of the taking of the Bastille by the people of Paris (July 1789). This great symbolic event was bound to react on the Belgian crisis. The Vonckist minority was strongly encouraged and the rest of the people saw in the event merely a victory of liberty against autocracy. Van der Noot had taken refuge in Breda, whence he had undertaken several journeys to secure the support of the Triple Alliance. Pitt had refused to grant him an audience, but the Dutch and Prussian governments, without making any definite engagements, had at least lent an ear to his proposals. The popular leader, rushing to hasty conclusions, announced that the Powers were favourable to the revolution. Vonck, on the other hand, had established his headquarters in the principality of Liége, where he had many friends and where he succeeded in enlisting a certain number of volunteers. When the Austrians entered the principality, he was obliged to leave for Breda, where he joined forces with Van der Noot. A retired colonel of the Prussian army, Van der Meersch, was chosen as the commander of the three thousand badly equipped volunteers massed along the Dutch frontier. On October 23rd he occupied Hoogstraeten, in the Campine, and issued a manifesto in which Joseph II was declared to have forfeited his rights. A slight success at Turnhout, a few days later, followed by the retreat of the Austrian forces, sufficed to provoke risings all over the country. Deserted by his Walloon troops, General d'Alton was obliged to leave Brussels for Luxemburg, the only town remaining loyal. On December 18th Van der Noot and Vonck made their solemn entry into Brussels, followed by a thanksgiving service at Ste. Gudule. Amazed by these events, Joseph II wrote to Count de Ségur: "A general madness seems to seize all peoples; those of Brabant, for instance, have revolted because I wanted to give them what your own nation clamours for." He was certainly nearer the truth than Camille Desmoulins, who, in his well-known paper, assimilated the two revolutions because they started almost on the same day. As a matter of fact, the Brabançonne revolution was far more conservative than progressive. The intellectual Vonckists, who had always been in a minority, were practically ignored on the morrow of the victory, and Van der Noot assumed power.

Belgium

SCENE OF THE BRABANÇONNE REVOLUTION.
(From an old print)
A delegation from Mons arriving at the Town Hall of Brussels.

"*BELGIAN UNITED STATES*"

The new Constitution, accepted, on January 11, 1790, by delegates of the provincial States, with the exception of Luxemburg, declared the "Etats Belgiques Unis" to form a confederation under the leadership of a Supreme Congress. The States General dealt only with questions of general administration and differences between the provinces. The Congress was responsible for foreign affairs, all local matters being referred to the provincial States. Though, at first sight, this Constitution seems to be strongly influenced by the American example, it marked merely the triumph of the particularist tendencies of the Middle Ages and a reaction against the dogmatic and centralized rule of Joseph II. It secured the predominance of the nobility and the clergy and the maintenance of the old States, while preserving the Church against any attempt at secularization. Any effort made by the Vonckists to infuse the new Constitution with the principles of the Rights of Man and popular sovereignty was not only resisted, but strongly resented, and soon a regular persecution of the progressive bourgeois and nobles was organized by the "statistes" led by Van der Noot. Vonck and his followers were obliged to fly to France, and Van der Meersch, who sided with them, was arrested by Baron de Schoenfeldt, placed by the Congress at the head of the National troops.

RETURN OF THE AUSTRIANS

The new emperor, Leopold II, who had succeeded his brother on the throne of Austria (February 1790), took the opportunity offered by these internal troubles to reopen negotiations. He promised a complete amnesty, the suppression of the reforms and the nomination of Belgians to all posts, even those of Plenipotentiary and of Commander of the National forces. Van der Noot had refused these offers on the ground that the Triple Alliance would support the Confederacy. On July 27th, however, England, the United Provinces and Prussia signed the Convention of

Reichenbach, reinstating Leopold II in his dominion over the Netherlands. This contributed to ruin the prestige of the Congress. The Belgian National troops could not offer much resistance to the invading Austrian armies. On November 25th, Marshal Bender reached Namur, and on December 2nd, nearly a year after their departure from Brussels, the Austrians re-entered the capital. The Reichenbach Convention had guaranteed complete amnesty. Leopold II kept his promise and, by the treaty of The Hague, restored all institutions as they had been in the reign of Maria Theresa.

Thus failed miserably a revolution begun amid fervent enthusiasm. The patriotism of the people cannot be questioned. They had only been reconciled to foreign rule in the sixteenth century because it had been the means of preserving their faith and their ancient traditions. As soon as this tacit contract was broken, they decided to shake off foreign tutelage and to make a bid for independence. But, if the people did not lack public spirit, they had lost contact with the times and were unable to use their liberty when they had conquered it. Public opinion was uneducated and regionalism had blinded the people to the advantages which they might have derived from a more centralized régime. They were not prepared to make any concessions to their political adversaries for the sake of unity; they had still to learn the motto of 1830: "Union is Strength." In this way, the terrible ordeal which they had to undergo under French occupation did not remain entirely fruitless. Neither the Spaniards nor the Austrians had succeeded in uprooting particularist tendencies. The French imposed a centralized régime and impressed the people with its social value. When, in 1830, the Belgians again rebelled against foreign oppression, they had learnt their lesson and did not again allow internal differences to deprive them of the fruit of their labours.

Chapter XXIII Liberty, Equality, Fraternity

One of the reasons of Joseph II's failure to reform Belgian institutions was that his monarchical power rested mainly on the nobility, the clergy and the peasants, who were bound to resent the sacrifice of their privileges and traditions. The French Republic and its outcome, the Napoleonic régime, were more successful, not because they displayed more diplomacy and moderation, but because, in spite of their excesses and autocratic procedure, they really brought a new idea into the country and based their power on a new conception of society. The bourgeois elements of the Vonckist school and the population of the great towns had by now been permeated with the spirit of the Revolution. They had adopted the principle of the Rights of Man and of equal citizenship, and, for the sake of such ideals, they were prepared to make some allowances. The first years of the French régime were nevertheless a bitter disappointment.

JEMAPPES

By the declaration of Pillnitz (1791), Leopold II, brother of the French queen, had laid the basis of the first coalition and manifested his intention of intervening in favour of Louis XVI. After his death (1792) Francis II pursued a still more aggressive policy towards the Revolution, and the Girondins, who had just come into power, obliged the King of France to declare war against Austria. The first attacks against Belgium were easily repulsed by the imperial troops, commanded by national leaders, but the victory of Jemappes (November 6th), won by Dumouriez with the help of a Belgian legion, opened the Belgian provinces to the revolutionary troops. General Dumouriez was a moderate and intended to remain faithful to the principles of liberty. He issued a proclamation, approved by the Convention, declaring that his soldiers were coming as allies and as brothers. When, on November 14th, he was offered the keys of Brussels by the magistrates, he refused them, saying: "Keep the keys yourselves and keep them carefully; let no foreigner rule you any more, for you are not made for such a fate." Greatly impressed by the warm reception given him in Mons and Brussels by the Vonckists, he did not realize that the country was far from being unanimous. The French general declared the Scheldt open, in accordance with a decree of the Republic which had proclaimed the freedom of the river.

Emile Cammaerts

BELGIUM UNDER FRENCH RULE.

While the Belgians hesitated to declare a Convention and to organize themselves according to the Republican régime, they began to feel the first effects of the occupation. The French army, in the region of Liége, lived only on requisitions. Cambon had presented to the Convention (December 1792) a decree suppressing all distinctions and privileges in the conquered territories, these being replaced by the sovereignty of the people. This sovereignty being without expression in Belgium, the provinces were practically administered by a number of Jacobin Commissaries, whose most important task was to confiscate the goods of the nobles and of the clergy and to enforce the circulation of the revolutionary paper money (assignats). These measures provoked a reaction in favour of Statism, and the conservatives obtained an overwhelming majority in the elections held in December. Meanwhile, England and the United Provinces, alarmed by the progress of the French in the Netherlands, had joined the first coalition (January 1793), and the Jacobins, dominating the Convention, had entered upon an annexationist policy, nothing short of the left bank of the Rhine being able, according to them, to secure France against the attacks of the reaction. In order to appease the scruples of the French moderates, the Jacobins endeavoured to provoke manifestations in favour of annexation in the Belgian provinces. A regular propaganda was organized by the Clubs. Orators, wearing the scarlet hood and armed with pikes, addressed the crowds in the market-places. The deputy Chepy, who had taken the leadership of the movement, declared that he was determined to obtain reunion by "the power of reason, the touching insinuations of philanthropy and by all means of revolutionary tactics." On many occasions crowds driven into a church were surrounded by armed "Sans Culottes" and obliged to manifest their attachment to the Republic by loud acclamations. In March 1793 a rising was imminent, ten thousand armed peasants being already concentrated near Grammont. It was prevented, at the last moment, by the return of Dumouriez, who ordered Chepy to be arrested, liberated hostages and enforced the restitution of the spoils taken from churches and castles. In a letter to the Convention, he protested against the mad policy pursued by the Jacobin Commissaries, and adjured them to read through the story of the Netherlands, where they would find that the good will of the Belgian people could never be obtained by force.

NEERWINDEN

Defeated at Neerwinden (March 1793), Dumouriez was obliged to retreat, and on April 28th the Austrians re-entered Brussels. The restoration was favourably greeted by the people, especially as Francis II adhered faithfully to the old privileges, abstaining from levying recruits, after the refusal of the States of Brabant, and personally taking the oath of the Joyous Entry (April 1794). This was the last time that this ancient ceremony was performed.

A few days later, Pichegru started a great offensive movement in Flanders, and on June 26th, the victory of Fleurus again placed the Belgian provinces in French hands. While Jourdan pursued the imperialists towards the Rhine, taking Maestricht on his way, Pichegru continued the campaign in Holland. Zeeland Flanders had already been conquered by Moreau, and the treaty of The Hague (May 1795) restored to the Belgian provinces most of the districts lost by the treaty of Münster, nearly a century and a half before. France obtained Zeeland Flanders with the left bank of the Scheldt, and, in Limburg, the key positions of Maestricht and Venloo. She obtained, besides, the right to place garrisons, in war-time, in Bois-le-Duc and other towns of North Brabant. Holland was promised compensation in Gelder.

REPUBLICAN RULE

While the internal policy of the Republic was veiled in so much ideology and marred by tyrannous cupidity, its foreign policy was based on sound realism. The French plenipotentiaries, like Joseph II, but far more clearly, perceived that the possession of the key positions on the Scheldt and on the Meuse was essential to the security of the country and to its commercial prosperity. A comparison between the clauses of the treaty of The Hague and of the treaty of Münster is particularly enlightening. Apparently, the demands of the French were moderate; in fact, they entirely reversed the situation created in the seventeenth century. No wholesale annexations would have given the French equivalent advantages. The choice of the Republic was dictated by sound strategic principles and determined by the same motives as had guided the Dutch in 1648.

But the Belgian people, suffering from all the evils of foreign occupation, could derive but scant satisfaction from the restoration of the lost districts. The Convention was waging war on the world and bleeding Belgium white in order to find the necessary resources. The provinces were obliged to pay a contribution of 80,000,000 francs, amounting to six times the previous yearly budget. Hostages were taken from the towns which could not contribute their share. Requisitions of all raw material were systematically organized. Cambon boasted to the Convention that the Netherlands not only provided for the upkeep of the Republican armies, but also enriched the national treasury. Under the management of the "Agence de Commerce et d'Extraction de la Belgique," the treasuries of churches, convents, corporations and municipalities were carted away, together with pictures, works of art and industrial machines. The Republican agents, nicknamed the "French sponges," even went as far as plundering private property. At the same time, the value of the assignats had fallen to a ridiculously low level, and in order to check the corresponding rise in prices the authorities had fixed a "maximum" and obliged the traders to keep their shops open.

All Dumouriez's promises had been long forgotten and no account whatever was taken now of the wishes of the population. Old charters were destroyed and people were obliged to plant "trees of liberty" in the market-places. The names of the streets were altered, the use of the Republican calendar enforced and the "decadi" (observance of the tenth day) substituted for Sunday. Religious festivals were replaced by feasts in honour of "Nature" or "Mankind," and most of the churches were closed or transformed into barracks, storehouses or temples devoted to the worship of the "Supreme Being." Finally, in 1795, a proposal was made to the Committee of Public Safety to annex the territory of the Austrian Netherlands. In spite of a few protests, the proposal was adopted, on October 1, 1795, and the country divided into nine departments—Lys, Escaut, Deux Nèthes, Meuse Inférieure, Dyle, Ourthe, Jemappes, Sambre et Meuse and Forêts.

The régime of the Directoire was equally hateful to the Belgians, who derived scant benefit from their annexation. The Flemish language was proscribed from official documents, all public manifestations of Catholic worship were forbidden, and the estates of religious communities confiscated. After the coup d'état of the eighteenth Fructidor, the Directoire exacted from every priest an oath of hatred against monarchy. Most of the Belgian priests having refused to take this oath, deportations and persecutions followed. Many churches were destroyed, among them St. Lambert, the cathedral of Liége.

By the treaty of Campo Formio (1797), Francis II submitted to the annexation of the Austrian Netherlands, but Great Britain refused to give up the fight, faithful to her traditional policy, which could not admit the presence of the French on the Belgian coast, which was all the more threatening now that they held the left bank of the Scheldt. The next year the second coalition was formed, and the Directoire applied to the Belgian departments the new law of conscription.

Up to that moment, with the exception of the rising avoided by Dumouriez, the Belgians had not attempted to rebel. Exhausted by the Brabançonne revolution, divided among themselves, they had merely shown a passive resistance to Republican propaganda and to the efforts made by their masters to induce them to take part in rationalistic worship. This last measure, however, provoked a rising among the peasantry. Many young men, liable to conscription, preferred to die fighting for their liberty than for the French. The movement was quite desperate. It could expect no help from outside, neither could it be supported by the nobles, who had fled the country, or by the high clergy, who were now powerless. The peasants were assembled in the villages, at the sound of the tocsin, wearing their working clothes and often armed only with clubs or forks. They raided small towns and villages, cut down the trees of liberty, destroyed the registers on which the conscription lists were based and molested those who were suspected of French sympathies. The rising, begun in the Pays de Waes, spread to Brabant, and especially to the Campine. The repression, entrusted to General Jardon, was merciless. Most of the leaders were shot and their followers dispersed after heavy losses.

NAPOLEON

The rule of Napoleon restored peace to the Low Countries. The emperor carried the war far from the Belgian frontiers. The United Provinces had become a vassal kingdom, under the sceptre of Napoleon's brother Louis (1806), and, with the exception of a British landing on the island of Walcheren which miscarried (1809), the Belgian provinces were spared military operations up to the eve of the fall of the imperial régime.

In spite of the aversion caused by incessant conscription levies and by the strict censorship which stifled intellectual life, the Belgians benefited largely from the stern rule of the emperor, who re-established discipline and succeeded in substituting many Belgian notables for the French officials who had, up to then, governed the country. Prefects were placed at the head of the departments, which were divided into arrondissements and municipalities, each of these divisions possessing its own councils and its own courts: justices of the peace, courts of the first instance, courts of assize with a jury, above which were installed Courts of Appeal and a Court of Cassation. A "general code of simple laws," still known as the Code Napoleon, was substituted, in 1804, for the confused and intricate customs and laws preserved from the Middle Ages, and the fiscal methods were similarly transformed, inaugurating a system of direct and indirect taxes.

The Concordat, signed in 1801, re-established religious peace, Catholicism being recognized as the State religion. Churches were reopened and the observance of Sunday re-established.

Already, as First Consul, Napoleon devoted great attention to external trade. Ostend, which had been bombarded by the British in 1798, was restored, and after the peace of Amiens Antwerp enjoyed a few years of remarkable prosperity. In 1802, 969 ships entered the port; in 1803 the customs receipts rose to over 6,000,000 francs, in 1804 to over 8,000,000, and in 1805 to over 15,000,000. But the emperor's decree of November 21, 1806, establishing the Continental blockade, after the Battle of Trafalgar, converted Antwerp into a powerful naval base and a great centre of naval dockyards, without any benefit to the rest of the country. The activity of the nation was again confined to agriculture and industry. In this latter domain the period is marked by the introduction of spinning machinery by the Gantois Liévin Bauwens, who succeeded in obtaining models of the new British jennies. This was the origin of the prosperity of Ghent. While, in 1802, only 220 persons were employed in this industry, there were over 10,000 in 1810. Another innovation was brought about by a British engineer, William Cockerill, who, in 1799, initiated the use of new carding and spinning machines in Verviers. Many French cloth manufacturers were sent to the Walloon town by the French Government in order to study the new process.

WATERLOO

There are no periods of Belgian history where intellectual and artistic production reached such a low level as under the Napoleonic régime. How could it be otherwise at a time when official patronage directed every activity towards imperial worship? In France, such worship, stimulated by brilliant victories, might have inspired some sincere manifestations, but in Belgium, where the people submitted to the French régime only as to a necessary evil, military glory could not provoke any genuine enthusiasm. It was more than compensated for by conscription and arbitrary imprisonments. According to La Tour du Pain, prefect of the Dyle, the Belgians were "neither English, nor Austrian, nor French—they were Belgian." In the way of administration and judicial organization, they learnt their lesson, but it was a distasteful lesson. They were too wise to disregard the benefit which they might derive from the simplification of procedure brought about by the reforms, and they remembered them at the right time, but they remained stubbornly hostile to a foreign domination which could not be supported by any dynastic loyalism, and most of them greeted with enthusiasm the arrival of the allied armies which penetrated into the country in January 1814, after the battle of Leipzig. This enthusiasm was considerably cooled by the time of Waterloo, when it was known that, in order to constitute a powerful State on the northern frontiers of France and to reward William of Orange for his services to the allied cause, Belgium's destinies would henceforth be linked with those of the Northern provinces. This decision, already declared in the secret protocol of London, was confirmed by the Congress of Vienna. From August 1, 1814, the Prince of Orange administered the Southern provinces on behalf of the Powers.

UNITED KINGDOM OF THE NETHERLANDS.

Emile Cammaerts

Chapter XXIV Black, Yellow And Red

The Vienna settlement, creating the joint kingdom of the Netherlands, suited the Powers which made it. It suited England, since it placed the Belgian provinces, and especially Antwerp, out of the reach of France. It suited Prussia, which acquired a strong foothold on the plateaux commanding the Meuse and the right to interfere in the affairs of Luxemburg. It suited Holland, whose position was considerably strengthened by the addition of rich and populous provinces. It suited Austria and Russia, since it created a strong buffer State acting as a bulwark against French annexionism in the North. It suited everybody but the Belgians themselves, who had never been consulted, in spite of their desire to be independent, made evident by the Brabançonne Revolution and their attitude under the French régime. They had been disposed of as being without legitimate owner, and if the idea of granting them the right to rule themselves ever occurred to European diplomacy at the time, it was promptly dismissed, under the assumption that Belgian independence meant, sooner or later, reabsorption by France.

The project of reuniting Belgium and Holland affords an excellent example of a scheme plausible enough on paper, but which could not resist the test of reality. It not only seemed sound from the Powers' selfish point of view, it ought to have worked for the common benefit of Belgians and Dutch alike. An end was made to the bitter struggle waged by Holland against the Southern provinces. The commerce of Antwerp ceased to threaten the Dutch ports, the Scheldt was open, the commercial blockade lifted at last, and Belgian trade able to regain its former importance after two centuries of stagnation. Belgium must benefit from the association with a strong maritime Power, possessing rich colonies and a limitless capacity for expansion. Holland's prosperity, on the other hand, must be largely increased through the agricultural and industrial resources of the Southern provinces. Even from a purely historical point of view the idea of reconstituting the Burgundian Netherlands must have appealed to those who had preserved the memory of their former grandeur. This was not a mere inert buffer State: it might become the strong central nation which European balance of power so urgently required, since the Renaissance, to relieve the tension of Franco-British or Franco-Prussian relations. Thus could be bridged the gap created, during two centuries, by the religious wars. The old tradition of Philip the Good and Charles V was to be renewed, and the Netherlands to take once more their rank at the outposts of European civilization.

THE JOINT KINGDOM

And, indeed, under exceptionally favourable conditions, sound union, if not "complete and intimate fusion," could have been the outcome of this bold experiment. Had the Powers formally recognized Belgian nationality and provided for the respect of the country's institutions under the new régime, the Belgians might have reconciled themselves to the idea of wiping away past grievances. The Dutch might have justified their attitude under the plea that they had not been fighting Belgium, but Spain or France, and that their policy had been dictated by the necessity in which they had been placed of defending themselves against foreign invasion. William I might have conciliated public opinion in Belgium by respecting scrupulously the country's customs, which had survived Spanish and Austrian domination, by avoiding all undue interference in religious affairs, by protecting the rights of the French-speaking minority and by placing the Belgians exactly on the same footing as the Dutch. In fact, his policy aimed at achieving the complete and intimate assimilation advised at Vienna from the Dutch point of view and without any consideration for the natural feeling of a people whose traditions and religion were different from his own.

The new Constitution was the Dutch Constitution adopted in 1814, revised by a commission including an equal number of Belgian and Dutch delegates. It provided for equal toleration for all creeds and a two Chamber Parliament where an equal number of deputies from both countries would sit. (This in spite of the fact that Belgium had 50 per cent. more inhabitants than Holland.) This Constitution or "fundamental law," as it was called, was adopted by the Dutch, but rejected by the Belgian States General. Instead of amending the law, the king considered abstentions as favourable votes and ignored all opposition, so that the new Constitution was passed, in spite of a strong adverse majority. This singular procedure was called, at the time, "Dutch arithmetic."

In several aspects, the policy of William I resembled that pursued thirty years before by Joseph II. It had the same qualities and the same defects. Though taking into consideration the material interests of the people, he ignored their character and traditions and the psychological problems with which he was confronted. Faced with opposition, he attempted to override all resistance by asserting his sovereign will, with little consideration for the democratic spirit which pervaded Western Europe at the time.

POLICY OF WILLIAM I

Like Joseph II, William I, very wisely, attached great importance to the economic revival of the country. The embargo once removed, Antwerp made surprising progress, its tonnage being increased twofold between 1818 and 1829. New canals were built between Maestricht and Bois-le-Duc, Pommerœul and Antoing, while through the creation of powerful banks, such as the "Société générale pour favoriser l'Industrie nationale," Belgian manufacturers received adequate credits. The king supported, also, the creation of several factories, such as the "Phœnix" at Ghent and "Cockerill" at Seraing. It was during his reign that Belgian collieries began considerably to increase their production and that the first blast furnaces were erected near Liége and Charleroi.

The Dutch king attempted also to develop national education. He placed the three Universities (Ghent, Louvain and Liége) under State control. Many secondary and primary schools were founded all over the country and public instruction made considerable progress.

Such measures would have been beneficial to Belgium, but they needed a deep knowledge of and sympathy for local conditions to be carried out successfully. Neither the king nor his Dutch ministers (the Belgians remained always in a minority in the Cabinet) were able to realize the difficulties which stood in the way and the legitimate grievances which might easily be created by hasty action.

Emile Cammaerts

When Holland entered the union, she had a debt of nearly 2,000,000,000 florins, while Belgium's debt was much smaller (30,000,000). The latter was, nevertheless, obliged to bear half of the total liabilities and the heavy taxes rendered necessary by the king's enterprising policy. Besides, in the distribution of such taxes the interests of Belgium, still almost entirely agricultural, were sacrificed to those of commercial Holland. The latter stood for free trade, the former for protection. It is characteristic of the situation that the first sharp conflict between Belgian and Dutch deputies took place in 1821 over a bill imposing taxes on the grinding of corn and the slaughter of cattle. These immediate grievances overshadowed, in the minds of the Belgians, the encouragement given by the Government to Belgian trade and industry.

A similar disregard for existing conditions and long-established traditions brought about the failure of the measures taken by William I to promote education. Not content with creating new schools, he endeavoured to give the monopoly of public education to the State and to subject the existing private establishments (almost all led by priests) to official control. He further increased Catholic opposition by establishing a Philosophical College at Louvain, where all those intending to enter a seminary were obliged to study.

These examples show how premature was the idea of a "complete union" between the two countries—an idea put forward, no doubt, owing to the necessity of creating a strong centralized State on the northern boundary of France. Had the Dutch Government possessed as much political wisdom as the Austrian Minister at the court of The Hague, they would have realized that the "kingdom of the Netherlands would never be consolidated as long as the constitutional and administrative union was not replaced by a federal system."

The same solution might have avoided a great deal of discontent with regard to the language question. The difference of language between Northern and Southern Belgium had created no difficulty in the last centuries, owing to the fact that the country was nearly equally divided, and also that the Northern provinces were bilingual, French being used by the bourgeoisie and Flemish by the people. The union with Holland placed the French-speaking population in a minority. On the other hand, twenty years of French occupation had left their mark on the country, and the prestige of French letters had never been so brilliant. It seemed, therefore, urgent to display a great deal of tact in any reform dealing with the language question, in order not to encourage pro-French tendencies at the expense of Dutch sympathy. The idea of introducing Dutch as the official language in Flemish-speaking Belgium seemed wise enough, since it was the language understood by the great majority of the people, but there was no urgent demand for it, and it could have been realized progressively with the development of Flemish education. King William, nevertheless, decreed that no officials or civil servants should remain in office in Northern Belgium unless they spoke and wrote Dutch correctly. Since a great many of these officials belonged to the Flemish bourgeoisie and had only a very incomplete knowledge of the popular language, they were obliged to resign their posts and were supplanted by Dutchmen. So that a measure which might have been popular in Flanders, at another time and under different circumstances, was considered as a mere pretext for turning Belgian subjects out of office.

Belgium

It must be made clear that this language question played a secondary part among the causes of discontent. It alienated the Flemish bourgeoisie without conciliating the working classes, whose influence in politics, at the time, was very small. It scarcely affected the French-speaking population, since only few Walloon officials were concerned in the matter.

BELGIAN GRIEVANCES

Scorning all opposition, William I had not even attempted to conciliate one of the two great parties which divided the Belgian population: the conservative Catholics and the Liberals, advocates of the "Rights of Man" and opposed to the influence of the Church. He had alienated the first by his attempt to monopolize education and the second by the autocratic manner in which he suppressed all opposition. The prosecution against a Liberal journalist, De Potter, who attacked the Government's policy in *Le Courier des Pays-Bas*, brought about the reconciliation of the two parties against the common enemy, in 1828, just as the harsh attitude of Joseph II had caused the alliance of Van der Noot and Vonck on the eve of the Brabançonne Revolution. From anti-Government, the movement became gradually anti-Dutch, and party grievances were henceforth merged into a revival of patriotic feeling, aiming first at administrative separation and later at complete independence.

The final outburst was no doubt hastened by the 1830 Revolution in France, when the legitimist dynasty was overthrown in favour of Louis Philippe d'Orléans, just as the taking of the Bastille determined a corresponding movement in Belgium against Austrian rule. But nothing could be more misleading than to attribute to French influence the popular demonstration which took place in Brussels, on August 25th, following a performance of Auber's *Muette de Portici* at the Monnaie Theatre. The song which stirred such wild enthusiasm in the breasts of the Brussels people was purely patriotic, and it was to defend the rights of their country that they sacked the house of Van Maenen, King William's unpopular minister, and the offices of *Le National*, whose director, a French pamphleteer named Libri, was looked upon as a Dutch agent. It is true that the French flag was for a short time hoisted at the Hôtel de Ville, but it was soon replaced by the three colours of Brabant.

French influences had been at work, but the French party remained a small minority. Every act of the leaders of the revolution shows that they were bent on obtaining first administrative separation, and later, after such a proposal had been made impossible through the king's stubborn attitude, complete independence. Never did the idea of a union with France commend itself to the people. From Brussels, standing on the language frontier, the revolution spread to Walloon Liége and Flemish Louvain. Most of the important towns, with the exception of Ghent and Antwerp, joined in the movement in both parts of the country. The Prince of Orange, whose popularity was used in order to calm the multitude, came to visit Brussels, but, unable to make any definite promise, he was obliged to fly from the city.

THE SEPTEMBER DAYS

Even at that last hour, the joint kingdom of the Netherlands might have been saved, since the most enthusiastic leaders, like Gendebien, only urged autonomy; but King William remained deaf to all advice of moderation and sent a Dutch army of 12,000 men against Brussels under Prince Frederick. The revolutionary leaders had preserved but small hope, owing to the unpreparedness of the defence. The Belgian success in the street-fighting which took place near the Rue Royale and the adjoining streets was nothing short of a miracle. After three days, Prince Frederick was obliged to leave the town, leaving 2,300 dead behind him, but the losses on the Belgian side had also been heavy, and all reconciliation had become impossible. A provisional Government was formed, a National Congress summoned, the complete independence of the country proclaimed and a new Constitution prepared, a special commission adopting the principle of constitutional monarchy (October 4th).

Meanwhile, the few towns, including Ghent and Antwerp, which had not already done so expelled their garrisons, the citadel of Antwerp alone remaining in Dutch hands.

The fascinating scheme endorsed by the Vienna Congress had completely miscarried. Though only a ruler of great political talent could have realized it, the story of the fifteen years of union between the two countries shows that the king and his Dutch ministers were unable to master the very elements of the difficult proposition they had to solve. Up to the last months several opportunities offered themselves to them of retracing their steps and retrieving the situation. They failed to seize them. A careful survey of events will show that the action brought against De Potter and the choice of The Hague as the seat of the Supreme Court did more to estrange the Belgian bourgeoisie from Dutch rule than the activity of French propagandists. The initial blunder of William I was to ignore the fact that Belgium was not merely a group of ownerless provinces, but a nation as strong in her soul, if not as happy in her fate, as the Dutch nation, deserving the same care and the same consideration. Had he acted as a national prince he would have succeeded, in spite of the sad memories of past oppression, as many princes had succeeded before. But he remained essentially Dutch in his manners and his political outlook, and as such he was bound to fail, as Joseph II, Maximilian and Philip II had failed before him.

MODERN BELGIUM (TREATIES OF 1830-1839 AND 1919).

Emile Cammaerts

Chapter XXV The Scrap Of Paper

Having failed to repress the revolution, King William appealed to the Powers signatories of the eight articles creating the joint kingdom. Lord Aberdeen answered that the independence of the Belgians was an accomplished fact, but a Conference was, nevertheless, called in London, in order to mediate between the two parties, to which France was invited to send a representative. On November 14, 1830, the conditions of an armistice were settled, according to which both belligerents were to withdraw their forces behind the frontier which divided the two countries before their reunion in 1814.

This arrangement would have restored to Belgium the left bank of the Scheldt, which she had lost since the Münster treaty. The Dutch king protested, and the line was altered from the frontier of 1814 to that of 1790—that is to say, five years before the annexation by the French of the contested territory.

Throughout the negotiations the autocratic Powers—Prussia, Austria and Russia—were opposed to the Belgians. They treated them as rebels who ought to be only too happy to buy their independence at any price. As a matter of fact, if the same wave of nationalism which had stirred Belgium had not, at the same time, caused serious trouble in Poland and Italy, it is doubtful whether England and France could have induced the Conference to accept even the principle of Belgian independence. But, owing to their internal troubles, both Russia and Austria were disinclined to take action, and Prussia would have found herself isolated if she had maintained an uncompromising attitude.

The Belgians, on the other hand, from the very beginning of the negotiations, placed themselves on an equal footing with Holland, and considered the Conference as a mediator, not as an arbiter. They gratefully accepted its intervention as "prompted by feelings of sympathy for the sufferings of Belgium and by humanitarian motives," but refused energetically to bind themselves by any engagement. When, on December 20th, Belgian independence was finally recognized, the Provisory Government remarked that "the balance of power in Europe can still be ensured, and a general peace maintained, by making Belgium independent, strong and happy. If Belgium were to be left without strength and happiness, the new arrangement would be threatened with the same fate as that of the political combination of 1815. Independent Belgium has her share of European duties to fulfil, but it would be difficult to conceive what obligations could be imposed upon her by treaties in the conclusion of which she had no voice."

Such a complete consciousness of their national rights on the part of the Belgian plenipotentiaries can only be explained by the fact that such consciousness had never ceased to exist. This was no new nation struggling for its birth, but an Old nation, as old as any of those who had assumed the responsibility of planning her future. The Belgian statesmen of 1830 had nothing to improvise. They had merely to pick up the threads broken through the vicissitudes of European struggle. Their new Constitution was based on the old Joyous Entry of Brabant, which Joseph II had vainly attempted to abolish, and whose memory forty years of French and

Belgium

Dutch centralization had not succeeded in obliterating. Their foreign policy was, in the same way, inspired by a firm attachment to their past and a firmer belief in their future. The London Conference was not long in realizing, when faced by such men as Lebeau, Van de Weyer and De Mérode, that they had not merely to deal with vague idealists or eloquent demagogues. It is not enough to say that Belgium was well represented. It would be more accurate to say that her delegates had a good case to defend.

THE LONDON CONFERENCE

Three treaties were prepared by the London Conference in the course of the negotiations. The first included a series of conditions formulated in January 1831 and known as "Bases of Separation." The second was the outcome of new negotiations which took place during the following months, and is known as "the Treaty of XVIII Articles" (July 1831). The third, framed after the defeat of the Belgian troops by the Dutch and the military and naval intervention of the Powers, is known as "the Treaty of XXIV Articles" (November 1831). Accepted by the Belgians, it was first rejected by William I, and finally sanctioned by him in 1839. This is the final settlement which popular history will remember as the "scrap of paper."

According to the Bases of Separation, Belgium lost the left bank of the Scheldt, but this stream was to remain entirely free. She also lost Luxemburg, which "would continue to belong to the German Confederation."

It will be remembered that, under the treaty of Vienna, this Belgian province had been converted into a Grand Duchy and given to King William, in exchange for his possessions in Germany, but the king had declared, at the time, that the "Grand Duchy would be considered as an integral part of the State." Accordingly, Luxemburg shared the political life of the rest of the kingdom, sending deputies to the Chambers and being, from every point of view, considered as a Belgian province. Luxemburgers had even taken a prominent part in the revolutionary movement. One of them remarked in Congress, during the debate which followed the Conference resolutions, that "national sovereignty was transferred from Brussels to the Foreign Office," and by an overwhelming majority (169 against 9) the Congress protested against any delimitation of Belgian territory made without the consent of the representatives of the nation.

BASES OF SEPARATION

A period of acute tension followed this refusal. King William had not raised the blockade of the Scheldt, in spite of the conditions of the armistice, and the Belgians consequently continued their military operations in front of Maestricht, which had not yet been evacuated. The Conference urged cessation of hostilities and prompt acceptance. The Government remaining obdurate, an ultimatum was sent fixing June 1st as the last date on which the Belgians had to submit and threatening military intervention. On June 6th, Lord Ponsonby, British representative at Brussels, and General Belliard, the French representative, were formally recalled by their respective Governments, but the action of the Powers was delayed owing to differences of opinion concerning the method of intervention. This allowed Belgium some time to reopen negotiations, and her delegates in London finally obtained the revision of the "Bases of Separation." A new agreement was drafted, on June 26th, known as "the Treaty of XVIII Articles," according to which Belgium became permanently neutral, while the questions of Luxemburg and Maestricht remained in abeyance, further negotiations concerning the contested territories having to be pursued direct between Belgium and Holland.

LEOPOLD I.
(Reigned 1831-1865).
From a portrait by Liévin de Winne. *Ph. B.*

Belgium

This diplomatic success was not only due to the perseverance of the Belgian delegates but also to Prince Leopold's wise decision not to accept the crown unless a satisfactory solution was reached. It must be recalled that, as soon as the Belgian Congress had decided on constitutional monarchy, the names of several candidates had been discussed. The conservative Powers favoured the candidature of the Prince of Orange, hoping thus to restore in the future the union of the two countries. But this proposal had met with an overwhelming opposition in Belgium. The candidature of the Duke of Nemours, son of Louis Philippe, had then been considered, and by a narrow majority of two votes the Belgian Congress decided in his favour. Such a choice could not be approved in England, since it would have meant, sooner or later, French hegemony over the Belgian coast and Antwerp. Louis Philippe, therefore, refused the Belgian offer. Prince Leopold of Saxe-Coburg-Gotha, widower of Princess Charlotte, was practically an English Prince, having spent most of his life in England; he was of German extraction, and a marriage was contemplated between him and Princess Marie Louise, Louis Philippe's daughter. He had already acquired a great reputation for wisdom, which gained him later the title of the "Nestor of Europe." It was felt that no better man could be found to fill such a delicate post, and both English and French diplomats were inclined to remove all obstacles which might prevent him from accepting the Belgian offer.

The Prince's influence and the Belgian diplomats' firm attitude succeeded in altering the Conference's views. The Belgians were no longer treated as rebels and ordered to submit, but as free people whose claims must be considered. "Everybody says," wrote Lord Palmerston to Lord Granville, "that the Belgians are mad and that it is useless to discuss with them. I have noticed that there is a good deal of method in their madness." Talleyrand, who was not too well disposed towards the Belgian emissaries and "their reticences," wrote on June 24th: "We have been in conference for forty hours, but the Belgian delegates are so little accustomed to this kind of negotiations, they create so many difficulties, that we cannot get on and I am tired out. A conference took place to-day at Prince Leopold's; it lasted until eight. It will continue at my house and last probably till late in the night." The next day, the XVIII Articles were signed.

Prince Leopold having accepted the crown, the new treaty was sanctioned by the Belgian Congress on July 9th. Less than a month later, on August 2nd, the Dutch armies, breaking the armistice, invaded Belgian territory and defeated the Belgian forces at Louvain. Owing to the armed intervention both of England and France, the Dutch were forced to retreat, but these military operations had set the seal on Belgian hopes.

THE XXIV ARTICLES

The Powers were now "firmly determined to stop, by all available means, the resumption of hostilities which would threaten Europe with a general war," and, on November 15th, King Leopold was obliged to accept, under strong protest, a new agreement, known as "the Treaty of XXIV Articles," which, though preserving the country's independence and neutrality, deprived her of her natural frontiers and tore from her territories whose inhabitants had shared her life since the early Middle Ages. The Scheldt was given the status of an international river, according to the General Act of Vienna, the supervision of pilotage, buoying and dredging operations being entrusted to a Dutch-Belgian commission. Belgium retained half of

Luxemburg (the area known to-day as the province of Luxemburg), while the other half, with the town of Luxemburg, remained in the hands of the Dutch king, and constituted a Grand Duchy attached to the German Confederation. "In exchange" for their portion of Luxemburg, the Belgians were obliged to relinquish their rights over Eastern Limburg and Maestricht, which became the Dutch provinces of the same name. Such were the "final and irrevocable" decisions of the Powers.

Though the compromise was entirely in his favour, King William refused to sanction it. From the beginning of the negotiations the Dutch had contended that, by the separation of Belgium and Holland, Article XIV of the treaty of Münster (that is to say, the right of Holland to close the Scheldt in time of peace or war) came into force again. Disregarding the liberal principles laid down at Vienna, they wanted to go back to the old régime of the seventeenth and eighteenth centuries which subjected Belgium to their control. Holding Maestricht, the key of the Meuse, and the Lower Scheldt, the key of Antwerp, they intended to treat independent Belgium as they had treated the Spanish and Austrian provinces.

Laborious negotiations proceeded during the following years, and, in 1838, King William declared himself at last prepared to sign the treaty on the consideration of the payment of a toll of one florin and a half per ton on every ship entering and leaving the stream on its way to Antwerp.

Meanwhile, Limburg and Luxemburg had remained Belgian, and the bonds attaching the sacrificed provinces to the country had become so strong that the forthcoming settlement provoked emphatic protests. Petitions were sent to the king, and delegations came to Brussels urging resistance. Once more, Belgian negotiators multiplied their efforts in London and Paris. But, this time, the friendly Powers remained adamant and the Government was made to understand that, if the Belgians created difficulties, nothing would prevent the German Confederation and the King of Holland from annexing Luxemburg and Limburg by force. In the spring of 1839 the Belgian Chamber was at last compelled to give its final decision. Three ministers had resigned from the Government. The Austrian and Prussian "chargés d'affaires" had left the capital. It was common knowledge that several Prussian army corps were massed on the Eastern frontier. Under such a threat, and this time without the support of England and France, the Chamber was faced with the cruel alternative of sanctioning partial annexation or seeing the very life of the nation jeopardized by foreign invasion. The deputies of Limburg and Luxemburg were the most emphatic in their opposition: "Suicide will follow fratricide," exclaimed a deputy of Maestricht, while a representative of Ruremonde urged armed resistance. "I would rather give my life a thousand times," protested a Luxemburger, "than a vote which would oppress my conscience until my last day." On March 12th, Mr. Metz, who was unable to walk through illness, was carried to his seat and declared that "neither the king, nor the Conference, nor the Government, nor the Chambers had the right to dispose of his life" by "a sacrilegious treaty which takes away four hundred thousand Belgians from the country of their choice and covers Belgium with eternal shame."

SUBMISSION

The Government's action was defended by Mr. Nothomb, who, though a Luxemburger and an ardent patriot, realized too well the danger of the situation not to urge submission: "We have not yet had the opportunity of rendering any service to Europe. She has no reason to be grateful to us. If it were not for our pressing need of independence, nothing up to now justifies our existence. What matter to her our national soul tempered by age-long traditions! If we resist, she will put an end to our existence as a free State with a stroke of the pen. In bending before the inevitable, Belgium will save her nationality, spare the disputed districts the horrors of war, and make a sacrifice which Europe will be obliged to take into account on the day when, bearing no responsibility in the outbreak of war, the country will be able to claim her revenge!" Another argument urged by some supporters of the Government was based on the fact that, though not legally bound by her former acceptance of the XXIV Articles, which had remained in abeyance for seven years, Belgium's faith had been pledged to it: "I believe," said one of them, "that international treaties have a real value, that they are not merely scraps of paper. I believe that Right more than Force governs the affairs of this world, and that, in the end, it pays to fulfil one's obligations, however painful these may be."

A tragic incident occurred on March 14th. Mr. Bekaert-Baekelandt, deputy of Courtrai, had first been opposed to the Government's policy. He had, however, been gradually convinced that all resistance had become useless. This conversion to the inevitable had broken his heart. He ended his speech by alluding to the return at a future date of the deputies of the sacrificed provinces to the Belgian Chamber. "Meanwhile," he said, "they will remain Belgians like ourselves, and they will be generous enough to consider that our votes are extorted by force, that they are a painful sacrifice imposed upon us by foreign nations. They will no doubt appreciate how powerless we are to avoid this sad obligation...." He did not proceed further, and fell dead.

NEUTRALITY

These manifestations have been compared with the heartrending scenes which took place at the time of the annexation of Alsace-Lorraine by Germany, but it would be wrong to draw too hasty conclusions from such a comparison. On the one hand, the annexation of Alsace-Lorraine is far more recent. On the other, Dutch administration and the Grand-Ducal régime did not provoke the same opposition among the people. If Belgian irredentism proved very strong at the beginning, it gradually diminished, owing mainly to the fact that the patriots, on both sides of the frontier, were unable to entertain any hope of reunion during the long period of neutrality which paralysed Belgian foreign policy. Recent manifestations which took place on the occasion of the revision of the 1839 treaties towards the reunion of Zeeland Flanders, Luxemburg and Limburg to Belgium must, however, not be misjudged. They must not be considered as the outcome of a crude instinct towards aggrandisement, following the military success of the Belgian army at the end of the Great War, or of a wild thirst for revenge, but merely as the outburst of irredentist feelings, nursed in silence during eighty years of neutrality, and revived, among a certain group of intellectuals, by the fierce struggle waged by the nation for the safeguard of its liberties. As for the demand of military guarantees made by the Government during these negotiations, a demand which must be clearly distinguished from the irredentist agitation just mentioned, it was merely prompted by the circumstances in which Belgium is placed at the present time. The territorial losses inflicted upon the country in 1839 were largely compensated for by the pact of neutrality entered into by the Great Powers, which provided Belgium with the strongest and most unequivocal guarantees respecting her territorial integrity. Provided these guarantees were observed faithfully, the closing of the Scheldt by Holland in time of war, the critical situation on the Eastern frontier created by the indefensible cul-de-sac of Dutch Limburg, and the supremacy in Luxemburg of a foreign Power, did not seriously jeopardize the country's security. The treaties of 1839 were considered as forming a whole, the moral safeguard of guaranteed neutrality counterbalancing, to a certain extent, the new territorial encroachments. With the disappearance of neutrality, the substitution of new guarantees of security for the old ones seemed obvious. The demands formulated at the Paris Conference by the Belgian people and Government—free access from the sea towards Belgian ports in order to ensure communication between the country and her allies in time of war, a military entente with Holland towards the defence of Dutch Limburg, and a rapprochement with Luxemburg—were therefore the natural outcome of the revision of the 1839 settlement.

Chapter XXVI Neutral Independence

From 1839 till 1914, Belgium lived under the régime of independent neutrality.

Her territory had been gradually reduced during modern times. She stood stripped of all her marches. In the course of the seventeenth century she had lost Walloon Flanders and Artois to France and Northern Brabant to Holland, while the conquest by the latter Power of Zeeland Flanders and some districts in Eastern Limburg had been confirmed and enlarged by the 1839 settlements. In 1816 Prussia had seized the districts of Eupen, Malmédy, St. Vith and Bitsburg, and the XXIV Articles had given half of Luxemburg to the German Confederation.

The same treaty granted Belgium independence. Within these narrow limits, she remained at least mistress of her destinies. She had her own king, her own Government, her own Constitution. As far as internal affairs were concerned, she enjoyed full sovereignty. She was diminished, but not deeply altered. She maintained, in the nineteenth century, all the main characteristics which had distinguished her history and civilization during the Middle Ages and the Renaissance. Two races, two languages, were still associated on her soil. Walloons and Flemings took an equal share in the framing of her future. The sea remained free for commercial purposes, and the great European roads, which had so largely contributed in the past to placing her in the forefront of European nations, still found in the country their natural and necessary meeting-place. This main fact must be made evident if one attempts to explain the causes of the Belgian renaissance during the nineteenth century. It is not enough to say that the Belgium of Leopold I and Leopold II followed the tradition of the Belgium of Charles V and Philip the Good. It must be added that modern Belgium, in spite of gradual encroachments, had remained whole. Such encroachments having taken place on all sides, the nucleus was untouched. Belgium preserved her great towns and her main streams. No essential organ of the national body had been impaired.

As far as internal affairs were concerned, Belgium then emerged free and sound from the turmoil of three centuries of European warfare. For external affairs, she was still subjected to the restriction of guaranteed neutrality. It is scarcely necessary to dwell on the distinction between self-imposed neutrality, such as that existing in Switzerland, and the régime of guaranteed neutrality imposed by the Powers on Belgium. The first is no restriction of the sovereign rights of the State upon its foreign policy, the second takes away from it practically all initiative in foreign matters. If the Powers bound themselves, in the 1839 treaty, not to violate the integrity of Belgian territory and to defend the country in case of attack, Belgium, on her side, undertook to observe strictly the rules of neutrality and to take necessary measures towards the defence of her frontiers. It might be argued, and it has been argued frequently in Belgium, that such neutrality could not prevent a nation from possessing colonies and concluding a defensive alliance for the sole purpose of safeguarding herself. But, as a matter of fact, rival Powers could not give such a liberal interpretation to the text of the treaties. First from the French side, later from the German side, Belgium was constantly held under suspicion. Any manifestation of public opinion concerning foreign affairs was deeply resented, her military policy was narrowly watched, she could not take a step towards self-defence or economic expansion without provoking some discontent among the Powers. Thanks to the firmness of her statesmen and, more than once, to the friendly support of Great Britain, she was able to resist urgent demands. But it goes without saying that the Belgian Government, anxious to preserve their dignity, avoided all possible cause of friction, so that Belgium scarcely ever made use of her legitimate right to determine, within some limits, her foreign policy. Neutrality, to all intents and purposes, meant paralysis. For many, it meant worse than that—carelessness and apathy.

FALSE SECURITY

After the eight years of uncertainty which followed the first signature of the XXIV Articles—eight years during which all parties joined under the permanent Dutch menace—two currents of thought divided Belgian opinion. The first attempted to minimize the military responsibility of the country, and, trusting blindly to the promise of the Powers, to reduce to a strict minimum Belgium's military charges in men and money. The second saw clearly that, without an adequate army and the necessary defences, Belgium would be unable to fulfil her obligations in case her integrity should be violated, and would suffer in consequence; it realized that any weakness in the country's defences increased the temptation of some Powers to break their pledge. It is easy to understand that the first school was generally more popular than the other, and rallied not only the sincere idealists who thought such a contingency as the tearing up of solemn treaties absolutely impossible, but many unscrupulous politicians only too anxious to use the popular catchword "Not a penny, not a soldier," or "Niemand gedwongen soldaat," for electoral purposes. The Belgians had always been stubbornly opposed to conscription; it will be remembered that they resisted all attempts at enforcing it in the past and that it was the main cause of the War of Peasants (1798) against the "Sans Culottes." To a people which, by tradition, was strongly adverse to militarism and centralization, it was only too easy to misrepresent measures of self-defence, urgently required by the European situation, as the first step towards autocracy and oppression. The partisans of military safeguards found themselves, therefore, in a minority, and their only support was the personal influence of the Belgian kings, who, from the first days of the new régime till the eve of the war, never ceased to emphasize the evident danger of disregarding the country's international responsibilities. It is true that, with the lapse of time, the danger became more and more threatening, but, on the other hand, the "anti-militarists" found a fresh argument in the fact that, during so many years, the country had been able to weather the storm.

MILITARY PROBLEMS

The first trouble arose in connection with the Socialist revolution which broke out in France in 1848. In the previous year, Marx and Engels had established their headquarters in Brussels, where they drafted the "Manifesto of the Communist Party." The Belgians, however, were not prepared to adopt it, and the revolutionaries decided to invade the country from the South. Bands organized in France and secretly encouraged by some French leaders attempted to cross the frontier near Mouscron, at Risquons Tout, but their advance was easily checked by the Belgian forces.

The only consequence of these disturbances was the vote by the Chamber of a new grant towards the reinforcement of the army: "No doubt," said the Minister Rogier on that occasion, "it will cost something to equip a greater number of men. But has one ever estimated the cost of an invasion, even if it only lasted a week?" In 1850, Leopold II wrote to one of his ministers: "Without means of defence you will be the plaything of everyone."

A greater danger loomed ahead. Louis Napoleon had, by the coup d'état of December 1, 1851, imposed his dictatorship on France. Many prominent exiles and refugees came to Belgium, and the Brussels papers openly expressed their opinion of the new dictator. So that Belgium, which three years before had been branded as ultramontane, was now denounced as a nest of communists and rebels. Pressure was even brought to bear on the Government to introduce Press censorship. It was duly ignored, and the relations between the two countries became strained. One year later, Napoleon became Emperor of the French, and all clear-sighted Belgians realized that he was only awaiting an opportunity to extend his power and authority towards the North. This was shown plainly by the French policy with regard to Luxemburg.

FRANCO-PRUSSIAN WAR

The emperor having approached the King of Holland in view of obtaining from him the cession of the Grand Duchy, a conference was called in London (May 1867) at which the independence, neutrality and inviolability of the duchy were placed under the collective guarantee of the Powers. Thwarted in this direction by European diplomacy, Napoleon III attempted to obtain a footing in Luxemburg by controlling the railways. In January 1868 the Compagnie de l'Est, under guarantee of the French Government, took over from the Compagnie Guillaume Luxembourg its railway lines both in Luxemburg and Belgian territory. Further negotiations began with the Belgian companies Grand Luxemburg and Chemins de fer Liégeois-Limbourgeois, which would have placed all the main railways of Luxemburg and South-eastern Belgium in French hands. Warned in time, the Premier, Frère-Orban, instructed the Belgian representative in Paris to declare that Belgium would never consent to such an arrangement. Napoleon's threats remained without result, the Belgian policy being strongly upheld by Lord Clarendon, and, in July 1869, a protocol was signed annulling the contracts of the Compagnie de l'Est as far as the Belgian railways were concerned. At the same time, Napoleon III, anxious to find at any cost "compensations" for the increased prestige which Prussia obtained from her Danish and Austrian victories, had sounded that Power regarding a project of partition of the Netherlands. His proposal, first kept secret and subsequently revealed by Bismarck on the morrow of the declaration of war in 1870, was to annex Belgium to France, while Prussia would be left a free hand in Holland. The publication of this revelation by *The Times* did more than anything else to alienate British public opinion, if not from France at least from the French emperor, during the Franco-Prussian War.

Baron Chazal, who had joined the Belgian ministry in 1857, succeeded in convincing the Cabinet of the necessity of reinforcing Belgian defences. In view of the superiority of the French army—for the threat came evidently from that quarter at the time—it was decided to give up the idea of defending the country by a cordon of inefficient fortresses, and to build round Antwerp a powerful "entrenched camp," where the Belgian army could retreat and maintain itself until reinforcements came from abroad. It goes without saying that the only country which would be in a position to send such reinforcements to Antwerp, in case of an invasion, was Great Britain, and Antwerp was purposely chosen as the only position where considerable forces could conveniently be disembarked from the sea. In view of the present interpretation placed on the 1839 treaties by Holland, which gives to the latter country the right to close the Scheldt in time of war, this scheme seems, to say the least, hastily conceived. But the Dutch exclusive sovereignty over the Scheldt did not appear nearly so definite at the time as it appears now. No mention being made of the matter in the 1839 settlement, many Belgian authorities considered that the stream was placed under a régime of co-sovereignty, and it seemed then incredible that the Dutch should stop the passage of relief ships.

In the face of strong popular opposition, the Chamber voted a credit of 50,000,000 francs for the Antwerp fortifications, and General Brialmont, one of the foremost military engineers in Europe, was entrusted with the work. After its completion, Antwerp was considered one of the strongest fortified towns in the world.

As soon as a conflict became imminent between France and Prussia, Great Britain, in accordance with her traditional policy as far as Belgium was concerned, demanded from the two Powers a declaration confirming Belgian neutrality. The situation in 1870 corresponds exactly to that in 1914, and the language used by Mr. Asquith during the first days of August of the latter year seems to echo the words uttered forty years before by his great chief. "It would be impossible for us not to interfere," firmly declared Mr. Gladstone, "should we witness the destruction of Belgium's liberty and independence." In both cases, British policy was inspired by the guarantee mentioned in the treaties, a guarantee which not only implied safety for Belgium, but also absolute opposition to any Power attempting to seize the Belgian coast. The motives were the same, the steps taken were the same, the outcome only was different. Both the French emperor and Bismarck confirmed, in 1870, the inviolability of Belgian territory, the latter stating that such a declaration was not required, the treaties being sufficiently explicit on the subject.

EUROPEAN POLICY IN 1870

Why did Germany respect in 1870 a treaty which she ignored in 1914? Even without taking into account the change in German mentality since her victory, military conditions were totally different. The strong chain of fortifications on the French Eastern frontier had not yet been erected, and the strength of the Belgian army appeared by no means negligible. Before the enormous increase of modern armies which took place during the twenty years of "armed peace," 80,000 men might have made all the difference one way or the other. It was approximately the strength of the French army which surrendered at Sedan. After this great defeat, German Headquarters declared their intention to pursue the fugitives into Belgian territory if the French forces attempted to escape being encircled by crossing the frontier. Such steps, however, were not rendered necessary. While showing their intense sympathy for the vanquished, the Belgians fulfilled most scrupulously all their obligations, and the European diplomats who had conceived the idea of

Belgium

neutralizing "the cockpit of Europe" could congratulate themselves. Their arrangements had worked perfectly, and for once Belgium had not been drawn into the conflict.

In the light of recent events, it is almost to be regretted that the test had been so successful. More than anything else, the 1870 experience allayed suspicion in and out of Belgium. The Powers refrained from pressing on the country the necessity for further armaments, and the hands of the anti-militarists in Belgium, instead of being weakened (as they ought to have been if events had been placed in their proper light), were considerably strengthened.

LEOPOLD II.
(Reigned 1865-1909). *Ph. B.*
ANTWERP, LIÉGE, NAMUR

Emile Cammaerts

During the long period of armed peace which followed, while the Powers formed, on one side the "Triplice" (1883), on the other the "Duplice" (1891) and the Entente Cordiale (1904), while armies and fleets were increased tenfold and German aggressive policy asserted itself more and more acutely, Belgium's defences were only slowly reinforced, in spite of the desperate efforts of disinterested patriots and of the stern warnings of the kings. The name of Leopold II must be associated here with that of Albert I. Both were prompted in their action by the same motives that inspired Leopold I's policy. They placed security on a level with, and even above, prosperity. Standing aloof from party intrigues, they were in a position to appeal to all patriots without distinction, and to make use of the services of a little band of clear-sighted citizens who saw the centre of danger transferred from France to Germany, and watched the young Empire's military and economic development with growing anxiety. Foremost among them stood Emile Banning, author of a prophetic report on the Meuse defences (1881-86). Nothing illustrated more clearly the crippling influence of neutrality on Belgian international thought than the way this man of genius was ignored by his fellow-citizens. In any other country, he would have exercised a considerable influence on public opinion. In Belgium, he was only heard by a few statesmen and, happily, by Leopold II, who no doubt had his report in mind when, in 1887, he warned one of his ministers of the necessity of Belgium not only safeguarding her independence, but "preventing the passage" of foreign troops through her territory. Germany had now become the main source of danger, but in order to avoid all criticism it was decided to build two bridgeheads, one at Namur and the other at Liége. The first commanded the upper valley of the Meuse, the second the middle course of the stream; one was facing France, the other Germany. The plan of defence was consequently developed, the forts enabling the army to make a short stand before retiring into the entrenched camp of Antwerp. It is largely to Banning's clearsightedness and to Leopold II's firm attitude that Western Europe owes the respite given by the resistance of Liége in August 1914. Had not General Brialmont's original plans of the forts been unduly curtailed, this resistance would have proved still more effective.

MILITARY REFORM

Credits for the defences of Liége and Namur, like those of Antwerp a few years before, were voted grudgingly by a Chamber lulled into a false state of security by the experience of 1870. But, if public opinion was little inclined to devote money to improve the country's defences, it became obdurate when experts advised a reform of the Belgian military system. Not only were the effectives ridiculously small, compared with the size of the German and French armies, but recruiting was managed through a system of drawing lots, to which was added the evil of "substitution"—that is to say, the sons of the bourgeois class who drew a "bad number" were entitled to buy a substitute, who took their place in the ranks. A campaign for personal and general service was launched, but in spite of the king's support it met with little success. A certain number of volunteers were added to the normal effectives in 1902, and in 1908, after the sensational journey of William II to Tangiers, new credits were voted for the development of the Antwerp defences. To those who objected that fortifications would be useless if Belgium did not possess a sufficient army to man them, the king answered: "Let us have the stones first. The men will come later." When the seventy-fifth anniversary of Belgian Independence gave him at last the opportunity of breaking the silence imposed upon him by the Congo campaign, he uttered a supreme warning to the nation: "Let us not be overconfident in our present prosperity; let us stand closer and closer together around our flag. Nations, like human beings, have to pass through a critical age which brings about old age or premature death. Its date, for young nations, falls *during the last quarter of the first century of their existence.*" Once more, on February 18, 1909, he imparted to a friend—for his lack of popularity had made public declarations useless at that time—his anxieties regarding the future: "It is indispensable that we should possess a good army, that we should be able to defend ourselves, and thus, in conformity with our international obligations, prevent the crossing of our territory by a foreign army, and *make such crossing as costly as possible, in order to remove the temptation from those who would be inclined to attempt it.... On my return from my recent journey to Germany, I warned all concerned that Germany is building more ships and increasing her military expenses. We must efficiently complete our fortifications and our equipment. You know that neither one nor the other can be improvised....*"

Leopold II attached such importance to the adoption of personal service, proposed in 1909, that he deliberately postponed an operation which might have saved his life, in order to be able to sign the decree which placed the Bill on the Statute Book. He died three days later.[1]

This supreme satisfaction was not unmixed. Important concessions had had to be made. The voluntary system was maintained to a certain extent, only one son per family being called up for a short time (fifteen months). The passing of the Bill was a victory in principle, but it only increased very slightly the strength of the Belgian army.

The Pan-German campaign was in full swing by then. Maps were published, beyond the Rhine, showing large portions of Belgium painted in imperial red, like the rest of the Reich. Pamphlets and books appeared claiming Antwerp as a German port and connecting East Africa with the German Cameroons through the Belgian Congo. Still the majority of the Belgians would not believe that such views were shared by the German Emperor and his Government. It was only after the Agadir coup (1911) and Algeciras (1912) that M. de Broqueville, Minister of War, strongly supported by King Albert, was able to carry through a Bill introducing general and compulsory service, which would have placed thearmy on a proper footing if its provisions had been rendered immediately effective. Unhappily, the Bill only provided for a gradual increase, the army reaching its full strength of 340,000 men in 1917. This last reservation proved nearly fatal to the country, for, when mobilization was ordered, in July 1914, the total forces available only amounted to 117,000 men, of which the combatant portion was reduced to 93,000 bayonets—an increase of only 10,000 over the effectives of 1870.

There are few subjects so depressing as the slow development of Belgian defences under the threat of invasion. Each time the situation became serious, as in 1848, 1852, 1908 and 1911, public opinion allowed some progress to be made. But it came always too late. The people were ready to face their responsibilities, but they could not be made to realize them. Blindly relying on the 1839 treaties, absorbed in their economic and intellectual development, they showed little interest in international affairs. Those who did, found themselves in the dilemma either of taking refuge in a fools' paradise or of powerlessly facing an ever-growing menace. Neutrality may have saved Belgium in 1870, full independence might have saved her in 1914.

Chapter XXVII Economic Renaissance

One month after the first outbreak of the Belgian Revolution, elections were already taking place. An almost equal number of Liberals (the successors of the Vonckists) and of Catholics (Statists) were returned to the Congress whose duty was to frame the new Constitution. It is typical of the spirit of patriotic union between both parties and of the adaptability of the Belgians to their new independent life that these deputies, most of whom had no experience of political life, succeeded, within two months, in drafting a Constitution which has since served as a model for several European nations. It was the result of various influences: the groundwork—based on individual liberty, equality before the law, freedom of the press, of worship, of public meeting, of association and of teaching—was no doubt inspired by the French. On the other hand, the preponderance of legislative power, represented by the Chamber and the Senate, over the executive, the principle of ministerial responsibility, placing the king outside and above parties, was the result of English influence: but perhaps the most interesting characteristic of the new Constitution was the way in which provincial and communal rights were safeguarded, the communes, in particular, preserving practical autonomy for local affairs, with the only restriction that the burgomaster was to be nominated by the king. The Belgian Constitution struck the balance between centralization, inherited from the period of French rule, and particularism, which had, from the Burgundian period, been the most striking feature in Belgian politics. If we associate, in our minds, particularism with the traditional conservatism of the Catholic peasantry and centralization with modern industrial developments and the intellectual culture of the large towns, we shall obtain a fairly good idea of the two general tendencies which divided public opinion in Belgium during the nineteenth century and whose main features may be recognized not only in politics, but also in the economic, intellectual and artistic development of the country.

LIBERALS AND CATHOLICS

The status of neutrality not only affected foreign politics, it reacted very strongly on Belgium's internal life. If it crippled her activity with regard to home defence, it developed to an abnormal degree party warfare. It shut the door on international problems and all questions which may be considered as national issues and before which party strife ought to cease in consideration for the common weal. Social, philosophic or religious differences were not balanced, in modern Belgium, as in other countries, by international consciousness. In the close atmosphere of the tutelage of the Powers, party politics absorbed the whole public life of the nation and external problems were practically ignored. It thus happened that the people who stood in the forefront of Europe, and who were more directly interested than any other in the fluctuations of European politics, were about the worst informed on foreign affairs.

From 1839 to 1885, the electorate being limited by a property qualification (only 35,000 electors out of 4,000,000 inhabitants taking part in the first election), the struggle was confined to the two middle-class parties, Catholics and Liberals.

Emile Cammaerts

Roughly speaking, the Catholics stood for the defence of religious interests, more especially in the domain of education and relief, the Liberals for the supremacy of a nominally neutral State in all public matters. It is easy to realize how this purely political quarrel could degenerate into a conflict of ideals, some ultramontanes distrusting the motives of "atheists" and ignoring the public spirit of men who did not share their creed, while some agnostics, steeped in the narrow doctrines of Voltaire and Diderot, made the Church the scapegoat of all social evils and even denied the wholesome influence of religion on social education.

During the first part of the century the conflict was not so acute, both parties possessing their moderate and extremist leaders and the so-called "Liberal Catholics" acting as a link between the two factions. From 1847 to 1870 the Liberals, representing the bourgeoisie of the large towns, were most of the time in power, while from 1870 to 1878 the Catholics, upheld by the farmers and the middle classes of the small towns, took the direction of affairs. The property qualification was progressively reduced, first for the parliamentary, later for the provincial and communal elections, and a larger share was given to the lower middle classes in the administration of the country. Meanwhile, party differences had developed through the gradual disappearance of the moderating elements on both sides, and the vexed question of education was coming to the fore. The 1830 Constitution was not very explicit concerning this matter, and both parties interpreted it according to their own interests. Many communes having neglected to keep up the official schools, religious orders had taken a more and more important part in primary education. When the Liberals came into power, in 1878, they passed a law compelling every commune to maintain its own schools, where religious instruction should only be given out of school hours. They also founded a great many secondary schools and training colleges, with the object of transferring education from religious to secular teachers. These sweeping reforms entailed heavy expenditure and unpopular taxation, and finally brought about the downfall of the Liberal régime in 1884. The Catholics proceeded to abrogate the 1879 law on primary education by giving State grants to the free Catholic schools, and suppressed a number of the secondary schools and training colleges established by the previous régime.

Feeling ran so high that King Leopold, who realized the harm which this "school war" was doing to the national spirit, warned Monsieur Malou (the Catholic premier) against the attitude he had adopted, as he had previously warned the Liberal premier, Frère-Orban: "The Liberals have acted as if there were no longer any Catholics in Belgium. Are you going also to act as if there were no Liberals left in the country, without any consideration for the disastrous consequences of such an attitude for the nation and for yourself?"

From 1885 to 1913 educational matters, though by no means forgotten, were entirely overshadowed by social problems and by the efforts made by the Opposition to obtain the revision of the Constitution and the adoption of universal suffrage. This change was brought about by the foundation, in 1885, by the Flemish printer, César de Paepe, of the Belgian Labour Party. Its action was from the first political as well as economic. While consumers' co-operatives, such as the "Vooruit" of Ghent, were founded in several large towns, Socialist clubs entertained a continuous agitation for electoral franchise, their aim being to use Parliament to

Belgium

obtain the sweeping social reforms inscribed on their programme. Here, again, we find French insistence on politics checked by the old spirit of association which had been so prominent in the Netherlands during the Middle Ages.

LABOUR PARTY

After the miners' strike of 1886, both Catholics and Liberals revised their programmes and paid more attention to social reforms. But the workmen, who were now powerfully organized, especially in the industrial centres of the South, wanted to take a direct share in political life. Under pressure of public opinion, the demand for a revision of the Constitution was at last taken into consideration in 1891, and in 1893 a new law granted universal suffrage tempered by plural voting. In 1902 a new campaign was launched by the allied Liberal-Socialist opposition in favour of universal suffrage pure and simple, without obtaining any result, but when, in 1913, a general strike supported the demand, the Catholic Government promised that the question should be examined by a parliamentary commission.

Before the war, Belgium was the most productive agricultural district of Europe. The secret of her prosperity is generally attributed to the small number of large estates and to the great area cultivated by small owners, 48 per cent. of the cultivated area being covered by farms of 2-1/2 to 7-1/2 acres. It must be added that, during the last twenty years, powerful producers' co-operatives, or "Boerenbonden," have grouped agriculturists and given them important advantages with regard to credit and insurance. The inbred qualities which have rendered this development possible are, however, to be found in the race itself. Again and again, in the course of centuries, the Belgian peasant has come to the fore under every political régime and every system of landholding. He has had to conquer the country from the sea, protect it against its incursions and to repair periodically the havoc caused by war. The memory of physical and social calamities has been handed down the ages, and the present system of small-ownership and co-operative societies is only the result of centuries of incessant toil.

The conservative spirit of the peasants and farmers is illustrated by the opposition made to the project of the Liberal Minister Rogier, in 1833, to build the first railway in Belgium. It was argued that this would be a considerable waste of fertile soil and would frighten the cattle. The first railway line, between Brussels and Malines, was nevertheless inaugurated on May 5, 1835, and since then, such enormous progress has been realized that, before the war, Belgium occupied the first place in Europe with regard to the development of its railway lines. All other means of communication have been similarly developed. In 1913 the country possessed 40,000 kilometres of roads, 4,656 kilometres of railway line, 2,250 kilometres of light railways, and 2,000 kilometres of inland waterways.

THE INDUSTRIAL REVOLUTION

The first consequence of the Revolution was to disorganize Belgian industry, which had lost the Dutch market, the powerful works of Cockerill, at Seraing, being among the few which did not suffer from the change. The introduction of machinery in a country so rich in coal-fields not only restored the situation but enormously increased industrial production in the Southern districts. In 1830 only 400 machines were used, with a total of 12,000 horse-power; in 1902 these figures had risen to

19,000 machines with 720,000 horse-power, without taking into account railway engines (718,000 horse-power).

The distribution of the various industries in the different parts of the country did not vary very much from that existing under previous regimes. Broadly speaking, no new development took place, every centre remaining in the situation determined by coal or the presence of raw material. The principal centre of the textile industry remained at Ghent, near the hemp-fields of the Lys; metal-works, glass-works, etc., were still grouped close to the four main coal-fields in the region of Mons, La Louvière (Centre), Charleroi and Liége; the number of men engaged on industrial production before the war had reached 1,500,000, among whom were 153,000 miners, over 149,000 metal workers, and over 129,000 textile workers.

But it is not so much to the number as to the quality of her workmen that Belgium owes her great industrial prosperity. This may be accounted for by the fact that a great number of industrial workers never lost touch with the land. Belonging, most of them, to agricultural districts, they do not settle permanently around their factories, and between the country and the great centres there is a continuous exchange of population. The hard-working qualities of mechanics and artisans are inherited from the peasants, and there is a considerable reluctance, on their part, to crowd into big cities, cheap railway fares allowing them to live around the towns where they work during the day.

TRADE OF ANTWERP

The condition of this wonderful economic development was the opening of the Scheldt. For nearly two centuries and a half the country had been cut off from the outside world and obliged to live on her own resources. We have seen how, during the fifteen years of union with Holland, the trade of Antwerp had made considerable progress, and how, in spite of Dutch resistance, the freedom of international rivers proclaimed by the Vienna Congress was applied to the Lower Scheldt. The 1839 settlement placed the river, below Antwerp, under the joint control of a Belgo-Dutch commission. The only obstacle still in the way was a toll of one florin and a half which King William had persisted in levying on all ships going and coming from the port. In 1863, after laborious negotiations undertaken by Baron Lambermont, Belgium was able to buy off these tolls from Holland for the sum of 36,000,000 francs. The stream was at last definitely free, at least in time of peace. Placed under normal conditions, with the help of numerous waterways spreading over the interior of an exceptionally rich country, Antwerp was bound to reconquer rapidly the situation it had occupied under Charles V. In 1840 about 1,500 ships, with a tonnage of 24,000, entered the port. In 1898 the annual tonnage had reached 6,500,000, and in 1913 over 25,000,000. Though such figures were undreamt of in the sixteenth century, the nature of the Antwerp trade remained very similar. The Antwerp merchants were really brokers or warehousers, and most of the merchandise brought to the port from all parts of the world was re-exported to other countries. So that in trade, as in industry and agriculture, the permanence of certain characteristics, determined by the land and the race, are preserved to this day. The absence of a national merchant fleet, which was equally apparent in the sixteenth century, did not affect imports and exports, which increased respectively from 98,000,000 francs and 104,500,000 francs in 1831 to 6,550,000,000 francs and 5,695,000,000 francs in 1910. The Government undertook various great public works in order to allow the country to benefit fully from this extraordinary activity. In 1906 a law was passed voting large credits for the extension of Antwerp's maritime installations. When these works are completed they will give to the port 60 kilometres of quays instead of 21. In 1881 the enlargement of the Terneuzen canal permitted large ships to reach Ghent; the new port of Bruges and the Zeebrugge canal were inaugurated in 1907, and an important scheme, whose result will be to connect Brussels with the sea, begun in 1900, is still in progress.

Economic renaissance was accompanied by a corresponding increase in the population. From 4,000,000 in 1831 it rose to 5,000,000 in 1870, and to 7,500,000 in 1911. With a density of 652 persons per square mile, Belgium became the most thickly populated country in the world and only consumed a fourteenth part of her industrial production. The necessity of finding new markets abroad and of discovering some substitute for the loss of the Dutch colonies, which had proved so helpful during the period of union with Holland, might have been felt by any far-sighted statesman. Leopold I had already devoted some attention to the problem. He encouraged several Belgian settlements in Rio Nuñez, where a regular protectorate was established for a short time, in Guatemala and in various parts of Brazil. None of these enterprises, however, bore fruit, and the problem was still unsolved when Leopold II ascended the throne in 1865.

FOREIGN ENTERPRISES

The search for a colonial outlet for the activity of the nation dominated the reign of the new king and absorbed all the energy he was able to spare from military problems. As Duke of Brabant, Leopold II had already drawn the attention of the country to the future development of China. He had formed several projects with regard to the establishment of a Belgian settlement at the mouth of the Yangtse-Kiang and on the island of Formosa. Their failure did not prevent him from taking, later on, an active part in Chinese affairs. The Imperial Government did not entertain towards Belgium the same distrust as it did towards the European Great Powers, and King Leopold several times had the opportunity of acting as intermediary between these Powers and the Chinese Government, in order to obtain concessions. He became thus, in later years, the initiator of the Peking-Hankow railway. The difficulty of finding a field of economic activity in foreign countries became, nevertheless, more and more apparent, and, without giving up his Chinese policy, the Belgian king endeavoured to ensure to his country some part of the vacant territories which had not yet been seized by other European nations. When his Congo enterprise was in full swing, he proposed to buy the Canary Islands from Spain (1898), and, after the Spanish-American War, opened negotiations with America with regard to the future development of the newly acquired Philippines. He was also concerned, for a time, with Korean, Manchurian and Mongolian enterprises, and nothing but the progress of the Congo scheme put a stop to his incessant search for new opportunities.

In 1876, when the Congo basin was still practically *terra incognita*, Stanley having just left Europe in order to determine the course of the stream, Leopold II founded the "Association Internationale Africaine." It was a purely private association, composed of geographers and travellers, its aim being to suppress the slave trade in Central Africa and to open this part of the continent to modern civilization. Two years later, on Stanley's return, the "Comité d'Etudes du Haut

Congo" secured his services in order to undertake, with the help of a little band of Belgian explorers, a complete survey of the Congo basin and to conclude treaties with the native chiefs. Within five years a region as large as a fifth of Europe, and eighty times larger than Belgium, had been brought under the influence of the Committee, and in 1883 the king founded the "Association Internationale du Congo."

If, instead of ruling over a small neutral State, Leopold II had ruled over one of the large nations of Europe, he would have reaped forthwith the fruit of his labour and the gratitude of his people. The Congo would have become a State colony, been subsidized by State funds, and the sovereign would have incurred no further responsibilities in the matter. But Belgium was not a Great Power like Germany, which acquired its African colonies at the same time, in a similar manner. Neither could she rest her colonial claims on historical grounds, like Holland or Portugal. She was not even fully independent, as far as foreign policy was concerned, and her right to break fresh ground might have been questioned at the time. Besides, popular opinion in Belgium, dominated by the fear of international complications, was not prepared to claim this right, even the capitalists considering the king's projects far too hazardous to give him the necessary support. Leopold II was, therefore, left to his own resources to accomplish an almost superhuman task: to obtain the necessary recognition from the Powers, and to sufficiently develop the resources of the Congo to persuade the Belgian people to accept his gift.

It was, therefore, not as a king, but as a private individual, that the president of the "Association Internationale du Congo" was obliged first to remove the obstacles created by French and Portuguese opposition, and, later, to persuade the other Powers to entrust him with the administration of the new territory. This first success must not be attributed to his diplomatic skill alone, but also to the enormous expenses implied by the bold enterprise, to the reluctance of the rich colonial Powers to incur further liabilities and to their anxiety to avoid international difficulties. Germany's attitude, in view of further events, may be described as expectant. Bismarck had only just been converted to colonial expansion, and found, no doubt, what he must have considered as the "interregnum" of King Leopold an excellent solution of his difficulties.

CONGO FREE STATE

In 1885 the work of the "Association" was recognized by the Congress of Berlin, the sovereign of Belgium becoming the sovereign of the Congo Free State. The treaty of Berlin stipulated that trade should remain free in the new State, that the natives should be protected and that slavery should be suppressed. Four years later, the king, in his will, left the Congo to Belgium, "desiring to ensure to his beloved country the fruit of a work pursued during long years with the generous and devoted collaboration of many Belgians, and confident of thus securing for Belgium, if she was willing to use it, an indispensable outlet for her trade and industry and a new field for her children's activity."

The work was pushed with indomitable energy. In 1894 a vigorous campaign against the Arab slave-traders was brought to a successful conclusion. In 1898 the first railway connecting Matadi, on the Lower Congo, with Leopoldville, on the Stanley Pool, opened the great waterway as far as the Stanley Falls. A flotilla was launched on the upper stream and its main affluents, while roads and telegraph lines spread all over the country.

The financial situation, however, remained critical. The enterprise had absorbed the greater part of the king's personal fortune. The credits voted by the Belgian Chambers were inadequate, and, though a few financiers began by now to realize the enormous value of the enterprise, their number was not sufficient to ensure the immediate future. Faced with considerable difficulties, which compelled him to severely curtail his personal expenses, Leopold II had formally offered the colony to the country in 1895. This offer had been rejected. Under the stress of circumstances, the sovereign of the Congo Free State decided to exploit directly the natural resources of the land, mainly rubber and ivory. The natives were compelled to pay a tax in kind and vast concessions were granted to commercial companies whose actions could not be properly controlled. This semi-commercial, semi-political system was bound to lead to abuses, even a few State agents betraying the confidence which their chief had placed in them and oppressing the natives in order to exact a heavier tax.

When the first protests were heard in this country, King Leopold committed the grave mistake of not starting an immediate inquiry and punishing the culprits. Distrusting the motives of the leaders of the campaign, and stiffened in his resistance by the tone they chose to adopt towards him, he allowed the opposition to grow to such proportions that the general public, whose indignation was skilfully nurtured by the most exaggerated reports, lost all sense of proportion. They ignored the fact that the king had given sufficient proof of disinterestedness and of devotion to his country not to deserve the abominable accusations launched against him. They forgot the invaluable work accomplished, under the most difficult circumstances, during twenty years of ceaseless labour, the suppression of slavery, of cannibalism, human sacrifices and tribal wars, and remembered only the gross indictments of Mr. Morel and the biased reports of Mr. Roger Casement (1913).

THE BELGIAN CONGO

When, the next year, three impartial magistrates sent to the Congo by King Leopold reported that the excesses had been repressed and advised a complete reform of the administration, their testimony was disregarded. When concessions were abolished and drastic measures taken against the criminal agents, the fact remained unnoticed. Even after the Congo had become a Belgian Colony (1908), under the control of the Belgian Parliament, when every scrap of authority had been taken away from the old king with the "Domaine de la Couronne" (whose revenue was to be devoted by its founder to public works in Belgium), when the colony had been entirely reorganized, the campaign of the Congo Reform Association went on relentlessly. Far from silencing his accusers, the king's death, a year later, was made the occasion of a fresh outburst of abuse.

The good faith of the public throughout the Congo campaign is unquestionable. That of its main engineers is at least open to doubt. They organized their efforts at the time when the greatest difficulties of colonization had been overcome. They pursued them after all cause for abuse had been removed. In one of his first books, *British Case in French Congo*, Mr. Morel suggests the partition of the Free State between this country and Germany. In his last books, written during the war, he warmly champions the internationalization of Central Africa in order to save the German Colonies. Neither can it be urged that those two men who roused the conscience of this country against the Congo atrocities were deeply shocked by more recent and far better authenticated atrocities committed in Belgium. If they were, the only remark an impartial observer might venture to make is that their actions, during the war, scarcely reflected such righteous indignation. It may be too hasty to conclude from this, and from the close association of Erzberger, Morel and Casement in the Congo campaign, that this campaign was engineered by Germany. We do not yet possess all the documents necessary to establish this fact. We know enough, however, to deplore that a movement which might have been so beneficial to all concerned was allowed to fall into the hands of unscrupulous agitators, who succeeded in estranging for a time Belgium from Great Britain, and incidentally in marring the last years of the life of one of the greatest Belgian patriots.

Chapter XXVIII Intellectual Renaissance

The remarkable revival of Belgian Arts and Letters which followed shortly after the 1830 Revolution is one of the most striking examples of the influence exercised by political events on intellectual activity. For over a century the nation had been devoid of self-expression, and during the fifteen years of Union with Holland scarcely any notable works were produced. No doubt this time, being one of economic recovery, was not favourable to the efflorescence of Art and Letters, but the intense activity of the period of independence appears nevertheless as an outburst of national pride and energy. It seems as if all the strength, subdued during the periods of foreign domination, had at last found an outlet, as if the Belgians had waited all these years to assert again their intellectual power, which could not or would not flourish for the benefit of foreigners.

PALACE OF JUSTICE, BRUSSELS. *Ph. B.*

Architecture no longer represents, in modern times, what it represented in the past, and it would be vain to search in modern Belgium, and, for the matter of that, in any modern country, for the manifestation of an original style expressing the spirit of the age. There are, however, symptoms of vitality which must not be entirely disregarded. The considerable number of public buildings erected and the more or less successful efforts of their builders are by themselves a remarkable testimony. It is characteristic of Belgian civilization and of its irradicable traditional spirit of regionalism that the Hôtels de Ville built in imitation of the Flemish Renaissance are particularly numerous, and even in some cases, such as the Maison communale of Schaarbeek, particularly impressive. Some reconstitutions were also attempted, as, for instance, the Antwerp Exchange and the Palace of Margaret of Austria in Malines. The only strikingly original monument is the Palace of Justice in Brussels, built by Poelaert (1870-79). It is the result of an extraordinary medley of styles, from the Assyrian onwards, and presents one of the most pathetic and gigantic efforts to create a beautiful monument under modern conditions. This huge building was intended by the Belgian people to be the apotheosis of Right. Not only of the Justice of everyday courts, but also of international Justice and of the right, so long violated on Belgian soil, of the people to dispose of themselves.

HISTORICAL SCULPTURE

Wandering through the most important squares and gardens of Belgian towns, the stranger will be astonished at the number of monuments raised to the great Belgians of the past and to the heroes of Belgian history. In Brussels, Antwerp, Ghent, Bruges, and even the small provincial towns, he will find statues dedicated not only to the modern kings and statesmen, but to the leaders of the various revolts against foreign oppression, to the great artists and communal tribunes. Almost every person mentioned in this book possesses his effigy, and the town of Tongres has gone as far as immortalizing the features of the Celtic chief Ambiorix in token of his resistance to the Roman Legions. All these statues are not necessarily great works of art, nor is the historical conception which their ensemble represents quite above criticism, but, if one remembers that they were almost all raised within fifty years of the declaration of Belgian independence, one may at least understand the reason of their sudden appearance. In spite of those who insist, in flattering terms, on Belgium's youth, she strongly maintains her right to old traditions and wants to keep her ancient heroes before her eyes. More or less consciously, the sculptors of these statues realized that their fathers of the Renaissance and the Middle Ages had as great a share in the making of the nation as present kings and ministers. Their sudden appearance in the midst of Belgian towns was not the result of official zeal, but the living symbol of the gratitude of new to old Belgium. Jacques van Artevelde in Ghent, Breydel and De Coninck in Bruges, Egmont and Horn in Brussels came into their own at last.

Beside these historical statues, the traveller will find some remarkable works of a more recent date which will recommend themselves for their purely artistic value and which are generally noticeable for their feeling for movement and muscular effort. In many ways, the qualities of Rubens were revived in the modern school of Belgian sculpture, and the Brabo fountain in Antwerp, the Death of Ompdrailles and the Riders' Fight in Brussels suffice to show the influence exercised by the seventeenth century school of painting on Jef. Lambeaux, Van der Stappen and J. de Lalaing. The most original of Belgian sculptors, Constantin Meunier (1831-1904), while possessing similar plastic qualities, opened a new field by his idealization of agricultural and industrial work. His miners, dockers, puddlers, and field labourers are known to all students of art and will stand in the future as the symbol of the economic renaissance of a people who could, even under modern conditions, find a kind of grim attachment to their labour.

Belgium

"THE PUDDLER."
By constantin meunier (1831-1904).

Cold academic compositions, painted under the influence of the chief of the Imperial French school of painting, Louis David, were the only productions of Belgian Art at the beginning of the nineteenth century. In no domain did the fashion change more abruptly, on the morrow of the Revolution, than in Belgian historical paintings. As early as 1833, G. Wappers of Antwerp exhibited a large canvas recording an episode of the recent Revolution. His example was followed by many artists at the time, and Belgian history became the subject of a great number of paintings, whose rather theatrical and pompous style does not entirely succeed in hiding their sincere and serious qualities. The French style of David was soon abandoned. Movement and colour, so inherent in the Belgian temperament, came again to the fore, and, though the influence of Rubens was overmastering, it was at least a national influence, and soon led, under the inspiration of Henri Leys (1815-69), to the production of historical works of great interest. The latter's frescoes of the Hôtel de Ville in Antwerp, illustrating the old franchises and privileges of the town, may still be considered as a striking expression of municipal freedom.

MODERN PAINTERS

At the same time, a great number of painters, reacting against the rather artificial style of historical paintings, went back to genre pictures, in which Teniers and his followers had excelled in the past. Henri de Braekeleer (1814-88) translated the simple, intimate poetry of modest interiors, while Joseph Stevens (1819-92) devoted his genius to scenes of dog life. Later, when social questions came to the fore and when the attention of the public was centred on the sufferings of the poor and destitute, De Groux, Léon Frédéric and, even more, Eugène Laermans (*b.* 1864) conveyed in their works a burning sympathy for the wretches and vagabonds straying through the towns and the Flemish country-side. The latter's work is strongly influenced by Breughel. Through an extraordinary paradox, Belgian Art, which only represented scenes of merriment during the darkest days of the Spanish occupation, gave far more importance to scenes of misery during the modern time of great public prosperity, so revolting did it seem that such prosperity should not be shared by all.

Another artist in whose works Breughel's inspiration is apparent is Jacob Smits (*b.* 1856). He is almost the only one who may be considered as a representative of religious painting in Belgium. Like Breughel, he succeeded in bringing the Christian story close to the people's hearts amidst Flemish contemporary surroundings.

A school of art in which colour and light play such a predominant part is bound to produce valuable landscapes. In this new form, the love of country expressed itself far more sincerely than in the earlier historical compositions. Under the influence of Henri Boulanger, Belgium produced, in later years, a number of first-rate landscape painters such as Verwée, Courtens, Gilsoul, Baertsoen and Emile Claus. Flemish landscapes exert a far greater attraction than the Walloon hills, and, generally speaking, the Flemish element dominates in the modern school as it did in the old. For the golden light lies on the damp fields of Flanders, and Flemish artists have not yet given up the hope of capturing it.

NATIONAL LITERATURE

The artistic Renaissance of modern Belgium might have been expected. The worship of colour and form had always been a strong characteristic of the race, and even in the drab years of the Austrian régime Belgian painters had never ceased to work. A far more startling development was the appearance, towards the middle of the nineteenth century, of a national Belgian school of literature. In the Middle Ages, Flemish and French letters in Belgium had produced some remarkable works. Owing to the scholastic character of these writings and to the predominant influence of French culture, they could not, however, be considered as a direct expression of the people's spirit. In many ways, the modern school of Belgian Letters was a new departure: French and Flemish influences were more evenly balanced, and, though they worked separately, Flemish and French writers, coming into close contact with the people's soul, expressed the same feelings and the same aspirations. For, if we make due allowance for the part played by purely Walloon writers, specially novelists and story-tellers, the main feature of the Belgian school of literature in the nineteenth century is the break up of the language barrier. Strange as it may seem, a comparison between writers in French and Flemish reveals a series of similarities so striking that, supposing an adequate translation were possible, there would be no difficulty whatever in including them in the same group. The main reason for this is, no doubt, that almost all the leaders of the movement in French, starting with De Coster and Lemonnier, up to the contemporary period of Verhaeren and Maeterlinck, are of Flemish extraction, and that their best works are imbued with Flemish traditions and Flemish temperament. Broadly speaking, one might say that most of the Belgian French writers are Flemings writing in French and are far closer to their Northern brethren than to the French whose language they use. Charles de Coster, who may be considered as the father of this particular branch of the school, published in 1868 the *Legend of Ulenspiegel*, which is nothing but a prose epic in which the legendary character of Owliglass is identified with one of the heroes of the sixteenth century revolution against Spain. Camille Lemonnier (1844-1913), in his best novels, deals with the manners and customs of the Flemish peasantry. The very soul of Flanders shines through the whole work of Belgium's great national poet, Emile Verhaeren, from his early *Les Flamandes* (1883) to the six volumes of *Toute la Flandre* (1904-12), and in all his earlier writings (1889-98), Maurice Maeterlinck remains under the influence of Flemish mysticism and miracle plays. This may seem a one-sided conclusion, and the names of many Belgian writers of great distinction may be quoted against it, but if we were to examine the question more closely, this conclusion would be rather verified than disproved. From a purely historical point of view, the general trend of inspiration is certainly towards the North rather than towards the South.

The main features which characterize the Belgian writers in French and confer on them a truly national originality are, on one side, a tendency to emphasize the intimate joys of life, and on the other, an intense feeling for mysticism, sometimes quite dissociated from any dogmatic faith. Just as Flemish Art is remarkable for the religious work of the fifteenth century and the sensuous productions of the seventeenth, so Belgian writing in the nineteenth oscillates between the spirit of Jordaens and that of Memling. In spite of some modernist tendencies and a great technical boldness, Belgian literature remains deeply influenced by mediævalism. It belongs to the twentieth century, even when written in the nineteenth, or to the fifteenth. The classical atmosphere of the French seventeenth and eighteenth centuries is totally absent. Those who care for the delicately poised balance of classical taste, for wit and brilliance of dialogue, will be disconcerted by childishness or fierce passion. It is an abrupt literature, but spontaneous and sincere, which has not been spoilt by formalism and scepticism, but which has not acquired, from a purely technical point of view, the perfection of the French. Having remained inarticulate during the two centuries of classical education, it has lost nothing and gained nothing through them.

Emile Cammaerts
THE FLEMISH MOVEMENT

It is significant that the movement started in Flanders before influencing the French-speaking part of the country. The Flemish novelist, Henri Conscience (1812-83) had devoted a series of books to the history of his country long before De Coster wrote his (*Ilenspiegel*). The Flemish language was, at the time, struggling against great difficulties. It had been entirely neglected, from the literary point of view, during the eighteenth century, and suffered now from the natural reaction which followed the 1830 Revolution. It had reaped little benefit from the fifteen years of union with Holland, and there was a general belief, among the Flemings themselves, that it would never recover its ancient position. The Flemish literary Renaissance was initiated by a small group of intellectuals, headed by Jan Frans Willems (1793-1846), who exerted all their energy to revive Flemish customs, collect folk songs and traditions, and obtain a liberal interpretation of the Constitution which proclaimed liberty of language. The Flemish Movement received a new impulse when the young poet Albrecht Rodenbach (1856-80) spread its influence to all Flemish intellectual circles. The Flemings began to realize that they possessed in Guido Gezelle (1813-99) a religious poet whose work could bear comparison with the best French writings in the country. They saw, growing up around them, a new school of writers of great promise, and they insisted on their language being recognized, not only in principle, but in fact, as the second official language of the country. In 1898 a law was passed removing some of the causes of grievances, such as the inability of judges and officials to understand the language of the people with whom they dealt. Progressively the Flemish language came into its own in matters of education and administration, and, before the war, the only large question still under discussion was the creation of a Flemish University. The principle of such an institution had been admitted, but the relationship between this new University and the old French University of Ghent had not yet been established.

COMMON TEMPERAMENT

It must be understood that the language question remained throughout a local quarrel between two sets of Flemish intellectuals. It was not a quarrel between Walloons and Flemings, and administrative separation was scarcely ever mentioned. It was not even, before the war, a quarrel between the Flemish people, who knew only Flemish, and the Flemish bourgeoisie, who preferred to talk French. It was a dispute between a few intellectual Flemings, who wished to restore the language to the position it occupied before the Spanish and Austrian régimes silenced it, and the Flemings who wanted to restrict it to the common people and treat it as a patois. It was, to put it bluntly, a discussion between those who ignored history and those who realized that the independence of the Belgian provinces was bound to bring about a revival of Flemish Letters, as it was causing a revival of French Letters. For two centuries the country had remained silent; she was now able to speak again and to use all the riches and the resources of her two languages. Instead of threatening national unity, bilingualism was its necessary condition. For real differences do not lie in modes of expression, but in the feeling and the soul of the people, and it matters little if an image or a thought is expressed in one language or another, as long as they reflect a common temperament and common aspirations.

Chapter XXIX Conclusion

The part played by Belgium during the war is well known. Those who knew the country and its history were not astonished at the attitude observed by King Albert and his people on August 3, 1914. Quite apart from any foreign sympathies, no other answer could be given to an ultimatum which directly challenged Belgium's rights. A modern nation might have been intimidated, but an old nation like Belgium, which had struggled towards independence through long and weary periods of warfare and foreign domination, was bound to resist. In challenging King Albert and his ministers, the German Government challenged at the same time all the leaders of the Belgian people, from De Coninck to Vonck and De Mérode, and the reply of the Belgian Government was stiffened by an age-long tradition of stubborn resistance and by the ingrained instinct of the people that this had to be done because there was nothing else to do.

GERMAN INVASION

History also accounts for the desperate fight waged by the small and ill-equipped army against the first military Power in Europe. Liége, Haelen, the three sorties from Antwerp, the ten terrible days on the Yser, are not due merely to the personal valour of the leaders and of their troops, but to the fact that they were Belgian leaders and Belgian troops, that they belonged to a nation conscious of her destiny and who had never despaired in the past, in spite of the ordeals to which she was subjected and of the scorn of those who questioned her very existence. The same thing might be said of all Allied nations. Even so fought the British, even so fought the French; the only difference lies in the fact that their heroism was expected as a matter of course, while that of the Belgians came to many as a surprise. For British traditions and French traditions were well known, while the past of Belgium was blurred amidst the confusion of Feudalism and foreign rule.

On the Yser, in October 1914, the Belgian forces had been reduced from 95,000 to 38,000 bayonets. These last defences, preserving about twenty square miles of independent territory, were maintained during four years while the army was refilling its ranks and reorganizing its supplies. It took its share in all the concerted actions of the Allies in Flanders, and when, at last, the final offensive was launched, on September 28, 1918, King Albert was placed at the head of the Anglo-Franco-Belgian forces.

Meanwhile the civil population, under German occupation, was undergoing one of the severest trials that the nation had ever experienced, not excepting revolutionary oppression and the Spanish Fury. The Germans used every means in their power to disintegrate the people's unity, break its resistance and enlist its services. Terrorism was used, from the first, at Aerschot, Louvain, Tamines, Andenne and Dinant, whilst the invasion progressed towards the heart of the country. Then, under the governorship of Von Bissing, the method was altered, and attempts were made to induce the chiefs of industry and their workmen to resume work for the greater benefit of the enemy. This policy culminated in the sinister deportations, pursued during the winter of 1916-17, which enslaved about 150,000 men and compelled them to work either behind the German front or in German kommandos. Enormous fines and contributions were levied on towns and provinces, the country was emptied of all raw material, private property and the produce of the soil were systematically requisitioned, and the population would have been decimated by famine but for the help of the Commission for Relief in Belgium. When it became evident, in 1917, that the passive resistance of the workers could not be broken, all the industries which had not been commandeered were entirely or partially destroyed and the machinery transported to Germany.

VON BISSING'S INTRIGUES

The most insidious attack of Governor von Bissing's policy on the Belgian nation was his attempt to use the Flemish Movement as a means to divide the Belgians against themselves. The governor, who explained his intentions in a remarkable document known as his "Political Testament," undertook this campaign under the assumption that Belgium was an artificial creation of the Vienna Congress and that such a thing as Belgian nationality did not really exist. German university professors had been at great pains to explain to the German and neutral public that nationality could only be created by unity of race or language, and that Belgium, possessing neither of these attributes, could consequently claim no right to independence. Following this trend of thought, the governor and his advisers considered the Flemish Movement as the outcome of internal dissensions between Walloons and Flemings, and hoped that, by encouraging the Flemings, they would succeed in dividing the country and in securing the protectorate of Flanders.

First the creation of a Flemish University in Ghent, replacing the French University, absorbed the attention of the German administration. Having secured the support of a few extreme "flamingants" known as "activists" and completed the professorial board with foreigners, they hastily inaugurated the new institution (1916). To their great surprise, all Flemish organizations protested indignantly against this action, contending that the occupying Power had no right to interfere in internal policy. The next step was a series of decrees establishing Administrative Separation, with two capitals at Namur and Brussels and a complete division of Government offices between the Flemish and Walloon districts of the country. This measure failed like the first, owing to the patriotic resistance of the Belgian officials and the inability of the Germans to replace them, and long before they were obliged to evacuate the country the Germans had given up the hope of mastering the absurd and unscientific decision of Walloons and Flemings alike to remain one people, as history had made them.

Professor Van der Linden has given to his valuable work on Belgian history the sub-title of *The Making of a Nation*, and shown conclusively how the present institutions of Belgium are the result of various contributions from the Middle Ages to the present time. But a book on Belgian history might just as aptly be called *The Resistance of a Nation*, since history tells us not only how the monument was built, but also how it was not destroyed in spite of the most adverse circumstances. From that point of view, Belgium may indeed be considered as the embodiment of steadfastness, rather than that of sheer heroism. She has succeeded in preserving, far more than in acquiring. From her fifteenth century frontiers she has been reduced to her present limited boundaries, which, nevertheless, contain all the elements of her past and present genius. She sacrificed territory, centuries of independence, long periods of prosperity, but she remained essentially one people and one land, a small people on a small land, combining the genius of two races and two languages and acting as a natural intermediary between the great nations of Europe. Her history, up to her last fight, is nothing but the struggle of a nation to assert her right to live, in spite of her weakness, in the midst of great military Powers. Unity, first constituted in the fifteenth century, is at once endangered by the rule of a foreign dynasty. During the first part of the sixteenth century the two influences, national and foreign, contend in the counsels of the nation. The latter tendency prevails, and, though remaining nominally independent in regional matters, the country passes under foreign rule. When, in the beginning of the nineteenth century, after the failure of several insurrections under the Austrian and French régimes, independence is finally granted, and when a new dynasty is at last inaugurated as a symbol of national unity, Belgium remains nevertheless under foreign tutelage. Her independence is bought at the price of neutrality; and it is only after the violation of this guaranteed neutrality by two of the foremost Powers which established it that the cycle of Belgium's trials comes to an end and that she is allowed to exert her sovereign rights in external as well as internal affairs.

TREATY OF VERSAILLES

Some may consider that Belgium has not reaped important advantages from the treaty of Versailles, and may be inclined to compare the small territories of the Walloon districts of Eupen and Malmédy with the efforts made during the last few years. But, quite apart from economic indemnities, which may prove a great asset if they materialize, Belgium has conquered a far more valuable possession than any territory could give. For the first time in modern history she has received full recognition. She is at last allowed to make friends with her friends and to beware of her enemies, if she has any reason to fear them. Through the bitter struggle of the last few years Belgium has conquered what other nations might consider as their birthright—the right to be herself, the master of her fate, the captain of her soul.

It becomes more and more apparent to foreign consciousness that her future is bound up with that of Europe. Her welfare will be Europe's welfare, her ruin, the ruin of Western civilization and Christianity. Unless through the League of Nations, or through any other means, justice prevails in international relations, the history of her tribulations is not yet closed, for only under a régime of justice may the weak hope to live in freedom and in peace.

Among the pantheon of monuments erected by modern Belgium to the heroes of her past history, the stranger will find, with some surprise, in the midst of the Place Royale in Brussels, an equestrian statue of Godfrey of Bouillon, who, nine centuries ago, sold his land to join the first crusade, and who refused to wear a crown of gold where his Saviour had worn a crown of thorns. Quite close stands the Palace where another Belgian prince returned lately, after four years' incessant labour at the side of his soldiers amid the sodden fields of Flanders. There is a great contrast between the civilization of the eleventh and that of the twentieth century, between the Great Adventure sought by the old crusaders and the Great War forced on Western Europe, between the mystic idealism of the Middle Ages and the practical idealism of modern times. On both occasions, however, Belgium was placed in the van, and found in Godfrey IV and Albert I two leaders whose courage and dignity will stand as the purest symbol of chivalry and national honour.

Norm the Normal by Ben Lemon

What happens when the most useless person in the world gets a reality show, he becomes the most beloved person the world has ever known of course. Now he can't do anything wrong. Bank robberies or attacking TV host must clearly be someone else fault. As the world steps in to help him nothing will ever be the same again. Just watch what happens when celebrity and popular culture starts butting heads with the political, justice and the world order, someone must lose.

The Meaning of Life and Other Useless Crap

This short pamphlet covers many topics that are some of the most important problems things we face in society today from stopping Hurricanes, Flooding and explaining The Meaning of Life. It will give you a new perspective into many of the problems that we face that are being ignored even though we already have a solution.

The Meaning of Life and Other Useless Crap is Perhaps our generations greatest work as it answers the age old question "What is the meaning of life?" Written simply and straightforward it is easy to understand why Ben Lemon is the most important living philosopher. It hasn't been since A Modest Proposal that a pamphlet can our perceptions so dramatically.

High Rants by Ben Lemon

Come and get it. There is no need to wait with this book you'll get Moral Deserts. For philosophy has never been this fun as you get to ponder the questions of the universe like you were doing it high. You'll go through the ups and downs of a drug induced euphoric bliss. It has never been this chill in philosophy since the hippies. Wow, look at that, I have solved the drug problems of the world. It took all this time but we now know how to do it. I have eliminated all the bad effects of experiencing God's little miracle that sweet Mary Jane. Now you'll be able to say that you have had multiple experiences and you just don't need any right now. Why would you, you are reading my book? No longer will you have that dazed head that always last not long enough or having to do anything to your body that would damage it. You can sit back and enjoy a completely clean, safe and fun experience with Mary Jane. With this solution to ending drug use across this nation will also need each and every one whose eyes have read this to start peddling it. I mean, get it into the hands of everyone in your life. Give them the first one for free, just to see if they like it. If you can stop your family from doing drugs don't you think that it is the right thing to do.

Made in the USA
Middletown, DE
09 April 2023